The Redgrave Murders

OTHER BOOKS AND AUDIOBOOKS
BY A. L. SOWARDS

THE LEY BROTHERS

The Rules in Rome

Defiance

THE ESPIONAGE TRILOGY

Espionage

Sworn Enemy

Deadly Alliance

STAND-ALONES

The Spider and the Sparrow

The Redgrave Murders

The Perfect Gift

The Redgrave Murders

a romantic suspense novel

A. L. SOWARDS

Covenant Communications, Inc.

Cover image: © Mark Owen / Trevillion Images. *Noose* © ftwitty, courtesy of istock.com.

Cover design copyright © 2019 by Covenant Communications, Inc.

Published by Covenant Communications, Inc.
American Fork, Utah

Printed in the United States of America
First Printing: July 2019

25 24 23 22 21 20 19   10 9 8 7 6 5 4 3 2 1

ISBN 978-1-52440-945-6

For Brad & Suzi

Praise for
The Redgrave Murders

A compelling love story blended with a suspenseful mystery and sprinkled with WWII history. *The Redgrave Murders* kept me reading into the early hours.

—Jennifer Moore, award-winning author of
Becoming Lady Lockwood and *The Shipbuilder's Wife*

A. L. Sowards does it again! In *The Redgrave Murders*, Sowards weaves a fantastic tale filled with relatable characters, a mystery that grows more intense with every chapter, and a romance that makes the heart cheer after each struggle the lead characters overcome. A terrific read for all.

—Gregg Luke, author of *The Healer* and *Plague*

Known for her award-winning historical novels, A. L. Sowards has ventured into a new genre, historical mystery, and proves that, yes, she can deliver compelling reads in both. *The Redgrave Murders* is a solid murder mystery highlighted with in-depth research of post WWII. I highly recommend it.

—Kathi Oram Peterson, author of *Bloodline* and *A Familiar Fear*

One of the best who-dun-it mystery/romances I've ever read—filled with enriching little-known historical details, fantastic characters, beautiful prose and powerful passages, heart-wrenching drama, and plot twists and turns that kept me turning pages long into the night.

—Charissa Stastny, blogger and author of
the Ruled Out Romances series

A. L. Sowards is a master at weaving stories set in the past. This time, she has crafted a murder mystery set in a post-World War II town laden with trauma and prejudices, resulting in a multilayered whodunit that will chill and intrigue both history and mystery fans.

—Stephanie Black, award-winning author of
Mind Games and *Not a Word*

Chapter One

November 9, 1943

Dear Evelyn,

I know we haven't always gotten along that well. That's probably my fault, but if you tell Mom or Dad that I'm admitting responsibility, I'll stop writing.

Maybe we can try to make things work better through letters. Part of my motivation is selfish—it's nice to get mail. I'm not homesick or anything, but the drill instructor trying to change us from mere recruits to Marines sure isn't saying anything nice. A word from home would be welcome. San Diego, California, is a long way from Maplewick, New York.

Do you remember that time I called you a spoiled princess? I think you were about seven, and I was about ten. Dad said no daughter of his was a princess. Princesses got married off to strangers to strengthen alliances. They ended up in lands where they didn't even speak the language, wed to former enemies, and died of infection at childbirth or because some fool medical quack bled them to death. He said his daughter would have a much better life. You could choose your own future. But, Evie, what do you want out of life? I've known you since you were born, but I don't know anything about what you like or don't like or what you want beyond graduating from Redgrave University. And do you really want Redgrave, or is that just what Dad's always wanted for you?

Your repentant brother,

Clive

April 16, 1948

THE BRAKES ON MY DAD's new 1948 Chrysler New Yorker gave out on the steepest hill in Maplewick. Panic traveled from my hands on the steering wheel, through my arms, and down to my feet in open-toed high heels as

I pumped the brake pedal. Despite my efforts, the car continued its sprint past the old houses that lined Pine Street, hurling me to my doom.

I stomped on the emergency brake. The tires squealed but didn't halt. I said something very unladylike under my breath, because at the end of the hill, Pine Street converged with Redgrave Avenue, where a steady flow of traffic raced past. If I couldn't stop the car, I was going to end up in a wreck.

The car slowed, barely, but it wouldn't be enough to keep me from crashing through the rapidly approaching intersection. Breathing grew difficult as I struggled to ignore my fear and find a solution. I gripped the wheel and drove closer to the curb, so close that the tires ran against it. I shuddered to think of the damage the car might take. Dad was not going to be happy. I glanced to the right, glad little Sarah Murphy wasn't out on the front lawn with a ball or jump rope as I flew past my boyfriend's place.

The tires shrieked as they skidded against the curb, but the car still wouldn't stop. I hesitated, then made a right turn into Mr. Garcia's gravel driveway. The ground was almost level there, and between that and the gravel, the car fishtailed, then slowed, then finally came to a halt.

I left the emergency brake set and switched the car off with trembling hands. Then I leaned my head on the steering wheel and took a few deep breaths. I needed to check the damage, but I wanted a minute to catch my breath. Maybe a few minutes.

Had I just ruined Dad's two-month-old car? I could buy him a new one, but repairing his opinion of my driving skills might be more difficult. He hadn't said the brakes were different from his prewar Ford, but I hadn't exactly asked. Had I done something wrong, or had the brakes really stopped working?

I jumped when a hand slapped against the car's roof and someone yanked the door open.

"Evie? Are you okay?"

I recognized Gary's voice. He'd probably been waiting for me to pick him up and had run after me when the car careened past. He sounded out of breath. I swallowed, trying to work some moisture around my mouth that felt as dry as the Sahara. Not that I'd ever been to the Sahara. Or anywhere outside the state of New York, for that matter.

"Evie?" Gary put his hand on my shoulder, gently, as if afraid he'd break me if he put too much pressure on me.

"I haven't seen it yet. How bad are the tires?"

"Who cares about the car—are you hurt?" His dark eyes scanned over me, probably checking for injury.

"I'm fine." I swung my legs from the car, and he backed up enough to let me climb out.

"Are you sure?"

If I could pick one word to describe Gary Redhawk, it would be *calm*. And that was true now, even in the wake of a runaway car. If I could pick a few more words to describe Gary Redhawk, they would be *loyal, steady, unbelievably handsome, hardworking, reticent to the point of secretive*, and *the best kisser I've ever met*.

I sighed. Gary wasn't panicked, but I was jittery, as if the fear I'd felt when the brakes had failed continued to surge through my body. And what would Dad say? "It's Daddy's new car. It's about the fourth time he's let me drive it, and I almost wrecked it."

"I think your dad would agree with me that you're a lot more important than the car." Gary glanced toward the traffic at the bottom of the hill. "Are you sure you're not hurt? Jerking to a stop like that—you might not feel it until tomorrow."

"I didn't stop that abruptly. That was kind of the whole problem, not being able to stop." I blew out a breath thick with frustration. The stench of burning rubber suggested I wouldn't like what I found on the other side of the car. I walked around the hood. It didn't look too bad. But once I got to the passenger's side, my stomach sank. The whitewall tires didn't look so white anymore, and the chrome hubcaps were dull instead of shiny.

Gary followed me. Black hair fell across his forehead as he crouched down to take a closer look. "I can buff most of the scratches out of the hubcaps." He examined the rubber next. "Not sure about the tires. You might want to have Monte or one of your cousins look at them to make sure they're safe."

He stood and walked around behind me, wrapping me in his arms. If he'd done that a minute before, I wouldn't have been ready, but now I was more worried than frustrated, and I didn't mind his arms. I liked them, actually. A lot.

Before driving over, I'd run into an old friend. Barbara had asked if I was still seeing that *aesthetically alluring Indian with the sensuous lips and winsome eyes*. I'd told her Gary was a Seneca of the Iroquois Nations, thank you very much, and yes, we were together. I snuggled in a little closer. Yes, we were definitely together.

"So the brakes didn't work?" Gary's whisper tiptoed along my ear.

"No. I kept pushing on the pedal, but the car wouldn't slow. The emergency brake helped but only a little."

"Did they work when you backed out of the garage?"

"It wasn't in the garage." The car had been parked in the semicircular driveway in front of the house, where I lived with Dad. I hadn't backed up. I'd just pulled forward. "I stopped a few times on the way over. The brakes felt a little weird. Squishy, almost. And it took longer than I would have expected to stop. But I thought I was just used to the old Ford."

"Squishy?"

I shrugged. "That's the best way to describe it."

"Does your dad have tools in the trunk?"

"Of course. Along with a mock-up of a Genoese crossbow and a couple French basinets." Dad was always prepared, for the practical and the less practical.

"More Hundred Years' War stuff?"

"Yeah. And he probably cares more about all of that than the car, so I hope none of it is damaged." Dad was a history professor with a special interest in the wars between England and France during the fourteenth and fifteenth centuries. *Interest* was probably too mild a description. *Obsession* was more accurate.

Gary walked around to rummage through the trunk. I looked over his shoulder as he pulled out a flashlight and an old blanket. I checked Dad's artifacts, housed in sturdy cardboard boxes. Felt surrounded the helmets, and coarse excelsior nestled the crossbow. He loved his old objects, even the ones that were reproductions instead of genuine antiques. Our house was like a museum, except my room. I didn't have anything pre-Edwardian in there.

Gary looked under the hood, then spread a blanket on the gravel so he could slide beneath the car.

"Should I come down too?" Crawling under the car in my skirt wasn't what I'd planned for the evening, and I didn't know what to look for, but I wanted to help. I'd tried to learn a few mechanical skills when my brother and cousin had fixed up an old car when we were teenagers, but Clive had told me to go away every time I'd asked.

"I'll just be a minute." Gary was under the car for a while before he slid out again.

"Did you see anything?" I asked when his face reappeared.

"Yeah, and I don't think you should drive it anymore. The brake line has a leak. It's been dripping all over."

"But it's only two months old!"

Gary's lips turned down. "It's a straight cut. I don't think it was just a bad part on the assembly line."

"Maybe Dad ran over something sharp. Or maybe I did."

"Maybe." Gary got to his feet. "Or someone might have done it on purpose."

Shock crept across my shoulders and made a chill seep into my spine. Ruining the brake line was asking for an accident. Why would someone intentionally risk a car wreck? "But that could have killed someone—and not just whoever was driving." I glanced at Redgrave Avenue. Had someone tried to hurt my dad by sabotaging his car?

Gary frowned again. "The cut seems intentional but not predictable. It could kill or injure, but if the brakes failed on level ground, the driver could probably still stop." He slipped his arm around my waist. "Or the driver might be smart enough to use the emergency brake, drag off the curb, drive onto gravel, and manage to stop, even on a hill."

Relief that the fiasco hadn't been my fault and that Gary thought I'd handled it well eased the fear I felt but didn't erase it completely.

"Your dad hasn't had any crazy notes from wronged students lately, has he?"

Dad's classes were legendary around campus for their difficulty, and he'd acquired a reputation as something of an ogre among the students. "Not since fall semester. But that was just a promise to complain to the dean. And Dean Roth doesn't mind if only two people pull A's a semester, as long as Daddy keeps publishing."

A line of worry grazed Gary's left eyebrow. "Will you be okay while I get some help to push the car?"

I nodded. As he left, I glanced at the glossy cream finish of the New Yorker. The color seemed so innocent, but whether it was mechanical failure or sabotage, I could have been seriously hurt or killed in that car. Not even the pleasant breeze and Gary's thoughtfulness could completely undo the lingering apprehension.

Chapter Two

November 27, 1943

Dear Clive,

Boot camp must be bad if you want to hear from me. I like the idea of trying to make things better, but if I'm going to write to you, I want your promise that you won't make fun of me anymore. You don't know how awful it is to have an older sibling always hounding you. Maybe now, with a drill instructor breathing down your neck, you can relate, a little.

GARY'S LANDLORD, MR. NORTON, AND another boarder, Charlie Murphy, helped push the car to Monte Frye's mechanic shop about a block away. Once everything was set, Gary and I walked back up the hill to Mr. Norton's house.

"Where did you learn to buff chrome?" I asked.

Gary gave me a wry smile. "Metal shop at reform school. They wanted to shift us from good-for-nothing Indians to good-enough-to-fit-at-the-bottom-of-the-labor-pool Indians."

"You don't believe that, do you?"

He shook his head. "Not now. But there were a couple years when it was hard not to."

Gary had started attending a boarding school for Indians when he was eight. According to Dad, schools like that were meant to integrate Indians into normal American society. Gary didn't talk much about it, but I'd gotten the impression that his experience there hadn't been pleasant. He'd run away a few too many times, and then he'd ended up in an institution for delinquent youth.

"Because of the schools?" I asked.

"Yeah. Do you still want to come to the warehouse with me? We can take the motorcycle." He'd promised to check an old warehouse for Mr. Norton, see if it could be turned into rentals because new housing had slowed to a crawl with the Depression and the war, and demand was still higher than availability. That was why the Murphy family of four leased one bedroom in Mr. Norton's, a pair of bachelors had another, and Gary rented the shed out back.

"I'd like to come." Exploring a warehouse might not be a normal date, but I didn't mind, and I saw no reason to change plans because of car trouble. "It's a ways out, though, isn't it?"

"Three miles."

"Can we stop by my house first so I can change into trousers?" My fitted skirt wouldn't do well on a motorcycle.

"Yeah."

We walked into Mr. Norton's yard. A clothesline hung with cloth diapers and small dresses told me it was wash day for Mrs. Murphy. I recognized the baby blanket I'd made for her son, Charlie Jr., and the bright socks I'd knitted for her daughter, Sarah.

Gary pulled his motorcycle around. "Want to walk to your house or ride?"

I didn't want to make him walk the motorcycle all the way to my house. I tested the give in my skirt and decided it could handle ten blocks. "We can ride."

He handed me the helmet, like normal.

"Your head is worth protecting too," I said.

Gary chuckled. "You're the only one who'd miss me."

"I doubt that." Sarah Murphy idolized Gary because he'd taught her how to play catch, and Mr. Norton relied on him to do most of the yardwork. Gary worked lunches at the Redgrave cafeteria and had a part-time job at a grocery store. Both his employers would miss him too.

"So, you wouldn't miss me?"

"You know that's not what I meant!"

The half-smile lighting up his face confirmed I was right. "I'll pick up a second helmet sometime." He'd been saying that for months, but it wasn't normally an issue. Maplewick was small, so we walked or I borrowed Dad's car. "You want to take the quickest route? Or the long way?"

"How about a path that doesn't involve driving anywhere near the history department?" I hiked my skirt up to climb on the back of the motorcycle, then slipped my arms around his waist.

"You sure? I think we should ride right past Dr. Fontaine's office. Then he and your dad would have something to argue about other than wars fought six hundred years ago."

I gave him a playful slap on the shoulder as we rode onto Pine. "Don't you dare!" Professor Lawrence Fontaine would relish telling Dad that I'd been riding about town with my knees exposed. Dad might let it slide in normal circumstances but not if Dr. Fontaine said something. Those two got along about as well as King Edward II and Robert the Bruce.

Gary stopped at the sign at the bottom of the hill. "I'm not staring at your legs or anything, but if you get sick of working in the bursar's office and it's around Christmastime, I bet the Rockettes would take you for their kick line."

My face heated as I tugged at my hemline. "I'm a respectable young lady, not a dancer."

"Nothing wrong with dancing for a living, is there?"

"Maybe not. But I think Daddy would die of embarrassment."

I couldn't hear for sure because the motorcycle engine went from a purr to a roar as he accelerated, but I think Gary was laughing.

* * *

Gary took me around the university, so neither Dad nor his rival professor saw me with my skirt hitched up. I needn't have worried. Dad was home, reading the paper in the parlor.

"Evelyn, I wasn't expecting you so soon." Dad smiled and stood. He was tall and bulky, with silver hair balding to look like a monk's tonsure. When I was younger, I'd pictured him as an armored knight, hefting his shield to protect me whenever Clive's insults started to feel like dragon fire. But our relationship had changed since the war's end, and the biggest reason why was painfully apparent as Dad turned to Gary, his smile gone. "Mr. Redhawk."

Even when I was a child, Dad told me I could make my own choices, but that hadn't stopped him from stating his opinion quite firmly the first time I'd brought Gary home. Dad didn't approve. He hadn't repeated himself, and he hadn't gone back on his promise that I could date whomever I wished. But nor had he ever shown Gary anything more than stiff politeness.

"Um, Daddy, I think I learned today how the Genoese crossbowmen felt at the battle of Crécy."

He raised an eyebrow in amusement, which was what I'd been hoping for. "Oh? You learned how it feels to be pierced with an English arrow, then trodden down by French horsemen who suspect you of treachery?"

"No. But I learned how it feels for equipment to fail when you're depending on it. Not wet strings on a crossbow but the brake lines in a car. They stopped working on Pine Street."

"Goodness." He stepped toward me and looked me up and down. "Were you harmed?"

"No."

"And my things in the trunk?"

"I checked them twice. No damage."

He nodded. "Good. I need them for lecture next week. And the car?"

"The brake line was cut," Gary said, answering that question for me. "Brake fluid was everywhere."

I left Gary to explain what he'd seen with the car. I didn't like leaving him to face Dad's hostility by himself, but the sooner I switched clothes, the sooner we could leave. Maybe car trouble would prove to be something the two men could discuss without tension. I walked past the suit of armor my family had named Sir Redgrave and trudged up the stairs, past a dozen medieval coats of arms, to my bedroom.

I changed into straight-legged gabardine slacks and loafers. They weren't as flattering as the tailored skirt and heels, but they were more practical for riding a motorcycle and exploring an old warehouse. I checked the mirror, wondering if my dark hair looked more wavy or messy today. Messy. I reapplied red lipstick, then grabbed a head scarf and wrapped it around my hair as I walked down the stairs.

"Professor Gerstner says you have potential, but you have a problem with tardiness." Dad's voice boomed from the parlor.

"I was late a few times. It won't happen again," Gary said.

"I would hope not. Valuable tax dollars have been allotted to give returning GIs like you a chance to make something of yourselves. I hate to see resources squandered."

"Yes, sir."

"Especially by someone like you. People expect you to step out of line. They'll question your loyalty if you're not careful. You can't afford to do anything that will make people think less of you."

"I think I proved my loyalty during the war."

"By surrendering and spending most of it in a prison camp?"

"That wasn't my fault." Gary's voice grew sharp. "Someone with a higher rank than me fouled up. And seeing as how you weren't there, I don't think you have any right to question how we fought."

I chose that moment to enter the parlor. It wasn't the first time the two of them had quarreled. It happened more often than not when they were in the same room.

Dad straightened to his full height. "Trousers, Evelyn?"

"Just for the evening. It's not like I'm wearing them to work."

"Since the car isn't working, I thought you might stay home tonight."

Dad had a way of suggesting things as though they were orders. I was twenty-four years old, but he still treated me like I was seventeen. I lived in his home, but I earned my keep—doing his laundry, cooking his meals, keeping the house clean. I probably would have moved out if there weren't such a housing shortage, or if he managed his diabetes better, but for now, I was keeping an eye on him and saving him the expense of a housekeeper.

I looked from my dad to Gary and back again. Dad should have been sitting in a restaurant with his wife or talking about baseball with his son, but Mom and Clive were gone. I was all he had left. I hated leaving him alone, but I didn't want to cancel my plans either. I'd spent the last four evenings at home, so why did I feel so guilty for going out tonight? "We're taking Gary's motorcycle, which is why I changed. I'm sorry about the car. Mr. Frye said he'll have it repaired in a day or two."

Dad crossed his arms. "Yes, I'll be speaking with Mr. Dailey about the car he sold me quite soon. To have something like the brakes fail within a matter of months is completely unacceptable."

I glanced at Gary, and he nodded. "I told him it might have been cut."

"Nonsense. Why would someone cut the brake line? Sloppy labor— that's the problem. And I'll see that Mr. Dailey hears about it."

Gary motioned toward the door with his head, almost in a plea.

"We're off, Daddy. Enjoy your evening. There's chicken from yesterday in the refrigerator. Put it in the oven for twenty minutes to heat it up."

"When will you be home?"

I gave him a hug goodbye and kissed his cheek. "I'll be home before midnight. And I'll make you your favorite breakfast tomorrow."

Dad looked at the grandfather clock and frowned. That morning, I'd told him we were exploring an old warehouse for Gary's landlord. I could see him itching to ask how we'd spend the rest of the night, but he held his tongue.

I headed for the door, and Gary followed me outside.

"I'm sorry," Gary said. "I was trying not to fight with him. I think I made it almost four weeks."

I grabbed the helmet from the motorcycle and strapped it on. "You've only seen him about twice in the last month."

"I'm sorry," he said again.

"It's not your fault." And it wasn't, but that didn't make it any easier to know my beau and my dad didn't get along. I didn't want to disappoint either of them, but most of the time, I felt like I was letting down one in order to please the other. I wasn't sure how long I could be pulled in two directions before something tore.

Chapter Three

Letter of November 27, 1943, continued

What do I want out of life, Clive? You might think it's silly, but I want to travel. That sounds so selfish to say while London's being bombed and Paris is occupied by Nazis. Daddy says we'll win the war, eventually, and maybe then I'll be able to see more of the world. I want to see if the Rockies are really that tall and if the Mississippi is really that wide. I want to see geysers in Yellowstone and palm trees in California and dip my toes in the Caribbean. It will have to wait, of course. I can't travel during the war. It would waste resources, and it might be dangerous. And I'm grateful for Maplewick. It will always be my safe place to come back to.

THE WAREHOUSE WAS EERIE IN its dilapidated state. The dead tree out front without a single blossom and the icy wind that picked up upon our arrival didn't help the mood much. I removed the helmet and looked around, half expecting to see a ghost.

"Doesn't look too promising, does it?" The edges of my scarf flapped around my face as I climbed off the motorcycle.

Gary grabbed his flashlight. "No. But people might be willing to do a lot of work to make it better if the price is right and if they can have a little space of their own."

"Is that why you live in a shack? To have a little space of your own?"

Gary nodded. "There were about thirty beds to a room in the boarding school. Same or worse in most of the POW camps." He glanced at me, and his mouth softened. "Don't get me wrong—I wouldn't mind sharing space with the right person but not with a bunch of other men grunting and snoring and mumbling in their sleep. Never again, if I can help it."

I took his free hand, wishing I could somehow wipe away all the bad things from his past—and because the warehouse felt like something out of a horror film. "Would you want to live here?"

"No." Gary's answer was immediate.

We walked around the outside, making sure there wasn't anything dangerous, like an old well a child might fall into or piles of broken glass. The weeds reached my hips in some places—impressive for this early in the spring. A cluster of birch trees looked as though they'd be pleasant in a month or so, but for now, they looked as rundown as everything else.

Gary was quiet, which wasn't unusual, but he seemed tense, and that wasn't normal. I kept looking at him, trying to figure out what was wrong, but he didn't meet my eyes. Mostly, he stared at the old chain-link fence topped by looped barbed wire.

"What type of warehouse was this?" I asked.

"Mr. Norton didn't say."

We finished circling the yard and stood in front of the sturdy metal door. Gary handed me the flashlight and fished the keys from his pocket. Daylight was starting to fade, but I could see strain on his face that I wasn't used to.

"Are you sure you want to go in?" I asked.

"I promised Mr. Norton I would. You can stay outside if you like."

"No, I'm fine. You just . . ." I didn't finish. What would I say? He was acting a little unusual but not weird. Not really. Besides, he'd grown up with people telling him something was wrong with him because he was Seneca, because he never knew his father, and probably a dozen other reasons. He didn't need to hear it from me.

Gary raised an eyebrow. "I just what?"

I shrugged. "You seem a little antsy."

He grunted. "The fences in Germany were a lot like this one, only double, with machine-gun towers."

I looked around again. There was a tower along the fence. No guard manned it, Nazi or otherwise, but a shiver ran down my back. I put my hand on his elbow, wanting to touch something safe.

The lock squealed in protest as Gary turned the key, then the metal door boomed as he pushed it open. I thought I felt Gary flinch, but I couldn't be sure because the noise startled me enough that I jumped.

I shined the light into myriad spider webs and a thick layer of dust. My throat felt dry as the beam pierced the darkness. A few spiders retreated into the shadows. I swallowed. I didn't like spiders—mostly my brother's doing—but they *probably* wouldn't hurt me.

"The owner's desperate to sell. Paid all the utilities for a month, so there should be electricity," Gary said. "See if you can find a switch."

I searched the walls for switches and finally found a row. I flipped them on, and a sickly dim glow gradually revealed a large, open space, shadowed by support beams and divided by partitions. I directed the flashlight's beam to the overhead structures, wondering if they were solid. It was hard to tell under all the built-up grime.

The lights gradually grew brighter, so I turned the flashlight off and walked forward, checking the floor as I went. Cracks lined the cement surface, but nothing seemed too damaged. I wouldn't want to live here, but I could see Mr. Norton adding walls to break up the space and laying down carpet to make it more comfortable. A single sink stood off to the side, but I supposed he would need more. Plumbing would be an expensive addition.

"Does he have a budget in mind for the project?"

"He didn't say." Gary's voice sounded strained.

We walked around the main storage area. In the back was a walled-off portion. "Offices?" I asked.

"Probably." His voice didn't sound any better.

I went through the doorway—there was no door. An uneven table, an old stove, and a few crates greeted me. The ceiling wasn't as high here, and the lighting from the main room didn't penetrate this room completely. I found a cord and pulled. A lightbulb above me flashed on, then exploded.

A startled cry escaped my throat as bits of broken lightbulb rained to the floor. I backed into Gary, clutching his hand. It was just a broken lightbulb, but my pulse pounded, and I wanted to either turn tail and run for the motorcycle or turn around and bury my face in Gary's chest.

"You got the flashlight still?" Gary reached for it.

I switched it on and handed it over. I followed him around the room, looking past the wooden crates and wondering how it would look if the place were cleaned up and given better lighting. I tried to picture something homey, but I couldn't get past how spooky and dusty everything seemed.

"No windows?" I asked.

Gary flashed the beam to where the ceiling and the wall met. There were a few windows, but they were tiny and so cloaked in grime that no light made it through. Maybe they'd been painted over during the war and never cleaned off.

"This place gives me the creeps." I folded my arms across my chest. I wasn't sure if it was the cold cement floor or the way everything looked, but it suddenly felt more like winter than spring.

One of the lights from the main room flickered, then faded, making the back room even darker. Then Gary dropped the flashlight. It spun a few times on the floor, showing first a pile of chains, then a poof of dust, then Gary. His back pressed against the wall, and his hand covered his eyes as he slid to the floor.

"Gary!" I ran over and crouched beside him. "What's wrong?"

He sat on the floor, his hand over his face. He didn't answer, but his breathing was shallow and rapid, and his shoulders were stooped. The flashlight's beam swung across his face again, stopping there, revealing a glint of sweat.

"Gary, what's wrong?"

He stared right past me, as if I weren't there.

"Should we go?" I asked.

No answer.

"Gary, do you want to leave?"

Still no answer.

I reached for his hand, but when I touched him, he flinched as if I'd burned him with a hot iron. He scrambled away from me, into the shadows.

What was happening to him? I thought about running for help, but the closest buildings were half a mile away, and I didn't think anyone would be there on a Friday night. I picked up the flashlight and turned it on him. He threw both hands up to shield his eyes, and then he curled into a ball.

"Gary, what should I do? Tell me how to help."

He didn't respond.

An old telephone hung on the far wall. The wires were probably still connected to the switchboard, but who would I have the operator put me through to? Mr. Norton didn't have a phone, so I couldn't call him, and Dad's car was in the shop—not that Dad would be much help with something like this. Besides, Gary didn't like being the center of attention.

I knelt next to Gary again, determined to try one more time before I called either my aunt or an ambulance. "Gary, it's me, Evelyn Hampton. Please let me help you."

He finally looked at me. His breathing was still too rapid, but he seemed to focus on my face, and that was better than before. "Evie?"

"Yeah. What's wrong?"

He ran a hand over his face and into his hair, sighing with what sounded like a mix of weariness and defeat. "I don't know what happened. It was like I was back in . . ."

"Back where?"

He shook his head. "Can we go outside?"

"Of course."

I stood and waited for him, wondering if he wanted the flashlight or not. He didn't take it but strode through the warehouse, checking to make sure I followed. I switched the lights off, and then we stepped outside. His hands trembled as he locked the door behind us.

I put my fingers on his arm. This time, he didn't jerk away. "Are you okay?" It was a stupid question, and I knew it the moment the words left my lips. Of course he wasn't okay.

He shrugged.

"What did you mean, that it was like you were back . . . I don't know. Back somewhere."

He hesitated. His lips moved a few times as if to answer, but then they stilled. Long seconds passed before he swallowed and spoke. "When I was a prisoner in Germany, we were locked in a warehouse a lot like this one when we weren't working."

"And the fences?"

"Those too. But the chains were what set it off."

"Did they chain you in Germany?"

He shook his head. "They chained the doors, not us. But when I was nine, I ran away from school. I just wanted to go home. Home felt safer. But they caught me and started chaining me at night."

"When you were nine?" I pictured a little boy in a little bed, scared and alone and clamped in big chains like the ones I'd seen in the warehouse office. "That's horrible."

"That and a good lashing was the normal punishment."

"And it was like you were there again?"

He nodded. "Yeah. Like I was in both places at once, living two nightmares at the same time."

I took his hand.

"I'm sorry, Evie."

"For what?"

He huffed. "For that. Whatever it was. I should have taken you to supper or a dance instead."

"I'm not angry. I'm worried about you. It was like you couldn't even see me."

He glanced at my face, then away.

"Could you see me? Or hear me?"

He shrugged again. I guessed that meant no.

"Do you want to talk about it?"

One side of his lips pulled up. "Maybe later." He looked back at the warehouse. "It's been a long day. I should get you home."

It was early for a date night, but if he needed time alone, I didn't want to press it, so I nodded.

He drove the motorcycle with more restraint than usual, slower around curves and not as fast up hills, as if driving were work rather than pleasure. He pulled around the semicircular drive in front of my house and turned off the engine. We climbed off the motorcycle, and I handed him the helmet. His hand was clumsy as he took it, and his lips were tight.

"Did I do something wrong?" I asked. He was usually so attentive, so present. But now it was like he was in another country.

"Of course not." He ran a finger along my jaw, and the warmth from his touch spread up onto my face and down into my chest. "You're perfect. I'm just . . . just . . ." He trailed off without finishing.

"Will I see you tomorrow? Lunch maybe?"

He started to nod, then stopped. "I can't do lunch. Can I take you out for supper? Make up for tonight?"

I nodded. "I told Aunt Janice I'd help with her garden tomorrow. Do you want to meet at her house?" That might prevent another confrontation between Gary and Dad. Aunt Janice cared who I spent my time with, but she didn't mind Gary the way Dad did.

"Sounds great." He gave me a hug and kissed my forehead. It wasn't much of a good-night kiss, more habit than tenderness. But given everything that had happened since I'd lost control of Dad's car, I would take it.

Chapter Four

December 24, 1943

Dear Evelyn,

I'm officially a Marine now. That's a lot better than some of the things they called us during training, but I won't repeat them, given my determination to treat you like a lady instead of an annoying little sister. I'm off to Camp Elliott next. Not much of a move. I think the next one will be more drastic.

I CAME TO BREAKFAST THE next morning with my hair still rolled into pin curls. I waited for Dad's normal joke about how I should try a sensible medieval style, like braiding my hair into ramshorns or covering it with a barbette and veil. I served him his omelet and a cup of coffee, but he just mumbled into the morning paper.

"Is something wrong?" I asked from the stove.

He turned the page of the newspaper sharply but didn't respond.

I cracked a pair of eggs for myself and added cheese and chives as the steam rolled off Dad's breakfast. He hadn't touched it. Maybe he was more upset about the car than he'd let on. I was more nervous than upset, wondering if someone had deliberately damaged it.

And I was worried about Gary. I'd never seen him fall apart like that. He'd never struck me as cocky, but he generally seemed comfortable with himself. That had disappeared last night. Something was off, and I hoped he'd be willing to talk about it. We'd been seeing each other for a year and a half—if we couldn't talk about his past and whatever had haunted him in the warehouse, what did that say about our relationship?

Dad folded the paper and put it to the side as I joined him at the breakfast table. "He has no business writing about the House of Plantagenet. He's always written about the Tudors before."

"What are you talking about?"

"Professor Fontaine announced that his latest book will be released in two months' time. A biography of Edward of Woodstock, Duke of Cornwall."

"Dr. Fontaine wrote a biography of the Black Prince?" I put my fork down. "Isn't that what you're working on?"

"Yes." He slammed his fist into the table. "And he knew it. But he wrote his faster than I wrote mine, and his will come out first." Dad folded his arms and sulked. "All that work for nothing. Two years of research, not to mention all the writing time. And I've already paid the typist! His probably isn't even as good as mine, but it will beat mine to press, and that's all the dean will care about."

I felt sick to my stomach. Dad had always had an uneasy relationship with Professor Fontaine, but this went beyond trying to win an award before the other did. This was taking three years of Dad's work and making it irrelevant. Worse, Dad was passionate about the Black Prince. This was a book he'd been planning to write for a decade, maybe longer. If Dr. Fontaine had scooped any of his other projects, it wouldn't have hurt this much. This one was meant to be his magnum opus.

"How soon could you have yours out?"

He huffed. "It won't come out now. What publisher would take a subject that's just been released by a professor from the same department at the same university? Sneaky knave wouldn't tell me what he was working on. Now I realize why. He's got a lot of explaining to do."

Dad didn't finish his breakfast.

I tried all morning to console Dad, but I didn't have much success. How could I? So much work, so much hope—and now it was gone. After lunch, I walked downtown, craving something other than gloom. A visit with my aunt sounded like a good antidote.

I paused on the sidewalk in front of the Ryder Café when I noticed Gary's motorcycle in the parking lot. I frowned. He worked Saturday mornings at the grocery store. Usually, he was done by lunch, but he'd said he had plans. Plans to meet someone else? I didn't have a monopoly on his time, but it would have been nice if he'd told me.

I glanced through the window. Gary sat across a table from a beautiful woman. She looked about my age—more than twenty, less than thirty, with the top of her hair pinned into ash-blonde rolls and the rest falling in soft curls around her neck. I glanced at the man again. I could see only the back of his head, but there was no question—it was Gary. I recognized the leather jacket and the way he nodded. And I recognized the sleek black hair. He'd made me laugh while I was trimming it a few weeks ago, and I'd cut it crooked.

Gary and the woman stood, and she put a hand on the muscles of his upper arm. Then she leaned in and kissed him on the cheek.

I inhaled sharply, as if I'd been punched. Why was she kissing *my* boyfriend? And why had he let her?

The woman glanced up, and I hurried off. I was moving away from my aunt's house now, not toward it, but humiliation kept me from walking past the café again. I stopped one building over, in an alley, and leaned against the wall of the pharmacy. I took a few deep breaths of musty garbage-scented air and blinked away the hot tears leaking from my eyes.

Why had Gary taken another woman to lunch? And why had she kissed him?

I liked Gary. A lot. And I'd liked him for a long time. We hadn't talked about marriage, but I'd certainly thought about it. What girl wouldn't after dating the same man for a year and a half? Things had always been so easy between us—whether it was a fancy night at a dance club or running errands for Mr. Norton. I'd trusted him, strained my connection with my father for him. Didn't our relationship mean anything to him?

An engine caught. Gary's motorcycle. A few moments later, the woman swaggered past the alley. I couldn't tell if the swing was from her high-heeled shoes or natural bounce or some combination. I knew what Gary's goodbye kisses felt like. If she'd kissed him again, after I looked away, and if he'd kissed her back, she was probably up in the clouds.

I wiped the tears from my eyes and forced my fists to relax. I wasn't as calm as Gary, but I had a mellow personality, most of the time. I wasn't feeling so mild as I left the alley to follow the woman.

I imagined marching right up to her and saying, "Excuse me, why did you kiss my boyfriend?" But then the humiliation came back. He'd let her kiss him. Maybe that meant there was something wrong with me, something that sent him looking elsewhere, something that kept him from caring for me the way I cared for him.

She headed for the train station, but my footsteps grew more and more hesitant, and the distance between us widened. I sat on a bench while she stood in line at the ticket office. I watched her board the train for Buffalo, but I never spoke to her. I guess I wasn't brave enough.

I wasn't sure how long I sat on the bench after the train rolled from the station. I felt hollow inside. I thought back to when Gary and I had first started dating and how shy he'd been. I remembered our first kiss and the way I'd thought everything was going to work out perfectly after that because his mouth had been sweet and gentle and enticing in a way I'd never known before. And I recalled all the times I'd thought I was in love with him.

It was hard to lose someone you loved.

But if I was about to lose Gary, at least I'd had practice. My mom had died three and a half years ago. Cancer. Seven months after her funeral, we'd gotten a telegram from the War Department. Clive had died on some island called Okinawa. After years of bickering, my brother and I had finally become friends—but just when we'd started to trust each other, he was gone. Sometime in between, I'd lost my fiancé, Roland, to another woman while he'd been overseas with the air force.

I knew about loss. But that didn't stop my chest from feeling like someone had pierced it with a pike.

Eventually, I pulled myself together. It hurt, but I wasn't going to let a cheating boyfriend ruin my life. I had a decent job and a considerable nest egg, and the world was a very big place. I could leave Maplewick whenever I wanted. Gary had been one of the things holding me here, but if he wasn't as loyal as I'd thought, maybe it was time to move on. I'd always wanted to travel. I hadn't yet because Dad needed me. But after two years of practice, he was getting better about managing his diabetes. Maybe it was time for me to finally chase my dream and see something beyond the borders of New York.

Aunt Janice always made me feel better, so I started the four-block walk to her home. She was my mom's older sister. She'd been engaged once, but her fiancé had gone overseas in 1918 and had never come back. Tragedy and disappointment surrounded her life like a moat around a castle, but Aunt Janice always remained cheerful. Right then, I needed some of that optimism.

"Evelyn!"

I turned to see my cousins Frank and Dale. I forced a smile and hoped it didn't look like I'd been crying.

"Evie, how are you?" Frank asked.

"Fine, thanks." Since Clive's death, Frank had stepped into the overprotective cousin role, but I didn't want to deal with that while the pain was still so raw. He and my brother had shared confidences, but Frank was Clive's best friend, not mine. When I was younger, I'd been jealous. I'd looked up to Clive, but what boy would want to play with his sister, three years younger than him, when he could play with his cousin, three days older than him, instead? Clive and Frank had been inseparable, and I'd been ignored or teased. "How's business?" I asked. After the war had ended and he'd gotten out of the navy, Frank had opened a music store.

"Already sold out of the new Nat King Cole song." He made a face. "But records are about the only things selling. The instruments are all gathering dust. If Clive were here, it would be different. He could always predict what people would like."

The music store had been Clive's dream too, and they'd always planned to work together. Frank had been the one with the big ideas, and Clive had been the one with the practical strategies.

"Maybe it just needs a little more time," I said.

It might have needed a location bigger than Maplewick too, but neither of us could do much about our town's population.

"Yeah, maybe."

I turned to my other cousin, Dale, who was a few years older than Frank and Clive. "And how's my favorite lawyer?"

Dale smiled. "No big complaints. Saw your aunt this week, actually."

"Aunt Janice?" Dale and Frank were related to me through my dad's side, not my mom's, but both sides knew each other well.

Dale nodded. "Yeah, she wanted me to redo her will. Not that it needed changing. I think she was just trying to support Maplewick's newest lawyer."

"That sounds like Aunt Janice." She wasn't a spendthrift, but I could see her stepping in to help a friend, even if she didn't have a pressing need for the service.

"Are you still running around with that Indian fellow?"

I'd been expecting—and dreading—that question. I'd spent over a year defending my relationship with Gary. And now, even though I suspected him of cheating on me, I wasn't ready to back down. "I think I've made it very clear that who I date is my choice."

Dale raised a hand slightly, as if in surrender. "Yeah, I know. I just worry about you." He gave me a look I'd seen countless times before. "And I think you could do better."

I wasn't sure if I should laugh or cry. Yes, I could do better than a two-timer, but that wasn't what Dale had against Gary. He wanted me to date a nice white boy with a dignified family and a large bank account. Gary had only his hard work and persistence to provide for himself and any future family, and I'd never met his relations.

I did my best to lighten the mood. "You just don't like him because he joined the army instead of the navy."

Dale chuckled. "Yeah, well. Be careful, huh? And, uh, Roland is back in town." He gave me half a smile. "He's still single."

I suppressed a groan. "Last time I tried that, it didn't work out so well." Roland Roth, the dean's son, had already broken my heart once. I saw no reason to date him again.

"People change. Maybe the timing was off back then. There was a war on—don't you remember?"

I changed the subject. "I developed the film from Easter. I got a few shots with all the boys looking at the camera at the same time. Stevie and Sammy are even smiling."

"Sounds like an Easter miracle. Thanks, Evie." Dale glanced at his wristwatch. "I've got to meet Fern and the boys at the park. See you around, huh?"

"Bye, Dale."

Frank didn't follow him. "You're not going to play with your nephews?" I asked.

Frank shrugged. "First, I wanted to make sure you're okay."

"I'm fine." I hoped he couldn't tell I was lying.

"Look, Evie, Mr. Redhawk has been through a lot. The war was hard on a lot of people, especially POWs. And I've heard enough about the Thomas Indian School to know it was no picnic." His eyes locked with mine. "Do you remember when you were little and you took in that stray cat?"

I nodded. "Clive hated it because it made him sneeze. But I loved that cat, even after it scratched me." I still had the scar on my right forearm. The fluffy tabby had lived with us for two weeks. Something had startled it, and it had drawn blood. My blood. Dad had gotten rid of it after that, and I'd cried for days—not because of my arm but because I missed my pet.

"Dale's like me. He wants to make sure you aren't taking in another stray because you feel sorry for it. Some people are too damaged by their pasts for you to fix, no matter how much you want to help. Broken strays can hurt, even if they don't mean to, and we just want you to be happy."

I didn't tell him that it was too late. I'd already let Gary into my heart. And I'd already gotten hurt.

Chapter Five

Letter of December 24, 1943, continued

It's strange, Evie, being away from home during Christmas. There's no snow here. I didn't realize how much I liked snow in the winter until it was gone. Have you heard that song, "White Christmas"? I think it came out last year. I know Christmas will be over by the time this letter reaches you, but next time you hear that song, think of me doing drills on the beach in San Diego. And, no, the beach isn't a pleasant place for drills. Sand makes everything twice as hard.

"IF IT WAS WHAT IT looked like and another woman really did kiss him, would you forgive him?" Aunt Janice eyed me over her china teacup. The weeding was done, and we were relaxing in her parlor.

I thought for a while before answering. Picturing Gary involved with another woman cut deep, but I couldn't forget all the good times, like yesterday when he'd helped with Dad's car. "Maybe. If he apologized."

"I know you like that boy."

I nodded.

A few thin wrinkles creased the skin around her blue eyes. "And I always thought he was thoroughly smitten. As he should be with a young lady as fine as my niece."

That pulled a smile out of me.

Aunt Janice set her teacup and saucer on the coffee table. "I've found that there are two sides to every story, Evie. Seems like a mistake to come to a conclusion before you know the whole truth."

"I saw her hold his arm and kiss his cheek."

"Did he kiss her back?"

"I don't know. I stopped watching." That painful feeling in my stomach came back.

"Evie, you always have choices. Sometimes people make mistakes. Often, the important thing isn't which mistakes we make but how we react to them. Someone who can admit they were wrong, even when they made a big mistake, stands taller before me than someone who keeps repeating the same problem over and over again and either can't see it or refuses to fix it."

"You think I should forgive him, then?"

Aunt Janice shrugged. "That's up to you. If you love him, and if he's sorry, it would be a shame to throw everything away over one kiss that he might not have initiated. But if you're just dating him because you're scared of being alone or because all your friends are married and you want to start a family, then maybe it's a good time to take a long, hard look at your relationship with Gary Redhawk. You don't throw away a perfectly good apple because it has one little scratch on it. But you don't hold on to it if what you really want is an apricot instead."

The doorbell rang, and I glanced at the clock. Quarter after five. "That might be him." Anger and anxiety twisted in my chest, but so did hope.

"If you want to invite him in, I can busy myself in the kitchen."

I trusted Aunt Janice not to eavesdrop, but the conversation Gary and I needed to have might turn lengthy. "I think we'll go on a walk or something."

"Do you want to let him in, or shall I?"

I needed another minute to compose myself, so I let her answer the door.

Gary greeted Aunt Janice politely, as always, asking about her carpal tunnel, then about her hat shop. She led him into the parlor.

"Hi, Evie." He stepped forward, and light from the window revealed a growing bruise under his left eye.

"What happened to your eye?" I stood to get a better look.

He shook his head. "Nothing much. I was clumsy."

I took his chin in my hand and pulled his face toward the light. His eye was swollen halfway shut. "It doesn't look like nothing much." And in my experience, being clumsy usually involved bruised shins and papercuts, not black eyes.

Aunt Janice took a few steps toward the kitchen. "Would you like some ice for it?"

"No, thank you, ma'am. I already iced it."

We left Aunt Janice's house after a few minutes. Maybe he didn't want to talk about the eye in front of my aunt, but I planned to ask about it as soon as I had a chance.

I caught a hint of his cologne as we walked along the street. He turned to me and smiled. His smile still did something to me, even when I was upset. It was as if I was the only thing important to him in the whole world, and it was hard to remember how much it had hurt to see someone else kiss him that afternoon.

"Evie, I want to apologize."

I sucked in a breath. Maybe bringing the conversation around to the woman in the café would be easier than I thought. I'd been uncertain before, but now I knew I'd forgive him. All he had to do was be honest and explain.

"About last night, at the warehouse. I shouldn't have taken you. I still don't know what happened, but I'm sorry if I scared you. Part of me's surprised you're willing to see me tonight."

He was worried about the warehouse? I studied his face. He was embarrassed. He needn't have felt that way. I wasn't upset about things he couldn't control.

"I'm sorry you have such horrible things in your past," I said.

He looked away. "Yeah. Me too."

I waited, wondering if he would explain the woman at lunch next. I almost asked him about it but decided to ask about his eye instead. "What happened to your face?"

His stride slowed. "Um, I can't really talk about that."

Silence enveloped us for several awkward seconds. He wouldn't tell me about his eye. He wouldn't tell me about the kiss in the café. An ache grew in my chest. I'd trusted him, but it seemed like I was losing him.

"I know it's early, but are you hungry?"

It was hard to stay mad at that soft, smooth voice. It didn't erase the hurt or the anger, but it lessened the sense of urgency. I wanted answers, but I could be patient and wait for the right time. Why would he take me to dinner if he was in love with someone else? Maybe I wasn't completely losing him.

I shrugged, trying to act calm and collected instead of hurt and insecure. "We may as well beat the rush, right?" None of the restaurants in Maplewick was ever packed, but places would be quieter now than they'd be in an hour or two.

"What are you in the mood for?"

I hesitated, then went for it. I wanted him to tell me about lunch, so I created the perfect opening. "I haven't been to the Ryder Café lately. How does that sound?"

He didn't answer right away. I waited for him to say he'd already eaten there or to suggest an alternative, but instead, he said, "Sure. That sounds good."

"We can go somewhere else."

"No, if that's what you want, let's go there."

"But it's kind of pricey."

He bit his lip. "I'm sorry I'm always on a tight budget."

"I don't mind the budget. I know you're working yourself through school." The GI Bill allotted only fifty dollars a month for living expenses, so there wasn't much to throw at nights out. "How about burgers?"

He took my hand and lifted it slightly. "How about whatever you want?"

We ended up getting hamburgers, but Gary seemed distracted the entire meal. He answered my questions, but he didn't tell me anything new about the café, his eye, or what had happened at the warehouse.

After we ate, we walked to the aging art deco movie palace to see what was showing. Last weekend, it had been a Western, but Gary didn't enjoy watching cowboys shooting up Indians. Neither did I, so we'd skipped it. This weekend, it was a war drama. "What do you think?" I asked.

He frowned. "It's been a long weekend with a lot of war stuff popping up. Maybe another time?"

I didn't press it. "What do you want to do instead?"

He shrugged. "Sorry I'm not very good company tonight. Maybe I should take you home."

That would be two nights in a row of him taking me home well before I was due, and midterms were several weeks in the past, so it wasn't because of school.

"I talked to Monte about your dad's car," Gary said as he walked me home. "He doesn't think it was mechanical error. Someone intentionally cut the brake line."

My chest felt tight. "Why would someone deliberately hurt us? I mean, Daddy's a hard professor to take classes from, but he's hard on everyone. It's not like he singles anyone out."

"You might want to report it to the police."

The gravel of the driveway crunched beneath my shoes as we reached home. I wondered if I should call the police myself or try to convince Dad to do it. He hadn't believed Gary yesterday, but he might believe a mechanic. Maybe it was just a prank that had gone too far. But what if it wasn't? I rarely drove, so Dad had to have been the target—but why?

"We should probably lock the car in the garage instead of leaving it out," I said.

Gary took my hand and led me to the detached garage. He studied it for a minute. "You should replace that lock. It would be easy to pick."

I raised an eyebrow. "You're an expert on locks now?"

He glanced at the ground. "I know some are easier to get past than others. And if someone is trying to hurt you or your father, you shouldn't count on one as flimsy as that to keep your car safe."

I grabbed the lock and yanked on it a few times. It felt solid. The screws connecting the hasp latch to the garage door were firm, and the padlock had a strong shackle. "Seems tough enough to me."

Gary took two skinny strips of metal from his pocket. The sun had set, so I couldn't follow his movements, but in a matter of seconds, the lock was detached and in his hand. "Looks can be deceiving." He passed the lock to me.

"Where did you learn to do that?" Surprise at his ability mingled with shock at his proficiency.

He shrugged. "Sometimes at the school, we got sick of nothing but porridge for breakfast and nothing but boiled potatoes for supper."

"So you picked locks?"

He nodded.

"And stole food?"

"I'm not proud of it," he whispered. "But a couple kids died every year. Usually, it was consumption or influenza that finished them off, but most of them wouldn't have died if they hadn't been starving. Thieving might have saved our lives."

I felt two kinds of horror. My boyfriend had been a thief. And my boyfriend had been stuck in a school that fed him so poorly he'd had little choice. "What was the school like?"

Gary frowned. "That's in the past. It's probably better if it's left there."

"Gary . . . you never want to talk about your past. It's like you don't trust me. And that makes it hard for me to trust you."

I saw the hurt in his eyes as he answered. "You don't want to hear about my past."

"Yes, I do."

"It's ugly, Evie. Trust me—it's better if you don't know." He walked from the garage toward the front porch, and I followed.

"You can't help what happened to you."

"It's not just what happened to me. It's who I was." He paused and turned to face me. "I'm trying to change. I want to be better than I was. I do. I want to be worthy of something better, good enough for someone like you."

"Someone like me, or me?" I thought of the woman from the café. She hadn't seemed so different from me.

"You, Evie."

"Then why are you dating other women?"

His face crinkled in confusion. "What?"

Was he going to pretend it hadn't happened? If he couldn't even tell the truth about lunch, maybe it was time for me to break things off, even though it made my heart feel like it was being scoured with chain mail. I walked past him and stepped onto the porch. "Maybe we aren't right for each other."

He looked at the ground as I turned back. "I've never been right for you, Evie. I'm broken in a way that's so deep and so permanent that I'll never be right for anyone. But it was working despite all that, wasn't it?"

I put one hand on the door latch.

"I'm sorry, Evie." His voice was quiet. "You deserve better than me. I've known that for a long time, but I've kept hoping that somehow things would work out anyway." He ran a hand across his face, wincing as he swiped it over his swollen eye. "I'm surprised you've stuck with me this long. I'm a former delinquent and a psychoneurotic case."

I'd heard that term before, mostly applied to veterans coming home with combat fatigue or the shakes. Gary was holding down two part-time jobs and going to school full-time. I wouldn't call him a psychoneurotic case. But a liar? I was thinking about it. And a thief? For good reason, but yes, at least in the past. I didn't mind that he'd stolen food. But it hurt that he'd never told me about it, that he still wouldn't give more than a few words as explanation.

"I watched that woman in the café kiss you." I folded my arms across my chest.

"You saw that?" Tension faded from Gary's posture. "Is that what's been bothering you all night? Why didn't you say something? I thought you were upset because you'd decided I'm crazy."

I waited for him to tell me more, still wanting a reason not to end things.

"Evie, I'm not sure what you saw, but Mrs. Armellino didn't mean anything romantic when she kissed me. She's Italian. It's a cultural thing."

"Who is she?"

"Just another piece of the past. I knew her husband during the war."

"Knew?"

"He died." Gary's voice was soft again, haunted almost.

Or maybe he wasn't haunted. Maybe I was a pushover, and he was manipulating me. "Good night, Gary." I pushed the latch down and shoved the door open. I needed time to consider everything before I cut things off with him completely, but I didn't think I'd make any rational progress tonight. I'd thought I loved him. But I hardly knew him.

I took one step inside and stopped. Sir Redgrave lay on his side at the foot of the stairs. He'd been in his proper place when I'd left, so that meant Dad must have knocked him over. But Dad loved that suit of armor. I couldn't see him leaving it on the floor like that.

"Evie, is everything all right?" Gary's voice called from the porch.

I glanced behind me. From where he stood, he'd be able to see the toppled armor. All the secrets he kept from me hurt, but I was practical enough to know I couldn't lift Sir Redgrave back into place. He was too heavy. Dad might try, but he wasn't as strong as he used to be.

"Do you want me to help?" Gary asked.

I nodded. Dad had already had a hard weekend—someone sabotaging his car and Dr. Fontaine ruining the prospects for his book. I didn't want damage to his most beloved artifact added to the list. I walked over to the side table to set my purse down and glanced along the hallway.

Then I screamed.

A body hung by its neck from the banisters.

Dad.

Chapter Six

February 13, 1944

Someone died today, Evie. A guy from my squad, in a training accident. We know we're being trained as cannon fodder, but we haven't even shipped out yet. Nothing like this is supposed to happen at Camp Elliott. It seems like death cuts deeper when it's unexpected.

GARY RACED UP THE STAIRS to cut Dad down. My legs no longer seemed to work, and my hands and shoulders shook. I took a step toward Dad, but my knees trembled, and I had to grasp the entry table for support. Gary bolted past me and knelt over Dad's stiff form for several long seconds before he looked up at me. His expression said it all: Dad was gone.

I vaguely noticed Gary calling the police, then calling my aunt. He took me into another room and wrapped a blanket around me, even though it had been a warm day. He wrapped his arms around me, too, and held me, and neither of us said anything. I cried a little, but I still couldn't believe what I'd seen.

I'd already lost Mom and Clive. What would I do without Dad?

Gary helped me into a chair when a knock sounded, then he answered the door to reveal three men, two in police uniform. The one in a suit seemed to be in charge. He had salt-and-pepper hair, fine lines about his eyes, and a firm, steady manner. He and Gary introduced themselves, then disappeared into the hallway, I suppose to examine the body. After a few minutes, the man in a suit came back to the parlor.

"Evelyn Hampton?" he asked.

I nodded.

"I'm Detective Joel Iverson. I'll be conducting the investigation."

"Please have a seat, detective." My voice was tight, uneven.

Iverson sat across from me.

I swallowed a few times, trying to work up the courage to ask my question. "Did someone kill him, or did he kill himself?"

"That's still under investigation. Based on what I've seen so far, it looks like homicide. It appears that his wrists were tied behind him, and then the rope was removed later."

I nodded. The result was the same: Dad was gone. But knowing I hadn't left him alone when he was desperate enough to take his own life lifted part of my burden.

"Can you think of anyone who might have wanted to harm your father?"

"No. Who would do something like this?"

Iverson asked detailed questions about when I'd last seen Dad alive and what I'd done in the interim. He took careful notes as I told him about the brake line and about what the mechanic had said.

"You spoke with the mechanic?" Iverson kept his expression impassive and his voice courteous and direct.

"No, Gary did." I glanced over at Gary, who was answering questions from one of the men in uniform. But in contrast to how Iverson was questioning me with polite precision, the officer interrogating Gary showed a clear lack of respect in his body language and tone.

"And then you cut the body down?" The officer raised one eyebrow and pulled his lips into a scowl.

"Yeah," Gary said.

The officer huffed. "And it didn't occur to you that you were interfering with a crime scene?"

"It just seemed like the decent thing to do." Gary met my eyes for an instant, then looked back at the officer. "I didn't want Miss Hampton to have to stare at her father's body hanging from a rope any longer than she had to."

The police officer frowned and grunted as he wrote something in his notebook. "And that bruise? Where did it come from?"

Gary's jaw tensed. "I'd rather not say. It doesn't have anything to do with this."

"I'll be the judge of what does and does not have a relation to this case. What happened to your eye?"

Gary gritted his teeth. "It got in the way of someone's fist."

"Whose?"

If Gary answered, I didn't hear the reply. Aunt Janice burst through the front door and ran to me.

"Oh, Evie. Is it true?" She pulled me into an embrace.

I nodded and started crying again.

Dad was dead, and I had no idea why.

* * *

Over the next few days, I spoke with Detective Iverson again several times, but I didn't do much else. I couldn't bring myself to go through Dad's things, I couldn't imagine who might have wanted him dead, and I couldn't concentrate on anything without the void of his loss consuming me. I missed his huffs and hums as he read the paper, missed the way he connected everything to the Middle Ages, and missed the smile he always saved just for me. Things hadn't been perfect with my dad, but we had a shared history, and I'd always known he loved me.

Now I couldn't help wondering if things might have been different if I'd come home earlier or if I'd made him recognize the threat the brake line foreshadowed. I didn't feel safe in the home where he'd died, so I stayed with Aunt Janice.

Dad was killed on a Saturday. We held the funeral the following Tuesday. I wore a dull black dress and a plain black hat and sat between Aunt Janice and Gary while the pastor, the college dean, and my cousin Dale spoke of Dad's life and achievements.

Only when the casket was in the ground did it feel real and final. I'd been to my mom's funeral, but this one was so much harder. When Mom died, we'd had time to prepare, and we'd known why. We'd thought the cancer unfair, but the disease had, in a way, been a convenient place to lay our blame and our sorrow. Murder was different. Murder involved hatred and injustice that made a disease seem almost tolerable in comparison.

I stood beside the grave and accepted condolences from well-wishers. Some I knew, like my boss and my coworker. A few friends came, but most of them had to hurry home to tend their children. I'd never spoken to the majority of the mourners. They meant well, but I wished they would hurry and leave. Exhaustion covered me as thoroughly as the dim April sun, and I longed to leave the cemetery. Aunt Janice stood beside me, and even though she was slight of frame, her presence was a support. Gary stood nearby too, behind me, where he wasn't in line for the hand pats and murmured words of sympathy but close enough that he could be at my side in a moment if I needed him.

Professor Fontaine and his wife were the last of Dad's professional associates to pay their respects. Dr. Fontaine was younger than Dad by about ten years but had the same manner about him—confident, cerebral, and slightly conceited.

"My condolences, Miss Hampton."

"Thank you." I struggled to be polite to the man who had ruined Dad's last morning on earth. Someone else had wronged my father far worse than Dr. Fontaine, but Dad's work had meant everything to him, especially since Mom's death. I couldn't help but think that the lesser wrong would have troubled him just as much.

"I'm so sorry, Evelyn." Mrs. Hollingback, our neighbor, took my hand in hers as the Fontaines moved away. "Such a brilliant man."

That was what most people focused on—my father's mind. That was what he was most proud of, so perhaps it was fitting, but more important to me had been his dry sense of humor, his calm ability to solve problems as mundane as the case of a missing doll, and his contagious passion for old things.

"Let us know if you want to sell the place off," Mr. Hollingback said. "We'll give you a fair price, save you a lot of trouble."

I nodded, somewhat absently. I didn't know what I was going to do with the house I'd grown up in or with all Dad's artifacts. Planning a funeral and speaking with the police had been as much as I could handle in the days since his murder.

Frank and Dale chatted a few yards away, while Dale's wife, Fern, held their youngest and tried to keep the two older boys from getting grass stains on their Sunday best.

I felt more than saw Gary step closer, so I turned to face him. I hadn't noticed before, but the black suit he wore was tight in the shoulders and loose in the waist. Maybe he'd borrowed it from someone. A strain between us still existed after Saturday, but by unspoken agreement, we were acting like it hadn't happened. I needed a friend who wouldn't expect anything in return for the support I craved, and that was Gary. He'd visited me at Aunt Janice's daily, often just sitting beside me while I thought or while I cried. The kiss in the café didn't bother me quite as much now, but all his secrets did. Did I love him, or was it time to say goodbye? I didn't know, and I didn't trust myself to sort it all out while I was grieving.

He took my hand, and I didn't resist. "Evie, let me know what I can do. I never knew my father, but I buried my mother not long after I got back from the war. We weren't as close as you and your dad were, but it was hard. I imagine what you're dealing with is harder. I want to help. I'll do anything for you."

I looked down at his hand holding mine. "Right now, I could use a hug."

A hint of a smile creased his lips as he stepped into me. I leaned against his shoulder, catching a hint of citrus and cedar as his arms enveloped me. Some things hadn't changed—I still felt safe and valued in his arms. And I believed him. I could ask anything, and he'd agree to it. Unless my request involved talking about his past.

He released me as a car pulled up not far from the new gravesite. I turned and noticed the police markings. Detective Iverson and one of the officers from the night of Dad's murder got out and walked toward us. Did the police normally come to funerals? If so, they were late.

Frank and Dale ended their conversation and came closer. Iverson had questioned them, so there was no need for introductions.

Iverson nodded to me. "Miss Hampton, sorry to disturb you."

I forced a smile, wondering if he had news.

Iverson turned to Gary. "Mr. Redhawk, you're under arrest for the murder of Professor Ernst Hampton."

Chapter Seven

February 27, 1944

Dear Evelyn,

Sometimes you reach turning points in life, events that alter everything that follows. Sometimes it's a choice you make. Other times it's forced on you. Tomorrow, we leave San Diego, heading west, and I have a feeling nothing will ever be the same again.

"WHAT?" GARY'S MOUTH TWISTED IN surprise.

Iverson motioned to the police sergeant, who approached Gary with a domineering posture. Gary backed away, a hunted expression on his face.

I looked from my boyfriend to the detective and then back again. Gary wasn't a murderer. He couldn't have done it. "No—this has to be some sort of mistake."

The sergeant ignored my protest and fastened a handcuff around Gary's right wrist and tried to pull his other arm around so he could shackle it too.

Gary jerked his hand away. "I didn't kill Professor Hampton!"

The sergeant grabbed Gary's free hand again and wrestled it back. Gary yanked harder, and the sergeant detached a truncheon from his belt and raised it in warning. Tombstones and policemen boxed Gary in, leaving no escape. His eyes darted around, seeking help and revealing panic.

I took a step forward. Gary might have a few illegal talents and a traumatic past, and he might not have gotten along with Dad, but he wasn't malicious.

Frank held my shoulder to stop me. "Careful, Evie."

Gary tried to jerk free again, and the policeman whacked him in the back of the head. I heard the crack and shuddered. Gary turned and met my gaze as the sergeant finished cuffing him and hustled him away.

"Evie, I swear I didn't kill your dad!"

I wanted to believe Gary as they shoved him into the back of the patrol car, but deep down, I couldn't dislodge a nagging doubt. Gary and Dad couldn't be in the same room without instant tension. I'd always thought that was more Dad's fault, but what if I'd been wrong? Gary kept so many secrets from me, and he'd been acting strange since Friday. Was it because he was guilty?

The detective and the sergeant drove away with Gary. Warm tears trailed down my cheeks, and it was hard to breathe.

Frank released my shoulder. "That snake. Making sweet with you all the while planning to kill Uncle Ernst."

I wanted to protest, but the sob lodged in my throat silenced my voice.

Aunt Janice glanced at my face, then at the disappearing patrol car. "Nothing has been proven yet."

I swallowed and sniffed. "I've known him a year and a half, and he's never done anything to hurt anyone. He can't be a murderer."

Frank's face softened. "Evie, I know this is hard on you. But they wouldn't have arrested him without reason."

"Let's ask the lawyer, shall we?" Aunt Janice motioned Dale over. He'd seen the arrest, but had kept his distance until now. He handed his youngest back to his wife and walked over to join us.

"Dale, what type of evidence would the police need to make an arrest?" Aunt Janice asked.

"Probable cause. They need a reason beyond a hunch." Dale hesitated. "Given Uncle Ernst's position at Redgrave University, the police are likely under pressure to solve the case quickly. Probable cause could be as simple as a history of arguments."

"That's not fair." I put a hand on my hip. "Daddy and Gary fought but not any more than Daddy and Dr. Fontaine fought, and I don't see them hauling him off to jail."

Aunt Janice straightened her back. "If the police have more than a reasonable suspicion against Mr. Redhawk, I would very much like to know what it is."

"I think I can ask some questions for you." Dale's words surprised me. He'd never been fond of Gary—or at least not of the idea of Gary dating his cousin. He seemed to recognize that more explanation was needed. "I don't want them electrocuting the wrong person just because they're in a hurry. Everyone deserves a thorough investigation, even if he's guilty."

Dale didn't believe Gary was innocent, but he was willing to at least look at the evidence. That was a start, one I'd take. I couldn't wipe away the fear that Gary was guilty, but like Dale, I wanted to search deeper before drawing any conclusions. "I'd like to come too."

* * *

"Why did we arrest that Indian? Several solid reasons." The police officer with the truncheon, Sergeant Horton, leaned back in his chair and gazed at Dale and me from across his desk in the tiny Maplewick police station. "This may be our first homicide case in seven years, but we know how to follow motive and evidence. According to several witnesses, the suspect never got along with the victim. The victim's body showed signs of a struggle, and the suspect had a black eye—still does. Further, the suspect had lock-picking tools on his person the day of the crime."

I folded my arms across my chest. I'd always thought the police were supposed to investigate all possibilities, not jump to the easiest conclusion. "None of those things prove Mr. Redhawk committed the crime." Horton's casual dismissal of Gary as "that Indian" irritated me. Regardless of what he might have done, Gary was still a man, just as much as Sergeant Horton. "If he were trying to kill my dad, why would he cut the brake line in the car when he knew I would drive it Friday night?"

"Maybe he expected your father to drive it before you did."

"But why would he point out that it had been sabotaged?"

Horton rolled his eyes. "Because the cut brake line would be discovered regardless. He might as well play the hero and throw you off the trail."

"Gary was with me the night Daddy was killed—"

Horton fingered a notebook. "The coroner places the time of death as that afternoon, not that evening. You weren't with Mr. Redhawk then, were you?"

I shook my head, losing some of my confidence.

"Do you know much about the suspect's past?"

I shrugged. "I know he attended a shameful boarding school as a child, a different one as a teenager, then served honorably in the United States Army during the war."

Horton smiled as if amused. "Do you know why he joined the army?"

"There was a war on. I assume he was drafted, like most men his age."

Horton leaned forward. "No. He joined the army because a judge gave him a choice. He could go to prison, or he could enlist."

Was that true? My throat felt dry, and my hands felt clammy. Like most things from his past, Gary had never brought up the details of his enlistment.

"Detective Iverson had a conversation with Sergeant Rumsey of the Irving Police Department. Our suspect and his cousin were involved in the assault of one Orville Brown, a teacher at the Thomas Indian School. They tried to cripple him. That's the kind of riffraff we're dealing with. He's been violent before."

I looked at Dale, tangible dread growing in my stomach, weighing me down. When I looked back, satisfaction glinted in Horton's eyes. He wanted Gary to be guilty. Maybe Gary had tried to hurt a teacher, but what if there was more to the story?

Anger—and fear—spurred my next words. "By all accounts, the Thomas Indian School is a nefarious institution, and the children incarcerated there were routinely abused. Planning violence against the violent is far different from hanging an aging college professor."

Horton huffed. "There are also concerns about the suspect's sanity. Spent time in a prisoner-of-war camp in Germany." Horton looked right at me. "Is reported to have had a psychoneurotic episode recently." Nausea washed over me as I remembered what I'd told Iverson about the warehouse. "He won't tell us where he was Saturday afternoon, and he resisted arrest." Horton relaxed a bit, as if those two factors proved guilt. "And he's not taking to captivity well. Crazy as a loon, if you ask me. Someone like that could have a fit and hang a man, easy."

Detective Iverson walked into the main office and frowned when he saw Dale and me. "Miss Hampton. Mr. Bingham. Can I help you?"

Horton straightened in his chair. "Sir, I believe everything is fine."

"May I see Mr. Redhawk?" I needed to hear his side of the story about his forced enlistment and whatever had happened with the teacher. And I wanted to apologize for telling Iverson about his disagreements with my father and the episode at the warehouse. I'd just been answering the detective's questions—I hadn't thought I was giving evidence against him.

Iverson frowned. "Under normal circumstances, I would allow it. But I don't think that would be safe at present."

"Gary wouldn't hurt me."

Iverson raised an eyebrow. "Miss Hampton, the answer is no. Mr. Redhawk is being most uncooperative. Psychoneurotic cases can be unpredictable and dangerous. I won't risk your safety."

I was about to argue when Dale broke in. "I thought you arrested Mr. Redhawk because of the lock-picking tools and his less-than-amiable relationship with my uncle. That sounds like something premeditated. Now you're suggesting the murder happened during a fit of insanity. Which is it?"

Iverson gave Horton a hard stare. "Discussing the case a little freely, were we?" Then Iverson turned back to Dale. "The investigation is ongoing. We're exploring both possibilities."

Both possibilities. Gary had made a plan and killed my father. Or Gary had gone crazy and killed my father. *Both* possibilities, but not *all* possibilities. They weren't looking at any other suspects.

Chapter Eight

March 15, 1944

Dear Clive,

I'm worried about Mom. She hasn't been herself lately. She still puts on lipstick and smiles at the right jokes, but she falls asleep in the middle of the afternoon and doesn't bother with the crossword puzzle anymore. She skipped her last two hair appointments. You remember how regular she was—every Friday morning for about twenty years. It's as if someone cut her energy in half. I want to help, so I'm trying to take over some of her normal tasks. But all my cooking and cleaning doesn't seem to be making her any better.

I WENT BACK TO AUNT Janice's house for the night. I took a few bites of a casserole one of her neighbors had brought over, but I didn't have much of an appetite. "He wouldn't have needed to pick any locks. Daddy didn't like that Gary was dating me, but he would have opened the door for him."

All evening, I'd been voicing random thoughts about the case, but I hadn't convinced myself of anything. I didn't want it to be Gary. I didn't want to live with the knowledge that I'd misread him so completely. Nor did I want him sent to Sing Sing Prison and executed.

But it could have been Gary—I had to admit that, especially when I considered his past and how he'd hid so much of it from me. "Why wouldn't he tell the police where he was all afternoon?" If Gary were innocent, why didn't he cooperate? And why had he resisted arrest?

Aunt Janice didn't seem hungry either. She'd pushed bits of casserole around, but not much had made it to her mouth. "Maybe he doesn't trust the police."

"Maybe not." Would I trust the police if I'd been forced into a horrible boarding school, then forced back to chains and the lash after finally escaping? "He said he was trying so hard to change, to leave the past behind him."

"A week ago, I would have told you he was doing an admirable job." Aunt Janice set her fork on the edge of her plate.

"And now?"

Aunt Janice shook her head. "I don't know. But I do know one thing. You like that boy. If they execute him for murdering your father and you aren't absolutely convinced that he's guilty, you'll always wonder. That's the type of doubt that can haunt a person the rest of her life."

"It sounds like Detective Iverson and Sergeant Horton aren't looking at anybody else. Just trying to decide if he was sane or crazy when he did it."

"The Maplewick Police Department is understaffed and underfunded. They're used to burglary and parking violations, not violent crimes. They think they have their murderer, so they'll move on to the next case. But if you were to prove that Mr. Redhawk couldn't have done it, they'll have to look elsewhere."

I clung to her idea. "You mean establish an alibi?"

Aunt Janice nodded.

I stood and grabbed a piece of paper and a pencil. After losing both parents and a brother, I wasn't going to let Gary go without a fight. I couldn't wait around for the police to have a change of heart—it might never come. "Daddy was alive when I left the house at noon. He was dead when I got home at . . . eight o'clock? Nine?" I hadn't had my watch on.

"Mr. Redhawk picked you up at a quarter past five. You just have to establish everything from noon to five-fifteen."

I wrote a few notes.

12:00—Daddy still alive
12:15—Gary leaves the restaurant
5:15—Gary at Aunt Janice's house

I had five hours to cover.

* * *

"Sure, I saw Mr. Redhawk on Saturday. Came in that afternoon wondering 'bout your car, Miss Hampton." Monte Frye used a rag to wipe at the grease on his hands.

"Do you remember what time?"

Monte's dark face looked thoughtful. "Right before closing. Between four-thirty and five."

"Did he stay long?"

"Maybe twenty minutes. He wanted to see the brake line, talk through the different ways it mighta been cut." Monte turned and rummaged through the odds and ends set on a bench along one of the shop's walls. He returned with a part—the brake line. "See, someone cut this. Neat cut, not all the way through, so anyone driving might not notice the brakes wasn't working at first. But you slam on them brakes, and the leak gets worse. Hard to control the car after that, ma'am."

I took the thin metal tube when he handed it to me. Had someone tried to kill Dad and make it look like an accident? Then gone a more direct route when that had failed and tried to make it look like suicide? "Could it have been a coincidence? Something sharp on the road? A problem from the factory?"

Monte pursed his lips. "Ma'am, I've been a mechanic for fifteen years. For two of those, I was over in Europe with the Red Ball Express. I've seen a lot of damage to cars, but I ain't never seen anything like that just happen, not even in a war zone with land mines and artillery shrapnel. Someone deliberately cut that line."

The spooky feeling I'd had after the car problems on Friday was back, stronger than ever. "Did Mr. Redhawk have a swollen eye when he came to see you?"

"Yes, ma'am."

"Did he say why?" He'd told the cops someone had punched him. If I could figure out who, maybe I could establish more of Gary's alibi.

"I asked, but he laughed it off, saying he poked a little too much into someone else's business."

"Did he say who?"

"No, ma'am."

I bit my lip. Gary wasn't the meddling type, at least not the Gary I knew. Who could he have provoked enough to earn a black eye? "Did he mention anything about where he'd been that day or where he was going?"

"He said he'd tell you 'bout the car when he saw you. Sounded like he was planning to see ya soon."

That was what I'd assumed, that he'd come to Aunt Janice's house directly from the shop. He wouldn't have had time to get to my house and back, let alone subdue and hang Dad in such a short time.

"The car's safe now, miss. I've repaired it, better than new now."

"Thank you for your help, Mr. Frye. How much do I owe you?"

* * *

Memory of the brake failure and certain knowledge of the saboteur's intent made me hesitate behind the wheel of Dad's New Yorker. I took a deep breath, started the car, and cautiously pulled onto Redgrave Avenue. A few blocks later, I concluded that Mr. Frye had been completely accurate—the brakes worked perfectly now.

I still needed to account for Gary's whereabouts from twelve fifteen until four thirty. But none of the students at Redgrave's library remembered seeing him at his usual study spot. His employer at the grocery store said he'd worked his normal morning shift but had gotten off at eleven thirty. Elva Ryder remembered seeing him at the café, but she didn't know the woman he'd met and hadn't overheard anything about where he might have gone afterward.

I drove up the hill on Pine Street and parked to the side of Mr. Norton's house. Gary's shack was in plain view as I got out, opposite the yard from the outhouse and a rusting water pump. The police might have already searched his room, but they would have been looking for evidence of guilt, not innocence. I knocked on Mr. Norton's door, planning to ask if he'd seen Gary on Saturday and if he'd let me look through Gary's things.

No one answered the door. I hadn't expected the two other bachelor boarders to be home, but I'd thought Mr. Norton might be around, or Wanda Murphy and the kids.

I knocked again and waited. If no one was home, my search for Gary's alibi was at a standstill. I turned to go but stopped when I heard a baby cry. The sound had come from inside the house, and though it was quickly hushed, it proved someone was home.

"Wanda?" I knocked harder. Maybe she was sick, and that was why she hadn't answered the door. But Gary's life was on the line. I needed to ask if she'd seen anything. "Wanda, it's Evelyn Hampton. Please, I need to talk to you."

A small sound drifted out to me, but no one replied.

"Please, Wanda. It's important."

When there was no response, I tested the doorknob. Locked. I went around back and climbed the two steps to the other door, the one that led to the kitchen. That knob was locked too, so I knocked. "Wanda? Sarah?"

I could come back later, but something was off. If Wanda was sick, why hadn't she sent Sarah to tell me to come back another time? And if they were all sick, maybe they needed help.

I rattled the back door, frustration and worry pumping through me. I had heard the baby cry, hadn't I?

I sat on the wooden steps and stared at the grassless patch where Gary usually parked his motorcycle. Maybe I'd wait for Mr. Norton or one of the others. I wasn't eager to go back to Dad's empty house. I guess it was mine now, or would be after probate. Strange how so many of my friends were struggling, squeezing in with in-laws or other couples, trying to find room for growing families in a place with few options, and I had a large, completely-paid-for home but no family to share it with.

Wind made the empty clothesline hum and the old hammock sway. Where would Gary go on a Saturday afternoon? He was thrifty, so I doubted he'd gone to the movies or the bowling alley. I'd never seen him drink, so that ruled out the bars. Besides, he would have reeked of cigarettes if he'd gone there, but he'd smelled pleasant Saturday evening. Could he have gone to a different spot in the library?

I let out a sigh. Who was I kidding? If Gary had an alibi with witnesses, he would have told the police already. My efforts were a crusade doomed to fail.

The door creaked as little Sarah Murphy pulled it open. The instant she saw me, she looked over her shoulder and ducked her head as if she knew she'd be in trouble.

I reached my hand out, and she came to sit beside me. "Sarah, why didn't you answer the door? Couldn't you hear me?"

"Mommy said not to say anything."

"Why not?"

Sarah frowned. "Because of Daddy."

"Is your dad home?"

"No. He went away."

"Did you see Mr. Redhawk on Saturday afternoon?" I wasn't sure if a four-year-old could tell Saturday from any other day, but I asked anyway.

Her petite face scrunched up in concentration. "Saturday. That was the day Daddy went away."

The first time she said her dad was gone, I'd assumed she meant for the day. Charlie Murphy was taking classes at Redgrave, in the same program as Gary. "He hasn't come back?"

Sarah shook her head.

"Did you see Mr. Redhawk?"

She nodded. "Daddy got in a fight with Mommy. Then he got in a fight with Mr. Redhawk."

"Sarah, come inside this instant!"

I turned at Wanda Murphy's voice coming through the window. Sarah stood and went inside. I followed her through the kitchen and into the dimly lit hall.

"I told you not to talk about that. And I told you to stay inside."

I'd seen Wanda a dozen times over the last year, and she'd always been kind, if shy. Today, her voice was different—there was a harshness in it but also worry. Something wasn't right.

"Mrs. Murphy?"

Silence.

"Mrs. Murphy, please. I need to talk to you. The police think Gary killed my dad. If I can't prove he was elsewhere Saturday afternoon, they might execute him. And I know they won't have the trial right away, but they're keeping him locked up, and I'm afraid he's not doing so well." The boarding schools of his childhood sounded little better than a jail, and then he'd spent part of the war as a prisoner of the Germans. Was the Maplewick jailhouse doing the same thing the old warehouse had done to him? Or worse? Was that why Sergeant Horton had said Gary was acting crazy?

Mrs. Murphy finally stepped into the hallway. I sucked in a breath heavy with surprise. Bruises lined her jaw, and her left eye was swollen and discolored.

She had a black eye, just like Gary.

Chapter Nine

April 3, 1944

> *Dear Evelyn,*
>
> *Do you ever feel like you have to relearn everything? We're doing more training here, with men who fought the Japs and know their latest techniques. If we get into a bayonet skirmish, we're supposed to hold our rifles differently than they taught us at boot camp so the Japs can't lock our blades. We're supposed to sleep with our hands by our knives because the enemy likes to infiltrate when it's dark and the guy over in the next foxhole can't see well enough to help if a Jap crawls in on top of you.*
>
> *Sometimes one little piece of knowledge from the right person can make all the difference. Knowledge, and a good knife.*

WANDA SAT IN THE PARLOR of Mr. Norton's home, rocking her baby. Sarah sat beside me on the couch. "Charlie's not usually violent. I'm not sure what happened on Saturday."

I hesitated. "Did he . . . did your husband give you those bruises?"

Wanda sniffed and nodded.

Charlie Murphy had always been polite to me. He took an obvious interest in his children, and he'd seemed extremely fond of Wanda. I wouldn't have suspected a streak vicious enough to leave bruises on his wife. "Has it happened before?"

Wanda didn't answer right way. "Once. He'd been back from the war about a month. We were happy to be together again, of course, but it was an adjustment too. We got married right before he joined the Air Corps, so we hadn't really lived together. Just a week here and a weekend there. I'd raised Sarah on my own up until then. There weren't many choices for housing, nothing we could afford, so we were living in my parents' attic. My brother and his wife were living there too, plus my little sister." Wanda shook her head. "They could hear every time we moved. We were trying to get to know each other again, but it was hard in a house so crowded."

Wanda turned to her daughter. "Sarah, why don't you go play outside?" Sarah raced for the yard.

Wanda hesitated, then spoke again. "He had nightmares. Still does. But he had a bad one when he'd been back four weeks. I tried to wake him up. He, uh, he grabbed my wrists and pinned me down on the bed, put his elbow into my neck." She reached up to rub her throat. "I couldn't breathe. I couldn't yell for help. I was terrified that he'd kill me right there in my parents' house."

"Did someone come?"

"He snapped out of it. Apologized. Promised it would never happen again. I asked him what'd been going through his head. He said he'd thought I was a Nazi. Me. In my nightdress." Wanda frowned. "It was like he wasn't seeing what was right in front of him. Seeing something in the past instead."

Her description reminded me of Gary in the warehouse, only Gary hadn't attacked me. "What did your husband do during the war?"

"He was a waist gunner on a B-17. His plane was shot down in late '44. He got captured. Sent to a camp. He doesn't talk about it much, but I think the civilians who captured him almost lynched him. Someone from the Luftwaffe came and took him before they finished him off. It didn't get easy after that, but the crash and the capture—I think that was the hardest time for him. Most of the crew didn't make it out, so he lost a lot of friends."

"What happened on Saturday?"

Wanda looked out the window. "We'd had a disagreement that morning. It's hard sometimes, living here, with no privacy. Four of us in one bedroom. Sharing a bathroom with four other men besides Charlie."

Guilt nibbled at me. I had so much space at my house. I'd talked about letting out rooms before, not because we needed the money but because so many people couldn't find a place to live. But Daddy hadn't wanted to take in boarders, and I hadn't pressed him. Now that he was gone, I supposed I could do what I wanted. But before I worried about the house, I had to search out Gary's alibi.

"After lunch, Charlie went outside with Sarah. He was supposed to be studying, but they played a while. Then he fell asleep on the hammock. I put the baby down for a nap and thought I'd try to ease the strain we've been having. Be playful, tease him like I used to when we were first married, before he went overseas. But I must have startled him. He started yelling in German, and he slugged me. I told Sarah to run inside and lock the door. Charlie pushed me, slammed me into the tree. That's how I got these." She pointed at her jaw.

"Mr. Redhawk heard us and told Charlie to stop. Charlie smacked him a good one, then Mr. Redhawk wrestled him to the ground and held him there until he calmed down."

"Did he snap out of it?"

Wanda nodded. "Started crying. Apologizing. He'd thought he was back in Germany, fresh from the crash. Said he didn't want to get captured again, that he'd die before he surrendered." Wanda sniffed. "The war's over. But he's still fighting."

Scary how certain memories could break a person open and make them feel like someone who loved them was their enemy. "Sarah said he went away."

"Yes." Wanda bit her lips. "We don't want word to get out. Nobody will hire a psychoneurotic case. But we've got the kids to think about. What if he'd attacked Sarah instead? Or the baby? What happens when Charlie Junior gets a little taller and surprises him? Will he see some German civilian with a pitchfork and hurt him? Kill him, thinking he's defending himself?"

Psychoneurotic case. That was why the term had been on Gary's mind Saturday night. "Where did Charlie go?"

Wanda shifted the baby. "Mr. Redhawk said Professor Gerstner is doing research on battle fatigue. They went to borrow Mr. Garcia's phone and called him. He told Charlie to come over and stay at his house for a few days. They'll try out some of the professor's ideas. Charlie's a good man." She nodded as if she needed to convince herself, not just me. "He'll get over this."

"What's he doing about classes?"

Wanda frowned. "Maybe he's going. I haven't talked to his professors because I don't want anyone to see what he did to me. And I don't want them to know he's still having problems. The war in Europe ended three years ago." She took a deep breath. "I had Sarah tell Mr. Norton that I was ill. I only leave the room when everyone's gone or asleep, send Sarah to put the diapers in the washroom and to fetch things. I figured Mr. Redhawk is in most of the same classes as Charlie. He can tell him what he missed."

"Gary's in jail. He's falling behind in classes too." And missing school seemed mild in comparison to what Horton had reported. Gary had seemed so fragile at the warehouse. What was jail doing to his mind? But I understood now why Gary hadn't told the police the truth about his black eye. He'd been protecting the Murphys. "I'm trying to figure out where Gary was on Saturday. If I can prove he was elsewhere, then he couldn't have killed my dad, and they'll release him." I glanced at the sleeping baby and caught sight of Sarah through the window. "I think he was trying to protect you, so he didn't tell the police how he got his black eye. They think my daddy gave it to him. I know it's hard, and it might affect Charlie's prospects, but will you tell Detective Iverson that Gary was here?"

Wanda nodded.

"When did it happen?"

"Not long after lunch. I'd finished the dishes and fed the baby, put him down for a nap. It was probably twelve thirty when I went outside. Mr. Redhawk's motorcycle was here then."

That meant Gary had come back after lunch at the café. "How long did he stay?"

"Three o'clock. I remember because I was surprised the baby had slept that long. I was worried we wouldn't get in and he'd cry."

"Wouldn't get in?"

Wanda smiled. "Sorry, I'm getting ahead of myself. When I told Sarah to lock the doors, she did. She's still young. Easy enough to slide the lock down. But it's an old lock, and it sticks. She couldn't push it up again. We couldn't get in the back door, and I didn't have my keys, so we couldn't get in the front door. We knew someone else would come home eventually, but maybe not before the baby needed to eat again. Mr. Redhawk went to his room and came back with some thick wires. Had the front door opened in no time. He and Charlie talked, then Charlie packed and left. Mr. Redhawk made sure the kids and I were okay, then he left too. Said he had a few things to do."

"Did he say where he was going?" If he left the house at three and didn't show up at Monte's until four thirty, his alibi was incomplete.

"No."

I knew why Gary had a black eye, why he'd been carrying lock-picking tools, and where he'd been for most of Saturday afternoon. But there was still a hole. Where had he gone between helping the Murphy family and checking on my car?

Chapter Ten

April 5, 1944

Mom broke her favorite china tea set this week. She dropped it on her way to the parlor when Aunt Janice came to visit. Said it was too heavy, but she's never had a problem with it before. I'm worried about her, Clive.

I can't believe I'm saying this, but you're missed. Are you ever homesick for Maplewick? Do you like being a soldier?

I HAD AN APPOINTMENT WITH Dad's lawyer that afternoon. Dale was waiting inside when I arrived at Mr. Montpellier's office. I gave him an embarrassed smile. "Seems odd, doesn't it, that Daddy made his will with someone else when he had a nephew with a law degree?"

Dale shrugged. "He probably made it before I passed the bar or while I was away during the war. Maybe there wasn't any reason to change it." Like Frank, Dale had joined the navy. He'd spent most of the war stationed at Pearl Harbor.

I sat next to him and glanced around the waiting room. Landscapes on canvas and lots of dark wood. Just the sort of place where Dad would do business. "I might have a job for you. Gary needs a defense lawyer."

Dale had grabbed a magazine, but he put it back down. "Mr. Redhawk? I'd like to help you, Evelyn. But I can't promise much. The evidence seems damning. And I don't have a lot of experience in criminal law."

"I know it's not your specialty, but there aren't many lawyers in Maplewick. And you at least have a sense of fair play. Sergeant Horton, on the other hand . . ."

Dale grunted. "Guilty until proven innocent, in his book."

"I'm working on that. I've figured out where Gary was most of Saturday afternoon. From twelve to about three, and from four thirty on." I told him about my visits to Mr. Frye's shop and Mr. Norton's boardinghouse.

He seemed impressed. "I'll be glad to defend Mr. Redhawk, but figuring out where he was for that hour and a half will help. A lot. That's enough time to arrange a murder."

"Maybe Detective Iverson will let you talk to him. Gary wouldn't tell the police where he was because he was trying to protect Charlie. But I talked to Wanda. She agrees that proving Gary's innocence is more important than keeping what happened a secret."

Dale took a pen from his shirt pocket and fiddled with it while he thought. "Maybe. Seems like an odd thing, though, to risk execution just to save a neighbor's reputation. The police might not ask for details. It might be enough to tell them he was there."

"Her bruises are still visible. And I don't think Gary trusts the police."

Dale nodded. "I'll see if I can get him to trust me."

The bell on the office door jingled as Frank came inside. I stood, and he gave me a hug. "Evie, good to see you. How are you holding up?"

"Mostly, I'm just trying to stay busy."

Dale chuckled. "She's trying to prove Mr. Redhawk innocent."

Frank raised an eyebrow. "Really?"

"Doing a good job so far. We now know how he got his black eye, and it wasn't Uncle Ernst's fist. And he used the lock-picking tools earlier that day when the neighbors locked themselves out of the house with the baby still inside. More heroic than sinister."

Frank crossed his arms. "But if he has nothing to hide, why didn't he just tell the detective?"

"Gary hasn't had good experiences with the police in the past," I said. "I think he puts them in the same category as Bureau of Indian Affairs officers. And there were complications with his neighbors. He probably didn't feel it was his place to say anything."

Frank grunted. "So, have you done it yet—found an alibi?"

"No. There's an hour-and-a-half hole."

"Plenty of time to hang a man."

"It wasn't him." I'd had my doubts at first, but not anymore.

"If you say so." Frank gave me half a smile. "How you really doing?"

I hesitated before I answered. First my mom. Then my brother. Now my dad. Before the war, a gathering of the Hamptons and the Binghams would have included eight. Now there were just three of us. "Right now, I'm trying to be brave. Maybe later, if I keep pretending long enough, it will start to be true."

Mr. Montpellier, a distinguished-looking man with white hair and impeccable posture, invited us back to his office to read the will. Dad had left $5,000 to each of my cousins. The remainder of the estate was to be equally divided among his living children. Since Clive was gone, that left me.

"It must have been an older will," I said as the three of us left. "From before Clive was killed."

"But after your mom died." Frank put a hand on my shoulder. "It's a sad business. I'm sorry, Evie."

I nodded, not trusting my voice. The funeral had felt final, but this . . . this made it even clearer that my family was gone. Grief had been like the ocean since Dad was killed, coming in waves—sometimes a gentle ache, sometimes an overwhelming despair. Right then, the pain was a tsunami.

"Have you been home much?" Frank asked. "I imagine that big house feels pretty empty."

I swallowed and took a few deep breaths. I could survive this. I knew I could. "I'm going over there now to pick up more clothes. I've been staying with Aunt Janice."

"How long will you be there?" Dale asked. "I'll go to the jailhouse and call you with any news."

"I'll wait there for your call."

* * *

When I pulled into the driveway, a middle-aged man waited on the front porch. As I stepped from the New Yorker, I recognized him from Dad's funeral, but I couldn't remember his name, not even when he removed his gray homburg hat. He was on the pudgy side, with long sideburns, perhaps to make up for the missing hair on the top of his head.

"Miss Hampton." He gave me a polite nod as I walked up to him, then stuck his hand out. I took it briefly. His palm was damp. "I'm Raymond Richards, Redgrave's chief archivist."

"What can I do for you, Mr. Richards?" I stood on the porch, not wanting to invite a stranger inside. Too many frightening things had happened lately for that, and I wasn't up to hosting anyone, even if it was just for a cup of tea.

"I don't want this to sound too forward, but have you decided what you'll do with your father's books and artifacts?"

"I haven't thought that far ahead yet." Until a half hour ago, I hadn't known for sure that they were part of my inheritance.

Mr. Richards ducked his head slightly. "Well, Miss Hampton, you should know that Redgrave University will gladly accept any donations. The broken pipe last winter damaged several of our collections, including a shelf of books on medieval Europe."

"You want my daddy's books?"

"We would be happy to accept them, yes. As well as any of his artifacts. I can't make guarantees, of course, but I could certainly petition for a collection to be named after him. Wouldn't it be grand? The Professor Hampton collection? With a suit of armor beside our medieval history section?" Hope lit his face.

I tried not to laugh. He was trying to bribe me—Dad's artifacts in exchange for a memorial on campus. Richards's delivery was tacky, and yet, Dad would have loved to have a section of the library named after him. I could hear him chuckling to himself and muttering, "Not even Professor Fontaine has part of a library named after him."

"I'll think about it, Mr. Richards."

"I admired your father a great deal, Miss Hampton. We spent a lot of time together, and he was ever so passionate about his work. And so careful with his research. If only all historians took such care to be as precise and accurate as Dr. Hampton."

"Thank you. He took great pride in his work."

Mr. Richards nodded. "Yes, he did." He took a step down, into the gravel of the driveway. "If you do decide to donate his library, we can only take unmarked books. I'm not sure you're aware, but your father sometimes wrote in the books he read." His face showed distaste, as if writing in books was a crime worthy of time in the stocks as punishment.

I looked away, hoping he wouldn't notice my amusement. Dad marked every book he read, though he bought them faster than he read them. I wondered if Mr. Richards was less interested in the books and more interested in Sir Redgrave and the other artifacts and reproductions Dad had collected over the years.

"Your father told me he was ordering a crossbow replica. Said he'd show it to me when it came. I don't suppose . . ."

My eyes wandered to the trunk of Dad's car, where the crossbow still lay in its cardboard box. I quickly looked away, hoping Mr. Richards hadn't noticed, but his eyes focused on the trunk with longing.

"I'm afraid I haven't made a decision about my daddy's things yet. I'll be sure to consider your offer."

Mr. Richards turned back toward me. "Thank you, Miss Hampton. I know your father would rather them be in Redgrave's care than sold at a pittance to private collectors."

I wasn't so sure, but I didn't reply. He replaced his hat and nodded his goodbye, and I watched him drive away. There was something unsettling about how he'd looked at the trunk, like a knight in battle craving his enemy's blood.

I hadn't been alone inside the house since Dad had died. I turned the key in the lock and hesitated, worried. The house was safe now, but someone had gotten in and murdered my father. Could they get in again?

My neighbor, Mrs. Hollingback, came outside and waved across our yards. I waved back, glad for a reason to postpone going inside but embarrassed too. This was my house. Was I scared to go inside the house I'd grown up in? The house I now owned?

Yes, I was.

I sighed and pushed down the latch.

Inside, the only sound was the ticking of the grandfather clock in the parlor. I closed the door behind me and stood before Sir Redgrave. Dad loved that suit of armor. He'd paid a lot for it back before the war. Money had been tight, and Mom had been furious. I liked Sir Redgrave, but I wasn't sure I liked him enough to keep him. I could picture him tumbling over onto a toddler and doing serious damage with his battle axe. More than a suit of armor, I wanted a home with a family. Maybe Mr. Richards would get his wish after all.

What would I do with the house? I didn't want to be reminded of the murder every time I saw the banisters. It wouldn't be hard to find boarders, but I didn't want to run a boarding house. I'd rather work at the bursar's office. Maybe I could hire someone to run the place in exchange for free rent. There were four bedrooms upstairs. I glanced in the parlor. It wouldn't be hard to change into a bedroom. Nor would the formal dining room or Dad's study.

I went there next. Twenty-four shelves of books stared back at me from four sets of six-tiered bookshelves that reached almost to the ceiling. Dad had probably read about a third of them. Some I would want to keep, but most I could let go with few regrets. Dad loved his books, and I read, but I preferred literature over history. He loved his music too, preferably at full volume. A record still lay on the turntable, so I moved the tone arm over and switched the player on. Dvorak's violin concerto filled the room.

I ran my fingers along the books. I'd turn the unread ones over to Mr. Richards and keep the ones Dad had marked up. Reading his annotations would be like having a conversation with him, so I'd pick up his favorites when I missed him.

I pulled out a book about medieval archery and flipped it open to find a note in Dad's tiny handwriting. *All fletchings on any given arrow must be from the same bird wing. All left or all right.* He'd circled the part of the text saying, "Goose feathers were a common source of fletchings," and drawn an arrow to his note. That was my father in a nutshell—full of knowledge, always wanting to correct, even when there wasn't an error, just a statement he could add more details to. He probably drove his students crazy. His fellow professors too.

I'd gotten used to it a long time ago. Whatever I said, there was something I hadn't remembered. Whatever I knew, it was only a start. It had kept me humble, I guess. But it had also made it hard to have confidence in my abilities. I didn't know *everything* about *anything*, so why should I try to discuss it? Why teach? Why write? Dad had given me freedom when it came to choosing where to work and who to date but not the assurance that I was wise enough to make a good decision.

I put the book back on the shelf, and the bookshelf tipped forward, toward me.

Books slid from the shelf and thudded to the ground. I threw my hands up to protect my face and scrambled back, but the bookshelf crashed down before I cleared the area. It landed on my right leg, just below the knee.

Pain made it hard to breathe. And so did fear. The bookshelves had stood in this room for two decades. Their contents had changed, but they'd never tipped before, not even when Clive or I had climbed them as children. Had someone done something to them, just like the car?

The sturdy bookshelf had me trapped and vulnerable. Was it the murderer again? And was he still inside? I had to get free. I tried scooting back, but the decorative upper molding of the shelf bit into my skin and held me. I tried to push the bookcase up, but the solid maple was too heavy. Heavy enough to kill had I been slower or had it tipped more quickly.

I tried not to think of how serious my injury might be, other than a hope that my leg wasn't broken. Warm blood trickled down my skin, but it hadn't pooled on the floor, so I didn't think the bleeding was dire. I stacked scattered books underneath the shelf on either side, hoping that would take some of the pressure off. I couldn't squeeze enough in to lift the bookcase, but the piles held the shelf as I turned my leg. I groaned as the pain flared, and I held back a sob. I had to twist and push on my skin, shaping my leg so it was flush with the ground, but after the initial torture, I could slide out.

I hobbled to my feet. More blood ran from the cut now. I grabbed the handkerchief from my pocket and pressed it against the gash, cursing at the pain. It hurt to put weight on my leg, but it hurt anyway.

My gaze swept the room. I grabbed the dagger-like letter opener from Dad's desk and held it in front of me because I was worried someone would come to finish me off.

I'd been using light from the windows, but it was nearly dusk. I switched on the lamp, and the lightbulb's glow filled the room.

The curtains fluttered.

Aunt Janice had gone around the house the night of the murder, making sure windows were closed and doors were locked. But the study window was open an inch. I tightened my grip on the letter opener and limped to the window. I pulled the curtains open completely, but there was no one there. At least not anymore. I pushed the sliding pane down, but something kept it from shutting all the way.

That was when I noticed a silvery strand of wire snaking in from outside. I reeled it in, about ten yards' worth. I tugged on it to test its strength, trying to break it, but it just bit into my hands. The wire led to the bookcase. It had been tied to a set of little nails pounded into the top, where the bookcase would have rested against the wall.

My throat went dry, and my heart rate spiked.

Someone had been watching, standing outside the window, waiting to pull the bookshelf over on top of me.

Chapter Eleven

April 10, 1944

Dear Evelyn,

Do you remember the time you locked the window in Dad's study so I couldn't sneak back in after I left to meet that blonde? I had to either knock on the door and wake up Mom and Dad, or get you to let me in. When I woke you up, you threatened to tattle unless I did all your chores for a month. You drove a hard bargain, Evie. That's why I hid the spiders in your sock drawer. Did you ever figure out it was me? I'm sorry now. It was petty and wasn't very nice. But it sure made you scream.

I LIMPED TO THE KITCHEN and traded the letter opener for a butcher knife. I wasn't sure I'd be any good with it if I had to defend myself, but I felt less vulnerable with something sharp in my hands. Clive's combat knife would have been better, but they hadn't sent his weapons home with his personal effects.

The bleeding from the cut was worse now. I tied a clean dish cloth around my leg and made an ice bundle to ease the swelling.

I hobbled into the hallway, planning to call the police. The party line was busy. I could have asked Mrs. Hollingback to get off the line—it was an emergency—but I hung the phone up quietly instead. I wanted a few minutes to think.

When I'd found out the car problems were intentional, I'd assumed Dad was the target. But what if I'd been the target all along? I hadn't given anyone reason to kill me—had I?

My next thought was bitter, like hearing that the city walls had been breached by a besieging enemy. What if Dad had discovered the murderer's intentions and had been hung to keep silent? What if his death were my fault?

I sat in the hallway with ice on my leg, a knife in my hand, and dread in my heart.

I wasn't safe. Assuming the same person was behind the car, the hanging, and the bookshelf, this was the third attempt. The police had it all wrong. It couldn't be Gary, because Gary was in jail.

The phone rang.

"Hello?"

"Evelyn?" Dale's voice came over the line. "I've been trying to reach you for a while."

"Did you see Gary?"

Dale didn't answer right away.

"Well, did you?"

"He wouldn't talk to me, or even look at me. They brought him into the interview room, and he just sat on the floor, legs pulled up to his chest and arms around his knees. For most of the visit, it was like I wasn't even there."

The same thing had happened at the warehouse. Chill beyond the ice on my leg crept across my skin. "For *most* of the visit?"

"Yeah. Eventually, I grabbed his shoulder. Thought maybe I could give him a shaking up, get him to focus. He pushed me across the room and grabbed one of the chairs, held it like a weapon."

"Did he hurt you?"

"No. Horton came in and whacked him a few times with a truncheon, then took him away."

Warm tears came to my eyes as I thought of Horton beating Gary.

"Evelyn, I'm sorry. It looks like Mr. Redhawk is guilty, but maybe I could convince a jury he committed his crimes while temporarily insane on account of what he went through during the war. He'd still get locked up, but he wouldn't be executed."

"Gary didn't do it."

"Look, Evelyn, not everybody talks about it, but a lot of men came back from the war crippled. And I don't mean missing a leg or blinded in one eye. I mean their head's not right. Just one of those things. Tragic for everyone involved. I saw it a few times in the navy. Some got better. Some didn't."

"Gary's going to get better. He's come so far."

"Maybe." Dale sounded unconvinced. "But even if he's innocent— and the evidence says he's not—I really think you should stop seeing him.

You're not safe with someone like that. He could have a bad day and kill you because he thinks you're some Nazi guard."

For a few seconds, Dale's warning hit a nerve. The Murphys were in love, but that hadn't stopped Charlie from hurting Wanda during a psychoneurotic episode. Was Gary dangerous? I pushed my doubts aside. Gary hadn't threatened me at the warehouse, nor at any other time in the year and a half we'd been dating. "Gary is innocent."

"There's an hour-and-a-half hole in his alibi."

"He's innocent, Dale. Someone tried to kill me tonight—and it couldn't have been Gary because Gary's in jail."

"What?" Dale's voice changed from his professional lawyer voice to his concerned cousin voice. "Someone tried to kill you? Are you all right?"

"They pulled a bookshelf over onto my leg. I've got a cut, nothing big."

"Stay there. I'm coming over."

Frank came to the door ten minutes later. "I heard you got hurt."

I showed him my leg and explained what had happened with the bookshelf and the wire. Frank rummaged through cupboards until he found the rubbing alcohol. I winced as he cleaned and bandaged the cut.

"Thanks," I said once he had finished.

"Yeah." He held up the box of Band-Aids. "Wonder how many of these your brother and I went through when we were younger."

"Enough to keep Johnson & Johnson in business, I imagine." The two of them had played rough, with each other and with me. "I miss him."

Frank put everything away. "Yeah, I do too."

Dale knocked, and I let him in. Then I went to the phone. "I'm calling the police. They have the wrong man in jail." Gary was innocent and ought to be freed. Beyond that, my worry for him was growing. I wasn't an expert on battle fatigue or psychoneurosis, but if being in jail was giving Gary flashbacks and making him unable to have a conversation with his lawyer, I wanted him out of there fast.

The line was busy again. I slammed it down.

"You could say you have to call the police." Frank gave me half a smile. "They'd probably understand."

"I came by to get clean clothes. I'll do that first."

"Wait." Dale put a hand on my elbow. "Let us look around and make sure it's safe."

I hobbled up the stairs behind my cousins. After Frank checked my closet and under my bed, I packed a small suitcase. When I came back down, Frank and Dale were elsewhere. I put a call through to the police station. "Can I speak with Detective Iverson, please?"

About the time I finished the phone call, Dale came in from the front, and Frank came in from the back.

"None of the doors or windows look forced," Frank said. "But they're old locks."

"It might have been someone Daddy knew well enough to invite inside the night of the murder. But that doesn't explain how he got into the study tonight." I folded my arms across my chest. Even with my cousins nearby, I was spooked.

"I don't suppose it could have been a woman?" Frank asked.

Dale shook his head. "It would take a lot of muscle to hang someone as heavy as Uncle Ernst from the banisters."

A knock sounded on the door. Dale went over and let Detective Iverson in.

"Good evening, Miss Hampton, Mr. Bingham, Mr. Bingham." Iverson's eyes went to the banisters where my father's body had hung, then to me. "You said it happened in the library?"

"In the study. Follow me." I led him past the kitchen, dining room, laundry room, and bathroom to what had been Dad's private sanctuary. I flipped on the overhead light, even though the desk lamp was still on. "I was looking through the books when one of the shelves fell toward me." The bookcase still lay on the ground, with books scattered about, some opened, some closed. "When I tried to shut the window, I noticed wire. One end led outside. The other was attached to the top of the bookcase."

I stood to the side while Iverson looked over the mess. "Where did you leave the wire?" he asked after a few minutes.

"It's still attached to the nails in the bookcase, isn't it?" I hadn't moved it.

Iverson scooted books out of the way and crouched down next to the shelf. "I don't even see nail holes."

"What?" I bent to take a closer look, wincing as the pain in my leg flared. Sure enough, the wire had disappeared. The back corner of the bookcase was angled rather than square, as if someone had sawed off a thin strip of wood to remove the wire and nails. "It was there." Had the man who set the trap come back to retrieve his wire? I'd assumed whoever was responsible had fled. My skin crawled. Had the man watched me ice my leg and use the telephone?

The detective seemed skeptical. "You're eager to see Mr. Redhawk set free, aren't you?"

"Yes." My stomach roiled. Gary was innocent, and even without a full alibi, I had hoped to get him released tonight, but now, the evidence that someone else had attacked me was gone.

"Eager enough to jump to the wrong conclusion?"

"What do you mean?" Did he think I was lying?

Iverson stood, his face set and unemotional. "You've had a rough few days. Losing your father, your boyfriend as the primary suspect. The incident with the car. And then a bookcase falling on top of you and hurting you."

"The bookcase didn't fall. It was pulled."

Iverson didn't answer.

"I saw the wire!" I could see the disbelief in his face. Worse, both my cousins mirrored his expression. They'd seemed to believe me when Frank had bandaged my cut and Dale insisted they search the house. But the wire's disappearance had brought in doubt.

"Then where did it go?" Iverson asked. "You've been here the whole time, haven't you?"

I nodded. "Yes. But I was in the kitchen. I turned the water on. I got ice from the deep freeze. I was on the phone and went up to my bedroom. I don't think I locked the front door when I came in, and a record was playing. Someone could have come inside and taken the wire without me hearing them." That was why Dad's study was back here—it was quiet, regardless of what was happening in the rest of the house. And the same was true in reverse—noise from the study rarely made it past the laundry room.

Dale motioned Iverson over. The two of them spoke with their backs to me, but I could hear every word.

"You aren't going to use this against her, are you?" Dale asked. "I know she's fond of Mr. Redhawk, but I can't see her pulling a stunt like this just to get him off."

Iverson shook his head. "I imagine the bookcase really did tip, but probably from normal causes rather than anything malicious." Iverson glanced at the overturned bookcase and the spilled books. "No doubt she saw something, and in a frightened state, thought it was wire."

I was furious, but I wasn't sure what to say to change their minds. I walked over to the window hoping to see wire or evidence of wire. But I saw nothing unusual. The window wasn't locked, but I couldn't recall if I'd locked it or not after I'd pulled the wire inside. I'd snuck in and out of that window before. Clive too. Most people over five feet tall could climb through from the ground below. Anyone could have waited outside the window, pulled the bookcase over, and then snuck back inside to remove the evidence. A thick forest lay beyond our property line where they could have hidden, or they could have ducked into the garage. Returning to take the wire and cut out the nails would have taken only minutes.

Someone had tried to hurt me. The detective—and my cousins, apparently—thought I was making it all up. And Gary was still stuck in jail with all the ghosts from his past.

Chapter Twelve

May 15, 1944

Yes, Clive, I assumed you were behind the spiders. Did you notice how often the temperature fluctuated while you were showering over the course of the next four months? There's a saying about revenge and serving it cold. If you're finally apologizing for the spiders, I guess it's time for me to apologize for stealing the hot water for dishes and flushing the toilet repeatedly while you showered.

THE NEXT MORNING, I WORE trousers to cover the bandage on my leg and drove back to Mr. Norton's home. He was there, and when I explained my purpose, he gave me the key to Gary's shed.

"I hope you can prove he's innocent. I don't think he'd do something like that."

I smiled my thanks. Mr. Norton knew the same Gary I did, not the Gary from the past who had tried to maim one of his teachers. Dale had told me about the case the night before, after Iverson had left. According to Sergeant Horton, in 1942, Gary and his cousin had knocked Mr. Brown in the head, then gotten caught before they could give him anything more serious than a headache. Gary had been capable of hurting someone then, and he'd fought in a war. But I knew what I'd seen. The wire had been real. Gary couldn't have pulled the bookcase over on me yesterday, and I didn't believe he'd killed Dad.

The shed was padlocked from the outside. I'd met Gary in the fall of 1946, but I'd never been inside his room, if it could be called a room. He always met me on campus, in the yard, or somewhere in town. When he'd first told me where he lived, I'd thought he was joking, but it wasn't really so odd, living in a shed. I'd heard of people living on old buses, in boxcars, or crammed into normal homes with a dozen people to a room. The shed was probably better than some of the barracks or tents he'd stayed in while enlisted.

I unlocked it and went inside. The shed had once housed Mr. Norton's gardening supplies and woodworking tools. That was all cleared out now, replaced by a surplus army cot, a small desk with a metal chair, a trunk, and an old sheet acting as a partition. His sketches caught my eye immediately. I'd given him drawing paper for Christmas, and it looked like he'd used every last sheet, then pinned them to the building's wooden walls. Murky light from the shed's only window revealed trees, flowers, mountains, birds, toads, and squirrels, all drawn in pencil, covering the walls.

Only one of the subjects was human. I looked at her, recognizing myself. It must have been a memory from winter, because I had a knitted scarf looped around my neck. My eyes were closed, and my face was tilted up. I'd expected to find pinups, not me, in what I suspected was the moment before he'd kissed me.

I pulled my focus from his drawings to his desk, hoping to find a note or a list saying where he'd been from three o'clock to four thirty last Saturday. My task wasn't going to be so simple. A pile of textbooks sat on one side of his desk, a stack of homework on the other. An empty tin can served as a pencil holder. I glanced through his work, but I didn't see any random notes written in the margins. I wondered how much of it was late because of the police. He'd pulled all A's last semester. Would his professors work with him? Or would his grades suffer because he'd been accused of a crime I knew he hadn't committed?

I looked around. Nothing in the small trash can. The nailed-up sheet hid a closet of sorts. He didn't have many clothes hanging on the closet rod, and only one spare pair of shoes lay on the floor. Wooden boxes screwed into the side of the shed held socks and other items of clothing. Nothing behind the peg that held his jacket. Nor was there anything under the neatly made cot. That left the trunk.

Going through his things without asking felt wrong. But I was doing it with the best of intentions, and I was curious. He kept so many secrets from me.

I lifted the trunk's lid and leaned it against the wall of the shed. It wasn't quite as neat as the rest of the room. The top was cluttered with blank stationery and lined paper, rent receipts, and check stubs. One side held out-of-season clothes: army-issue boots, an olive-drab Eisenhower jacket, a knitted cap, a few pairs of gloves.

I held the hat, remembering a walk we'd taken in January. He'd noticed I was shivering, so he'd taken the cap off his head and pulled it over mine, then leaned in to steal a kiss, banishing the chill with his lips.

I searched further, past a pair of wool blankets. A small box held a lapel pin issued to servicemen for honorable discharge—it was an eagle, but everyone called it a ruptured duck. In the same box was a campaign ribbon, a combat infantry badge, checkerboard insignia patches for the 99th Infantry Division, and dog tags. I also found a bundle of letters, a beaded sash, and a pair of moccasins. The moccasins were in good condition—but child sized, far too small for Gary's feet. A folder contained his birth certificate, discharge papers, and a diploma from the reform school. A jar tucked into the corner held about ten dollars in coin and bills.

I flipped through the letters—about two dozen of them. I didn't have any right to read them, nor did I know how they would help me find an alibi. But I wondered—who did Gary write to? He rarely spoke about his family. He'd never met his father, his mother was dead, and he had no known siblings.

I hesitated, then pulled the top letter from an envelope with a return address in Provo, Utah.

March 3, 1948

Dear Red,

My first question won't surprise you. Are you taking good care of my motorcycle? I know I always joke about wanting it back when I finish school. Now I'm not sure I'll need it. It's one thing to drive your wife around on the back of a motorcycle, but when you add in things like groceries and a baby, maybe it's not the best option for a family man. Yeah, that's an announcement.

The next question won't surprise you either. Have you proposed to that girl of yours yet?

I paused. Had Gary written to someone about *me*? I checked the return address again. Gary had never mentioned a Lukas Ley, but I assumed he was someone he knew from the war because anyone else would have called him *Gary* or *Mr. Redhawk*. As far as I knew, Gary hadn't even thought about marriage. Was I completely wrong, or was his friend just teasing him?

I hear you about the nightmares. Yes, I still have them. And, yes, I wake my wife up sometimes. Belle says it's good practice for when the baby comes.

Did Gary have nightmares? He'd never told me about them. Was it because he didn't trust me? Because he was ashamed?

The letter went on from there, talking about Mr. Ley's classes at Brigham Young University—mostly business and science—and plans to welcome a baby to the family in the summer.

I sorted the rest of the letters, looking at the return addresses on the opened envelopes. Three from Mr. Otetiani Amedon. Eight from Mr. Lukas Ley. Two from Mr. Winston Monson. Five from Mr. Chuck Samson. Three from Mr. Edwin Cooper. And two from Mrs. Cora Armellino.

Mrs. Cora Armellino. The woman who'd kissed Gary at the café on Saturday. I wasn't sure I wanted to know what she wrote to him, but she'd seen him the day of the crime. No one else seemed to know where Gary had been during that missing hour and a half, but maybe she did.

I opened the first letter with trembling hands.

January 17, 1948

Dear Mr. Redhawk,

We've never met before, but I tracked down your address through Lieutenant Cooper. I believe both of you served with my husband, PFC David Armellino, in the 99th Infantry Division during the war. I received the telegram that he was missing in late December 1944. Then one telling me he was killed a month later. Both promised to send more information as it became available, but I've never learned the conditions of his death, aside from what the newspapers reported about the Battle of the Bulge.

Some days, that was enough. My husband died somewhere in Belgium fighting against the Nazis. But lately, Davey Jr. has been asking about how his daddy died. He's almost seven. I don't know how much I should tell him, but at present, I can't tell him much of anything because I don't know what happened.

Were you there the day David died? I've been reading through his letters again, and you're mentioned in many of them. He always called you Red. It sounds like you knew each other well, from training and into Belgium. I know it's been a few years, but I am driven to find someone who can tell me more about how David died. You would do much to ease a widow's grief if you could provide me with more information.

Sincerely,

Cora Armellino

I read the next letter right after.

April 5, 1948

Dear Mr. Redhawk,

I thank you sincerely for your reply of March 27th. David always spoke well of you. He said he felt like he could depend on you to keep him safe in the foxholes, but when you didn't answer right away, I must confess I gave up hope of hearing from you. I understand you've been busy with school, and I appreciate your willingness to tell me about David.

I can meet you at the Ryder Café in Maplewick on Saturday, April 17. I'll leave Davey with my mother, as I'm not sure how much he should hear at his young age. I'll plan to be there at half past eleven.

Until then,

Cora Armellino

That explained why he'd met Mrs. Armellino. She'd thought Gary could tell her how her husband died. That didn't explain the kiss, but I understood why he'd agreed to see her. How could someone say no to a plea like that?

I wished he would have told me. He'd never shared any details about the war, and while part of me knew the details would be awful, part of me wanted to hear them anyway. I wanted to know what he'd been through. I wanted to understand him better, and knowing his past seemed the best way to do that.

I looked at the return address on the envelope. Mrs. Armellino lived in Buffalo. I could write to her, ask her if Gary had told her anything about his plans for the afternoon. But it would take a few days for the letter to arrive, it would take time for her to answer, and it would take time for the letter to return to me. All the while, Gary would be sitting in jail, bombarded by whatever memories left him in another place and another time. I could call or send a telegram, but I wasn't sure she had a phone, and it would be hard to ask my questions in a telegram.

Or, I could take the car. The drive was just under two hours.

Chapter Thirteen

June 10, 1944
> *Evelyn,*
> *You were behind the crazy showers that summer? No, I didn't know it was you. I thought it was just problems with the boiler. The spiders only lasted a few minutes—don't you think punishing me all summer was a little harsh?*
>
> *What I wouldn't give for a real shower now, even one interrupted by bursts of cold, then scalding water. I'm on a little island. Just arrived a few days ago. We're not supposed to give specifics, like names, but suffice it to say it's warm, and we see a different set of stars at night. Rainstorms are abrupt here, and strong. Almost as strong as a shower. So when it rains, we all strip down, grab our soap, and try to get clean before it ends. The storms leave as suddenly as they come. Last time, I got caught with soap on me when the rain stopped. My scalp still itches.*
>
> *And for the record, I'm not a soldier. I'm a Marine. There's a clear distinction. You wouldn't call some peasant with a crossbow a knight, would you?*

I parked Dad's New Yorker on a side street in Buffalo. My leg had been aching since the run-in with the bookcase, and it was worse after driving for nearly two hours. The pain built as I locked the car and took the first few steps, then seemed to quiet down a little as I walked along the street of narrow row houses, looking for number 105.

As the throbbing in my leg decreased, the anxiety in my chest skyrocketed. The letters had seemed innocent enough, and Gary had said the kiss wasn't romantic. But I still felt threatened. My heart was vulnerable when it came to Gary. What if he didn't care for me the way I cared for him? What if "that girl of yours" Mr. Ley had mentioned in the letter wasn't me but Cora Armellino? Logic told me I was being ridiculous. Mrs. Armellino's first letter hadn't arrived until January. Gary hadn't written back until March, after the date of Mr. Ley's last letter, so he couldn't have meant Mrs. Armellino.

Maybe I was perpetually insecure because I'd been jilted before. The boy I'd fancied in high school had flirted with me, then asked another girl to Prom. The man I'd been engaged to during the war had broken things off when he'd secured a different fiancée in England. Clive had told me I was better off without someone like Second Lieutenant Roland Roth. I'd wanted to believe him, even when the pain had been fresh and raw, and now I was glad I hadn't married Roland. But sometimes I wondered if things would have been different if I'd been prettier or more interesting or if I hadn't been so distracted and sobered by my mother's illness.

I took a deep breath and knocked on Mrs. Armellino's door. Part of me hoped no one would answer. Then I wouldn't have to face the woman who might have beaten me in an unspoken competition for Gary Redhawk's heart. But worry for Gary was bigger than my fear of getting hurt again.

A little boy of about seven answered the door.

"Davey?" I asked, remembering the name from the letters.

He grinned and nodded.

"Is your mother home?"

The boy turned from the door. "Momma!"

She wore her soft curls unpinned today, but it was the woman from the café who approached a few moments later. "Hello?"

Awkwardness heated my face. "Are you Mrs. Cora Armellino?"

"Yes."

"May I ask you a few questions about your lunch last Saturday with Mr. Gary Redhawk?"

Her eyebrows scrunched together in confusion. "How do you know about that?"

"It's kind of complicated. But Mr. Redhawk has been accused of a crime, and I'm trying to establish an alibi."

"Really?" Her puzzled expression grew more pronounced. "He seemed so nice. And my late husband spoke so highly of him. I never would have suspected he's a criminal."

"I don't think he is a criminal." I blatantly ignored the assault incident from before the war and the theft. "But the evidence is against him, and he's an easy target."

Mrs. Armellino nodded. "I guess I ought to invite you in, Miss . . . What did you say your name was?"

I hesitated, but I didn't want to lie. "Miss Hampton." Would she recognize my name from her conversation with Gary?

"Come in, Miss Hampton." I didn't notice much of a reaction. I guess that meant Gary hadn't mentioned me. She pulled the door open and led me into a cluttered sitting room. "Have a seat. I'll put the kettle on."

While she was away, I glanced around the room. A framed picture of Mrs. Armellino and a young man in formal clothing sat on a small table, next to a lamp and a folded newspaper.

"My late husband," Mrs. Armellino said when she returned. "He was killed during the war."

I nodded, not wanting to admit I already knew that because I'd read her letters.

When I didn't say anything, she continued. "That's why I tracked Mr. Redhawk down. He and my husband served together. I wanted to know what happened. Mostly for my son's sake, but also for mine."

"You hadn't met Mr. Redhawk before?"

Mrs. Armellino shook her head. "No. We exchanged a few letters. My husband mentioned him when he wrote home."

"Did you learn what you wanted?"

She nodded.

"Will you share it with me?"

She glanced down the hallway, perhaps making sure her son was out of earshot. "They knew each other during training, were friends even then. The whole division went to England in the fall of 1944, then crossed the channel and went to Belgium. They arrived in November, I think. Everyone called them the battle babies because they were new and inexperienced. I knew all that already, but Mr. Redhawk confirmed it."

The teakettle whistled, and she excused herself to go get it.

"Mr. Redhawk shared a foxhole with my husband," she said when she returned. She sat and poured a cup of tea for me. "He said they were spread thin because no one thought the Germans were strong enough to attack again. But they did. Hit them hard. They held, then pulled back to protect these villages. Krinkelt-Rocherath. They're near Elsenborn Ridge. Mr. Redhawk said it was an important position because if they held, they'd stop the German advance. But if they didn't hold, the Germans would have access to the road, and they'd capture supplies and such."

Mrs. Armellino took a sip of her tea. "Everyone was retreating to Elsenborn. My husband's squad was helping to hold the villages until everyone withdrew. They were among the last to retreat, took a lot of fire from the Nazis. David died. Mr. Redhawk and Mr. Cooper ran out of ammunition, and then they got captured."

"Did he say much about his capture?" I'd always wondered about it, but Gary had never elaborated.

"No. Just that they got separated from everyone else and didn't have much of a choice." She sipped her tea again. "It was important, Elsenborn Ridge. Mr. Redhawk called it the northern shoulder of the bulge. Everywhere else along the line, the Germans pushed us back. But Elsenborn held."

I smiled softly, admiring Gary even more. He'd told Mrs. Armellino just enough for her to know her husband's death had been worthwhile, that he'd fought for something vital.

"And now you know what to tell your son?" I asked.

"Yes." She frowned. "I think it was hard for Mr. Redhawk to talk about it. But it means so much to me, to know that David's death wasn't in vain."

Gary would have paid a price for that conversation. Discussing the memories afresh would have made them fester. Then he'd gone home and been punched by Charlie Murphy. No wonder he'd seemed out of sorts on Saturday and hadn't wanted to watch a war movie.

I sipped my tea—it was strong and a little too sweet. "Do you have any idea what Mr. Redhawk was planning for the rest of the day? I have most of the afternoon and evening filled in, but I'm missing more than an hour. If I want to prove him innocent, I need to account for everything."

"Can't he tell you?"

"I'm not allowed to visit him."

Mrs. Armellino nodded. "No, I don't suppose they'd let a reporter in." I hadn't told her I was a reporter, but I didn't correct her assumption.

"What is he accused of?"

"Murder."

Mrs. Armellino gasped. "It can't be true."

"Help me prove it."

She nodded. "It's just that some of it was supposed to be secret. He was taking his girl out to supper that night. You could track her down, and I'm sure she'll confirm she was with him."

"There's still a hole."

She pulled her lips to the side. "I'm not supposed to say."

"Mrs. Armellino, if you don't help establish his alibi, he could be convicted and executed. I'm not sure what the secret is, but I think you had better tell me."

"If you promise not to print it."

"I promise."

She smiled. "He had an item on layaway at a jewelry store. He said he was going to make a payment."

Gary, buying expensive jewelry? That didn't sound like the Gary I knew. "May I ask how that particular information was brought up?"

Mrs. Armellino brought her hands into her lap and glanced at the ring on her left hand. "My husband has been dead for three and a half years, and I haven't lived with him for five. I miss him, and I wish he had come home, but I'm also getting lonely. I might have suggested we meet again. Davey needs a father." Her gaze went to the hallway, where I assumed her son was, somewhere farther in the house. "Mr. Redhawk was making it clear that he's already in a serious relationship. Pity. Good-looking man, in his way. Seems nice enough." She looked at me again. "What newspaper did you say you were from?"

I'd been hoping she wouldn't realize her mistake. Now she would feel I'd misled her, and I guess I had. "I didn't tell you I was a reporter. I'm a friend trying to help."

Her eyes narrowed. "What's your given name, Miss Hampton?"

"Evelyn."

She let out a bitter chuckle. "Of course. You're the girlfriend. You needn't worry. He's quite devoted to you."

"If he's so devoted to me, why did he let you kiss him?"

"You can't blame a girl for trying, can you? I shouldn't have. I think it made him uneasy." She fiddled with her teacup. "I'm sorry. It's just that I recognize a good man when I see one, and good men who aren't already married seem to be in short supply lately."

Chapter Fourteen

June 15, 1944

Dear Clive,

Mom's still acting tired all the time. You know how compulsive she's always been about keeping the house clean? I found cobwebs in the dining room and sticky spots on the kitchen floor. I wouldn't call the house unkempt, and I'm trying to keep things up to her normal standards. But she's always been so clean. You've seen her beat rugs and polish silver and scour sinks—like she's going to war against dirt and tarnish. She still cleans, but it seems like it's all halfhearted now.

IT WAS PAST CLOSING TIME for all the Maplewick jewelry stores when I made it back from Buffalo, so I resumed my search the next morning. It was Friday already, and I was due back at work on Monday. I was running out of time to investigate, but more than that, I was worried about Gary. He'd been in jail for parts of four days now. I wanted him free.

I took along the picture Gary had given me a few months ago when I'd asked for one.

"I don't know why you want my picture, but here it is," Gary had said as he'd handed the photo to me. It was a few years old, of him in his army uniform, facing the camera with a soft smile. "Do I get one of you now?"

"Maybe if I had any recent ones that I thought were even slightly flattering."

He scoffed. "You're telling me a pretty girl like you doesn't have any good pictures?"

"None that don't make me cringe." Or that didn't include an ex-fiancé.

"Then I guess I'll have to make one in my mind." His eyes caressed my face, and his fingers played along my neck. He held me for a long moment, then kissed me, one of those kisses that left me feeling all dreamy and content and wanting to snuggle up next to him for the rest of the day.

"There," he'd whispered. "That's my favorite of all your expressions. I'll keep that in my head."

The fancy jeweler on Main Street looked at the picture and shook his head. "No, I don't recognize him. And Saturday was slow. I would have remembered."

I got nearly the same response at the watchmakers and at the other jewelry store closer to campus.

Finally, I went to Baumgartner's Jewelry. The bell on the door jingled softly as I went inside. Mr. Baumgartner shuffled out from the back room. He was probably in his sixties, a widower with tufts of white hair on the sides of his head but none on the top.

"Can I help you, miss?"

I handed the picture to him. "Was this man in your store last Saturday?"

Mr. Baumgartner pulled a pair of glasses from his shirt pocket and put them on. "Ah, Gary Redhawk. Good lad, that one. Yes, he was here. Why do you ask?"

"He's been accused of a crime, and I'm trying to establish an alibi. Do you remember when he came?" The store sold clocks and watches as well as jewelry. I hoped that meant Mr. Baumgartner paid attention to the time customers came and left.

Mr. Baumgartner took off his glasses. "Yes, he was later than normal. Usually comes by at about noon. But I didn't see him until seven minutes past three last Saturday."

"Does he come by often?"

"Oh yes. Every other week, when he's gotten a paycheck. He makes a payment and does any odd jobs I might have for him. I put his work against the cost of the ring. He ought to have it paid off soon. Doubt I'll see as much of him when that happens," Mr. Baumgartner chuckled.

I took the picture back when he handed it to me. "He's buying a ring? By doing odd jobs for you and making layaway payments?"

"That's right. He wants it paid off by his sweetheart's birthday. He's ahead of schedule, I believe." Mr. Baumgartner looked from the picture I held of Gary to my face. "Say, when is your birthday, miss?"

"June."

"And your name is Evie?"

I nodded.

He chuckled. "Then I'd wager that ring is for you, isn't it? And I've said too much."

Gary was buying a ring for me?

Oh. *A ring.*

I wasn't the only one who had thought about marriage. Gary hadn't just been thinking about it; he'd been doing something about it. My knees no longer felt like they would support me as thrill and surprise and a hint of regret swirled around inside me. "May I sit down?"

Mr. Baumgartner motioned to a stool. "Of course. Please have a seat, Miss Evie. I suppose that's short for Evelyn?"

I nodded as I sat in front of a display of gold chains and pearls. How could I have doubted Gary? He was every bit as serious about our relationship as I was. Or at least he had been. I might have ruined it Saturday night when I'd told him we weren't right for each other. Yet, despite my hurtful words, he'd done all he could to help me in the days after Dad's murder, at least until he'd been arrested.

Gary didn't have time for odd jobs around Mr. Baumgartner's shop. He had homework and two part-time jobs. But he was sacrificing his time and his money, two things he had in short supply, for me. I hoped he wasn't getting anything too fancy. I didn't need something expensive. "Can I see the ring he's buying?"

"Absolutely not. I've already ruined most of the surprise." Mr. Baumgartner sat on a stool next to me.

"How long has he been making payments on it?"

"Since October."

Six months. That felt like a long time. "He's never talked to me about getting married. I was beginning to think he wasn't interested."

Mr. Baumgartner frowned slightly, a sad expression that made him look even older. "He has worries, you know."

Gary was quiet around most people, so Mr. Baumgartner's assertion surprised me. "Does he talk about his worries with you?"

Mr. Baumgartner's face softened into a smile. "It takes a long time to polish all the glass in this shop, and he's been coming in for six months."

"What does he worry about? Does he think I'll say no?"

"He doesn't tell me everything." Mr. Baumgartner glanced out the window at a couple passing by. "My son served in the Great War. Came home with a few ghosts, if you will. I think Mr. Redhawk has a few ghosts too. Nightmares that wake him up at night. That's why he lives in a shed. He jokes about it, but he likes his privacy when he wakes up screaming."

"Does he wake up screaming often?"

"Often enough to hesitate before he asks a woman to share his bed."

Would that matter to me? No. I would take Gary, nightmares and all.

Mr. Baumgartner leaned an elbow on the display case. "He's a little worried about other things too. Finding a place to live. Providing for a family. Knowing how to be in a family. We learn a lot from how we're raised. It only takes one person to break the pattern, but those things we see from the time we're small—it's hard to change them." Mr. Baumgartner straightened his spine and met my eyes. "He said a few things last Friday and Saturday made him worry. Moments in time he couldn't remember because it was like he was in the past. A friend doing something similar and harming someone. He's worried about those ghosts—he doesn't want to hurt anyone."

"I was there on Friday. He didn't get violent."

"Good. For both your sakes. I'm afraid that lad's had a hard past."

"A hard past doesn't rule out a happy future."

Mr. Baumgartner smiled again. "I like you, Evie. You might be just what Mr. Redhawk needs."

I held back a laugh. "You're just saying that because you want Gary to buy me a ring."

"No, I'm just saying that because I want Mr. Redhawk to be happy."

That was something we had in common, and I was grateful for his kindness. "How long was Gary here on Saturday? You said he arrived a little after three?"

Mr. Baumgartner nodded. "Yes, and left around four thirty."

Gary's alibi was complete.

Chapter Fifteen

Letter of June 15, 1944, continued

I'm sorry if I insulted you by calling you a soldier instead of a Marine. I promise I won't do it again. But you both use rifles, don't you?

Dorothy got married last week. She barely knows the man, but he's shipping overseas soon, and they didn't want to wait. Lois got engaged, but they haven't set a date yet. Roland still writes, and he expects a furlough after training, so I'll see him in the fall. Daddy seems to like Roland, maybe even more than I do. Mom is more indifferent, but she's indifferent about a lot of things lately.

I WAITED ON A LONG bench at the police station. The clock on the wall showed one o'clock in the afternoon. I'd been there for two hours while Detective Iverson double-checked the alibi. I suppose he wanted to make sure I wasn't lying. Or maybe he wasn't ready to admit that he'd arrested the wrong man.

Sergeant Horton walked past me, a smirk on his face. "Ah, Miss Hampton. Anyone try to kill you lately?"

I folded my arms across my chest, seeing no humor in his question. Someone had pulled that bookcase over on me. I'd been foolish not to keep a better eye on the evidence, but I hadn't made it up. Dad would have said something scathing in return, but I couldn't think of anything, so I gave Sergeant Horton my best glare and didn't answer.

I fiddled with the cuffs of my blouse and waited some more. I should have brought a book. A newspaper sat on the bench beside me, but I'd already read it cover to cover. I hadn't thought it would take so long for Iverson to call Mrs. Murphy, Mr. Baumgartner, and Mr. Frye. Or maybe he was visiting them in person—Mrs. Murphy didn't have access to a phone. What if she'd decided to protect her husband instead of protecting Gary? It would take only one person changing their mind to doom Gary to more jail time—maybe the electric chair.

Finally, Detective Iverson opened the door to his office. "Miss Hampton?"

I stood.

He motioned me inside and offered me a seat across from his desk.

"Miss Hampton, the alibi checks out. Under normal circumstances, I would be ready to release Mr. Redhawk, but there are a few things you should be aware of."

"What things?"

"He hasn't tolerated jail very well."

"I don't imagine he has, not after his time in the residential school and as a POW."

Iverson frowned. "It's more than that. I believe he is suffering from severe psychoneurotic episodes. I'm not sure it's safe to release him. It might be better to send him to an institution."

"An institution? Like an asylum for the insane?"

Iverson nodded.

I sat back in the chair, stunned. The police had arrested the wrong man, and they'd broken him. An ache grew in my throat—somewhere deeper too. "Locking him up is what triggered all this. You can't put him in an asylum. That'll make it worse. Give him his freedom and a few days to recover, and I'm sure he'll be fine." I wasn't sure he'd be fine, but I wasn't about to share my doubts with the police.

"Miss Hampton, he may not have murdered your father, but he's dangerous, capable of malice. The Irving Police Department made that clear."

"That was six years ago. He was a broken teenager back then. Now he's a veteran and a college student. He's trying to put the past behind him, and if everyone will just give him a chance, he'll do good things now. I know he will."

Iverson pursed his lips. "You aren't a neutral source when it comes to Mr. Redhawk."

"And you are?"

"I've tried to be."

"And Sergeant Horton? Has he tried to be fair when it comes to *that Indian*?"

Iverson didn't answer. I hoped that meant he recognized his department's shortcomings.

"Will you release him now?"

Iverson stood. "Yes. But I want you to be careful. He might not be the same person you remember."

That last line was like a dagger twisting in my heart. I loved the Gary I remembered. More now, after I'd dug into his past and seen how kind he could be to the Murphys and the Armellinos. Things had been going exactly where I wanted them to go—Gary was planning to propose. But then a murder had robbed me of my father, and a false accusation had hijacked and changed the man I loved.

The man I loved. I hadn't used that phrase before, not even in my head. But now that I was uncertain he'd be returned to me without permanent damage, I freely admitted it, at least to myself.

I waited while Iverson and Horton went back to the jail cells. When they brought Gary out, he still wore the black suit from the funeral, minus the tie. When I'd last seen him, he'd had a black eye. Now I counted four distinct bruises, just on his face. They'd beat him. Anger at the injustice churned in my stomach, and it was soon joined by fear when Gary looked blankly around the room, his eyes scanning right past me as if he didn't know me.

I walked closer. It was too much to hope for a joke, but some hint of recognition, some spark of life would have been welcome. Horton tried to hand Gary a manila envelope. When Gary wouldn't take it, he handed it to me instead.

"His wallet. Keys. Things that were in his pockets."

I took the envelope. Then I faced my boyfriend. "Hello, Gary."

He didn't respond. I hadn't noticed until I was closer, but his breathing was unnaturally quick. Sweat beaded his forehead, and the muscles of his jaw kept his mouth tightly clamped.

"Gary?" I reached out to touch his hand, but the instant my skin met his, he jerked his hand back. His eyes seemed blank, emotionless. The back of my throat grew tight, like I might start crying if I wasn't careful. I wanted to yell at Sergeant Horton and chastise Detective Iverson for what they'd done to him. But it wasn't completely their fault. Countless traumas had left Gary vulnerable. It was up to me to figure out how to make him strong again.

It would be easier without a hostile audience. "Gary?"

No response, almost like he wasn't hearing me.

"Miss Hampton," Iverson began. "Let me know when you'd like me to call the asylum."

"I'm sure he just needs a little time, detective. And maybe a little fresh air." I was scared of being rejected again, but I slipped my arm under Gary's elbow and began guiding him toward the door. He was stiff, but after some initial resistance, he let me lead him. I breathed a sigh of relief. I didn't want to cause any more of a scene in the police station. Once I got him outside, everything would be easier.

At least I hoped it would be easier.

Chapter Sixteen

Letter of June 15, 1944, continued

I'm finally twenty-one, Clive. I was going to join the WAVES now that I'm old enough. I've been looking forward to it—a chance to get out of Maplewick and see someplace new, do something to help the war effort. But I don't think I can leave right now, not when Mom's been so sick. How can I leave someone I love when they need me so badly?

GARY BLINKED IN THE BRIGHT afternoon sunlight and lifted a hand to shade his eyes. I doubted they'd let him outside since Tuesday, and I hadn't ever seen the jail cells, but I assumed they were poorly lit.

I slowed, waiting for his eyes to adjust. He looked around, and his breathing slowed a bit, but not to normal. His eyes stopped on my face. I still didn't see recognition, but at least he looked at me.

"Gary? Should I take you home?"

He didn't answer. I gave him a few moments, then walked him to the New Yorker. Normally, he was the one getting doors, but this time, I opened the passenger side of the car and said a silent prayer that he'd get in without a fuss.

"Gary, will you get in the car?"

He hesitated, but eventually, he sat. I closed the door gently, then walked around and joined him inside.

I sensed we needed time, but Maplewick was a small town. It was a quick drive from the police station to anywhere we might go. I studied him as he looked out the window.

"You can roll it down, if you want."

He turned from the window to give me a blank stare, then turned back.

What was I supposed to do with him?

If I could just get him to respond, maybe things would snowball back into place. "Gary, do you remember much of what happened on Saturday?"

No answer.

"Do you like living in Maplewick?"

Silence.

"Do you remember who I am?"

More silence.

I drove. I went from one end of Maplewick to the other, then I continued to drive for another twenty minutes or so, and then I turned around and repeated the process. I drove the circuit another two times. Gary's breathing returned to a normal rate, but he didn't talk.

I finally parked outside a grassy field. I was wasting gas, and I wasn't making much progress. Would sleeping help him? I could take him back to his shed, but I wasn't sure he could take care of himself. Leaving him alone in his current state felt like leaving a small child to climb all over a trebuchet.

"Are you hungry?"

Warm tears ran down my cheeks when he didn't answer. Almost three hours had passed since we'd left the station, and he hadn't said a single word. I turned the car back on and drove around a little more.

"It's 1948, isn't it?"

I nearly slammed on the brakes when I heard him. His voice was different—softer, scratchier. Out of use, I supposed. "Yes, it's 1948."

I drove halfway to the neighboring town and back again before he next spoke.

"We're in Maplewick?" Each word seemed uncertain, hesitant.

"That's right." I glanced over at him. He stared straight ahead, not at me.

"And I was arrested . . . for killing your father."

"Yes, but you didn't do it."

"I didn't?"

I turned to face him. Didn't he already know that? I looked back at the road. "You couldn't have. He was killed sometime between noon and nine o'clock at night. You were with Mrs. Armellino, then the Murphys, then Mr. Baumgartner, then Mr. Frye, then with me. Don't you remember?"

Out of the corner of my eye, I saw him shake his head. "No." He looked out the window and was silent for minutes that felt like hours. "I remember parts but not all of it. You're certain it wasn't me? Horton said it was."

"Horton was wrong. And Detective Iverson wouldn't have released you without a solid alibi."

"What day is it?"

"Friday."

"I was arrested Tuesday?"

"That's right." I glanced at him. He was watching me now. There were so many things I wanted to ask him, but I decided to wait. I would take it slow, let him come back at his own pace. "There's an envelope with your things in it." Maybe holding familiar items would help his memory.

I took peeks at him as I drove. He examined the keys and the wallet. He paused when he pulled out a black tie.

"I don't remember this."

"I think you borrowed it, and the suit. For the funeral. Probably from Charlie Murphy or maybe from Herbert Morgan or Jack Dickens."

He glanced at his clothes. "I think they're Jack's. I hope he didn't need them this week."

"Do you want me to take you home?"

"Yeah."

"Do you remember where you live?" I glanced at him.

His eyes were on me again. "Yeah. With Mr. Norton. Don't . . . don't you know that?"

"I do." I felt my face grow warm. "I just wanted to see if you remembered."

"I remember a lot of stuff. It's just not all in the right order, and I'm not sure how much of it's true."

We drove in silence for a few moments. I wanted to ask him what he remembered and what he was confused about. But something told me to give it time. I turned into Mr. Norton's driveway and stopped the car.

Gary looked around. "You had car trouble here."

"Yes, last week."

"Do I call you Miss Hampton or Evie?"

I smiled, relieved he remembered who I was, even if he was having a hard time remembering how formal our relationship was. "You call me Evie."

His lips turned up, softening his face. "I've got all these images in my head. I'm just not sure if they're memories or wishes . . . We . . . I've kissed you before, haven't I?"

I nodded. Part of me hurt that he didn't know for himself, but part of me was glad I was still in his head, somewhere.

"And I've told you I'm in love with you and want to marry you?"

I took in a sharp breath. That was in his head? He'd imagined it rather than saying it. But either way, I had a feeling he'd wanted to say those things, and warmth filled me at the thought. Gary was broken at the moment, but he was still in love with me.

"Um, Gary, you haven't ever said that to me."

"Oh." He looked away, confusion and embarrassment showing on his face.

I leaned over and put my hand on his. When I'd done something similar at the police station, he'd jerked away. But this time, he stayed still. Maybe he remembered enough now. "Gary, you've had a rough week. What can I do for you? Are you hungry? Do you need to rest?"

He ran his free hand over his face. "I think I should start with a shower and some clean clothes." He looked at Mr. Norton's house. "But I don't know if I'm ready to face a crowd."

I glanced at the house. It might be empty. Or it might be full of seven people who would want to know all about what had happened, when Gary himself was still sorting everything out. I almost offered to check to see who was home, but I wasn't ready to turn him over to the care of his housemates. "Why don't you grab some clothes, and I'll take you to my house. You can shower there, and nobody will bother you. I'll cook something, and we can have a quiet supper."

Gary looked at the house again and nodded.

Chapter Seventeen

July 15, 1944

Dear Evelyn,

What's happening with Mom? The first few times you mentioned it, I thought she was just feeling a little under the weather, but now it sounds more serious. Even Dad wrote about it in one of his letters.

It's hard to be so far away. I worry about Mom, but I'm glad you're there to help, Evie.

I'd trade you chores, if I could. In addition to our normal training, they send us out on work parties around the island. The worst is picking up the half-rotten coconuts. Coconut smells good when you sprinkle it on ice cream, but when it starts to decompose, it's absolutely vile. I'm never going to eat it again. If coconut trees are on your list of things to see when you travel, cross them off.

I'D NEGLECTED GROCERY SHOPPING THAT week and had spent more time at Aunt Janice's house than at mine. The refrigerator had predictably disappointing results when I opened it, but I managed to find everything I needed for chicken noodle soup. It wasn't fancy, but it was cool outside, and soup sounded comforting.

I added noodles to the simmering broth, chicken, and vegetables about the time I heard the water in the upstairs bathroom switch off. I'd told Gary to take as long as he wanted. He'd probably been in there a half hour. I was washing dishes when he came into the kitchen.

He picked up a dish towel and dried what I'd washed—the cutting board and knife, a mixing bowl, and the rolling pin. We'd cooked together before, and I took it as a good sign that he slipped back into our routine.

"How are you feeling?" I asked.

He didn't answer immediately, as if he needed time to gather the right words. "I think I've got most of my memories sorted out now. Which are real, which are far enough in the past that I can ignore them, which are things Sergeant Horton said that aren't true."

"Did he give you those bruises?" The top button of his shirt was undone, exposing discoloration on his neck that his other collar had hidden. There were a few bruises on his arms too.

"The last few days are still a little fuzzy."

"I'm sorry, Gary."

"It's not your fault." He spread the damp cloth out to dry. "You just lost your dad, Evie. How are you holding up?"

I stirred the soup, even though it didn't really need it. "Better, now that you're free."

He stood behind me and put his hands on my arms. Part of me softened at his touch, but another part of me was nervous, because I wasn't sure he was the same man I'd fallen in love with.

"Most of my mind seems to be working now, but there's one thing I can't figure out."

"What's that?"

"Why is a classy lady like you spending so much time with a guy like me?"

I turned around to face him. He was close enough that I could smell the lingering scent of soap and see each of his eyelashes. I reached around to run my fingers along the hairline at the back of his neck. "I cut your hair crooked. You said there wasn't any way you could get a different date with a haircut like that, so I was stuck with you until it grew back. Do you remember that?" It was probably long enough that I could trim it again now, but I liked the idea of being stuck with him awhile longer, at least until we settled into whatever new dynamics we would have after my dad's murder and Gary's time in jail. I wondered, too, what the impact would be of all I'd learned when I was looking for an alibi. I'd invaded his privacy. I liked what I'd found, but there might be repercussions when I confessed what I'd done.

He gave me one of his half smiles. "I remember the haircut. But that doesn't explain why we're close enough that you cut my hair and bring me to your house to shower. It's not that I don't remember. I just don't understand."

He was asking a serious question, and given all the sleuthing into his past that I'd done, I thought he deserved an honest answer. "I guess, for my part, we're together because all my life I've felt like everyone has wanted me to act a certain way, be a certain type of person. I'm always trying to fit into their mold. The professor's daughter, the officer's perfect fiancée, the efficient office worker. With you, I feel like I can say whatever I'm thinking and do whatever I want without worrying about how you'll judge me. Everyone else wants to change me. But you just accept me."

He brought his hand up and played with the end of my hair. "Why would I want to change perfection?"

My cheeks grew warm. "I'm not perfect."

"Closest thing to it I've ever met."

"Actually, I've been really nosy the last few days while I was trying to establish your alibi."

The expression on his face grew thoughtful. "That's why they let me out. Because you figured out where I'd been."

I nodded.

"I should have told them." He swallowed. "I was just . . ." He trailed off.

"I spoke to Wanda. You were trying to protect Charlie?"

"Yeah. And then everything was mixed up in my head. I didn't know if I was in New York or Germany or what year it was or who was asking questions."

I ladled soup into bowls and took them to the breakfast alcove instead of the formal dining room. While we ate, I told him what I'd done. I confessed to reading some of his letters and driving to see Mrs. Armellino, told him I'd talked to Wanda, Mr. Baumgartner, and Mr. Frye to establish where he'd been. And I told him what Sergeant Rumsey from the Irving Police Department had reported. I felt like I'd dug too much into his past and had done it behind his back, so I ended with an apology.

He shook his head. "No, it's my fault." He met my eyes. "Thanks for getting me out." He was quiet for a few moments before speaking again. "I was going to tell you, eventually."

"Tell me what?"

"About what happened in Irving." He glanced at the table. "It's just you haven't ever made any big mistakes. I wasn't sure you'd understand."

"I've made plenty of mistakes."

"You haven't broken the law."

I was silent for a moment. "I think I've had a few traffic violations. I just didn't get caught."

"Traffic violations?" He chuckled softly. "I've been a petty thief most of my life. It didn't seem that wrong back when I was a kid. We were strapped if we snuck into the larder and stole food, but we were strapped for all sorts of stuff. We got beat if we spoke Seneca instead of English, and that never seemed like something we should be punished for. I had to sleep in chains because I ran away, and running away hadn't seemed evil. But stealing things didn't stop there."

"Did you get caught?"

He shook his head. "Not since I was little, at the school, even before. I, uh . . . well, I guess I had a talent for it. And I was hungry." One side of his mouth turned up. "It came in handy in Germany. They didn't feed us much over there either. Worse than in the schools. I think a few men might not have made it if I hadn't been good at scrounging food and firewood and odds and ends, like wire clippers."

"Wire clippers? Did you escape?"

"Once. Didn't make it very far before they caught us again. After that, I think I was too worn down to try again. 'Bout wasted away before the war ended." He put his hands in his lap and watched my face. "Then I came home and hit the bottle pretty hard. I was a no-good drunk for about a year."

"But I've never seen you drink."

"This guy I knew during the war came looking for me when I didn't write back. He poured all my liquor down the drain. If I hadn't been so drunk, I would have punched him. Then I got sober, and he was still there, filling out college applications for me. He told me he'd lend me his motorcycle for a few years if I stopped drinking. Haven't touched the stuff since. Not because of the bike. He just convinced me to stop wasting my life, that I could be more than a drunk. I'm not a thief anymore either. I stopped when I got back from the war." He paused for a bit, thinking. "I was going to come clean with you about the past, eventually. But when we first started dating, I was worried it would scare you away. And the longer I put it off, the more I had to lose."

Gary had come a long way. I'd never seen him less than sober, and I couldn't imagine Mr. Baumgartner keeping him on at the jewelry store if items had gone missing. I felt like he'd overcome the drinking and the thieving, but there was one thing that still worried me. "And the teacher— Orville Brown? Was that the only time you planned an assault? Or just the only time you got caught?"

He looked at his hands. "There was one other time. In Germany. We clobbered a guard so we could escape. He was awful. I watched him beat one of my friends almost to death once—that guard deserved it." Gary looked up, and there was an anger in his eyes that I'd never seen before. "And Mr. Brown deserved it too."

Chapter Eighteen

Letter of July 15, 1944, continued

I complained to one of the old salts about the rotting coconuts, said I hate the way they fall apart into stinking chunks as they decay. He gave me this look and said I'll find out what hatred really is when we get into battle.

I'D NEVER BEEN SCARED OF Gary before, but the intensity of his emotion was unsettling. I tried to keep my voice level, not wanting to sound angry or frightened. "What did Orville Brown do to *deserve* being crippled?"

Gary was quiet for a bit, and the silence felt ominous. When he finally spoke, it was only a whisper. "He liked to come into the dorms at night."

That didn't seem so bad to me, not at first. But I suspected Mr. Brown hadn't come into the dorm rooms to tuck the children in or to read them bedtime stories. The longer I thought about it, the worse it sounded. "And he hurt them?"

Gary nodded.

"Not with a strap?"

"A strap wouldn't have been so bad."

I couldn't speak for a few moments as horror filled my chest. Those poor children. "Did he hurt you?"

Gary wouldn't meet my eyes. "Evie, I'll answer any question you have about my past. I owe you the truth. But please don't ask me that."

That was enough of an answer, and I felt sick to my stomach. I pictured Gary as a boy. Frightened, abused, powerless. "So Orville Brown was a pedophile."

Gary nodded. "When my uncle died, my aunt hit the bottle. She was deemed an unfit parent and was ordered to turn her youngest son over. He was sent to the Thomas Indian School. So his brother and I made our plans.

We thought maybe if Mr. Brown couldn't walk, he wouldn't be able to hurt anyone."

"Couldn't you have gone to the police?"

Gary huffed. "We tried. But we were just two delinquent teenagers, Indians to boot. No one believed us. And it was . . ." He sighed. "It was difficult to talk about." He took a breath, and his hands fisted in his lap. "It's one thing to lose our land, lose our culture. But do you know how hard it is, as a people, to not be able to protect our own children? I can't think of a more wretched condition to be in than to know your children are being taken away from you and being abused, and there's nothing you can do to stop it."

Gary had expressed frustration with the Bureau of Indian Affairs before, but until now, I hadn't fully understood. "Is Mr. Brown still at the school?"

Gary shook his head. "No. The judge knew. He didn't want word to get out, and he didn't want a scandal, but he knew we were telling the truth. I was a month shy of eighteen, so he was lenient with me. I joined the army. Mr. Brown went into early retirement. And Otetiani went to prison."

"Otetiani—your cousin? The older one?"

Gary nodded.

"The judge didn't let him enlist?"

"The judge gave him a choice. Otetiani said he couldn't serve a nation that had broken so many treaties and suppressed his people. I guess I'm . . . I don't know. I guess I'm not as idealistic as him." He fingered the edge of his empty bowl. "But I still ended up a prisoner. The Germans gave us worse food than the school. And we had worse beds, but at least they left us alone at night."

I stood and walked to the window, looking out but not really seeing much. "Do you have anything good in your past?"

"For a while, there was you."

My heart hurt. Gary had been a thief and a drunk, and he'd tried to cripple a man. But I couldn't blame him for stealing food when he was hungry, nor for plotting against Mr. Brown when he was trying to protect a child.

I went to church every week and listened to the preacher tell me people could change, that Jesus could fix everything, that the past could be forgiven. I'd always believed it, at least for me and for the prodigal son. But did I believe it for Gary, believe it with enough faith that I'd risk marrying him, if he asked me, believing that the past wouldn't somehow destroy us?

"I should probably go." Gary stood and cleared our bowls. He filled the sink with water, like he was going to wash the dishes, so I guess he was cleaning before he left. "Thanks for the food. And thanks for getting me out of jail."

I almost asked him to stay, but I needed time to process all I'd heard. "I'll drive you back."

"I can walk."

The doorbell chimed. I left Gary in the kitchen and went to see who it was. When I pulled the door open, Roland Roth stood on the porch in a tailored suit, a bouquet of flowers in his hands and his most charming smile on his face. I hadn't seen him since he'd gone overseas in 1944, and my stomach did a little flip of surprise.

"Evelyn!" With a flourish, he swept the fedora from his head, revealing glossy, combed-back waves. Roland had never skimped on the hair tonic during the war, and it seemed that hadn't changed.

"Hello, Mr. Roth."

"You can call me Roland."

I didn't reply.

"Look, Evelyn, I'm in town for a few weeks. I thought maybe I could take you to supper. Catch up on the last few years."

"I thought you got married while you were in England." That was what his letter had said when he'd broken off our engagement.

He looked at his shiny brown oxfords. "We got it annulled. She was married. Thought her husband was dead, but he showed up again when the war ended, and she chose him over me." He handed the flowers to me. Tulips and freesia. "These are for you. I'm sorry I hurt you. The war just lasted a long time. I was far from home, and I was lonely. Could we try again? Pick up where we left off?"

"I think it's too late for that."

"I heard about your father. My condolences. He was a brilliant man." Roland grinned again. "He always liked me. I don't think he'd object to us seeing each other again, even if his death is recent."

I shook my head. I wasn't entirely sure where I stood with Gary, but I wasn't ready to return to Roland any more than France was willing to turn Aquitaine over to England. "I'm seeing someone else."

"I heard. But we had it so good. And your dad liked the idea of us being together. Remember how thrilled he was when we got engaged?"

"I've changed. And Daddy isn't here to be thrilled anymore. If you'll excuse me." I stepped back so I could close the door.

"You aren't even going to invite me in?" Roland still had that deep melodious timbre to his voice. He could have made it as a radio broadcaster, but last I'd heard, he was in law school. His eyes narrowed at something behind me.

I glanced around. Gary stood in the hallway, hands in his pockets, with a none-too-friendly look on his face. I turned back to Roland. "I already have company."

Roland frowned. "I see. Well, perhaps another time. Good evening, Evelyn."

"Good evening, Mr. Roth."

I closed the door and leaned against it with the flowers still in my hands. I stared at Gary, and he stared at me.

"So that's Roland Roth," Gary said.

I nodded. I'd told him I'd been engaged before, that Roland had broken it off during the war. I didn't have to explain, but I still felt awkward. "I guess he's in town for a bit."

"And he wants you back."

Gary's words were a statement, not a question, so I didn't answer.

"Can't say I blame him." One side of Gary's mouth twisted up.

I smiled back and tossed the flowers on the table in the entryway. Roland Roth was handsome, but Gary Redhawk could melt my heart with one little grin. There was more to a man than looks, of course, but Gary came out on top in most of those categories too. "I think he's going to be disappointed."

Gary glanced out the window as Roland's car drove away. "He probably has a less complicated past than I do. And I don't plan on living in a shed my whole life, but I doubt I'll ever be rich."

"I think there's something admirable about overcoming a difficult past." As I said the words, their truth hit me with full force. Gary's experiences would have crippled most people, but he was a good man now, despite his past. "Have you really not drunk any alcohol since you made that promise to your friend?"

"Stone-cold sober."

"And stealing?"

He glanced away. "I scrounged a few things in Europe, even after we were liberated. It was habit, taking anything that might be useful later. Food. Red Cross pencils. Wooden boards. It took some time to break it. I stopped by the time I got back to the States." He folded his arms and met my eyes. "Except once."

"Oh?"

"Do you remember the day we met?"

"Yeah." He'd come into the bursar's office asking for an extension on his tuition payment. The GI Bill was supposed to cover it, but the VA had been late sending the check. It was a common enough occurrence, one we dealt with routinely, but I'd taken my time sorting it out because I'd enjoyed having him seated in a chair across from my desk.

"I stole your pen."

"No, I remember. You handed it to me. And our fingers touched." Contact with his skin had sent a pleasant warmth all the way up to my elbow. His good looks and our easy conversation had already caught my attention, and that sensation had cemented it.

"Yeah. I gave it back to you. And then I swiped it. It's in the crate with my socks."

I tried to remember using the pen again after we'd met, but I couldn't. It had disappeared. "Why did you steal my pen?"

He shrugged. "I guess to remind me that there are people who are beautiful on the outside and kind on the inside."

I felt my face heating up. I'd always known our first meeting had been exceptional, at least when it had come to my memories. Apparently, I'd affected him enough that he'd wanted a pen as a memento. "I have a confession too. You remember how you asked me to supper that night and I said I was busy, so you asked if we could meet the next night instead?"

"Yeah. And you insisted we meet at the restaurant. Which ended up being a good thing because I might have chickened out if I'd come to pick you up and seen how big this house is."

"I was busy that night too. We had a family supper planned, which is why I wanted to meet elsewhere. But I was afraid you wouldn't ask again if I turned you down twice."

A smile softened his face. "After two rejections, I probably wouldn't have tried a third time." He laughed softly. "What a pair we are. The first time we met, I stole something, and you lied."

I pushed away from the door.

Gary's face sobered. "Evie, is that a bandage on your leg?"

I looked down. My skirt covered the bandage at the moment, but it must have shown when I moved. "Yeah. Someone tried to pull a bookcase over on top of me."

"What?"

Chapter Nineteen

Letter of July 15, 1944, continued
Our island is inhabited by two main life-forms.
One—the men of the 1st Marine Division. Some are replacements, like me.
Others fought at Guadalcanal and Cape Gloucester, and I'm trying to learn all
I can from them.
Two—land crabs. They're enormous and like to crawl into my boondockers
at night. They stink almost as much as the coconuts when they rot.

GARY STUDIED THE STILL-OVERTURNED BOOKCASE. "This part isn't varnished." He ran his fingers along the back corner where the nails had been cut away. "That fits with your version of what happened. Iverson should have done something."

It was nice to have someone other than Aunt Janice believe me about the wire. "He thought I was trying to get you out of jail. Which I was, but I was telling the truth."

Gary ran a hand along the top of the fallen bookcase. Then he stood and did the same for a bookcase still standing. He looked at his fingers.

Mortification at the dust made my face burn. Mom would have never let the dust build up like that, not when she'd been healthy. "I need to do some spring cleaning."

He shook his head. "I'm not inspecting your housekeeping. Just looking for clues. The one that tipped is clean. The other one isn't. Like someone wiped it down either when they were putting nails into it or after they sawed off the back part."

"To hide the wood shavings? And fingerprints?"

Gary pushed the fallen bookcase up, angling it back into place. Then he got down on the ground. He swiped a finger along the hardwood floor and showed me the result. Sawdust.

I had known someone pulled the bookcase on top of me, but seeing additional evidence made me cold inside. Gary looked through the wastebasket for a rag, but whoever had sneaked in must have taken the cloth and shavings with them.

He looked along the window, where I'd told him the wire had been, then walked back to the bookcase. "It doesn't seem like a sure way to murder someone. Kind of like the brake line. It could kill, but it's more likely to injure."

"What does that mean? That the murderer isn't very smart? Or he's not sure he wants to kill?"

"The hanging was no accident." Gary wiped his hands clean on his pants.

I folded my arms across my chest, chilled at the memory. Gary must have guessed my emotion, because he put an arm around me. It was harder to feel threatened when he was close, but his next words weren't exactly comforting. "Whoever it is might try again."

I leaned my head into his neck. "Why would someone want to hurt me?"

"I don't know." He put his other arm around me and pulled me closer. "But I'm going to do everything I can to make sure he doesn't succeed."

I lifted my head to look him in the face. "That sounds very protective, Mr. Redhawk."

"Well, Miss Hampton, based on what I said in your car today, I think you have a very clear idea of how I feel about you."

I smiled. That was a bright spot in a week full of tragedy and danger. Gary was in love with me. I stared at his lips, remembering that I hadn't kissed him in a week. I met his eyes. I wasn't exactly sure what had happened to his mind while he'd been in jail, but he was back now, and we'd finally breached the wall of secrets he'd built to hide his past. I wound my hand around his neck and brought his mouth down to mine.

Gary's lips sent tingles along my skin and focused all my attention on him. The rhythm of his mouth and the warmth of his breath and the steadiness of his arms drew me in. We were so near that I could feel his pulse. He deepened the kiss, bringing in more passion, a new, unfamiliar heat. I welcomed it. I wanted to follow it, explore it, get so caught up in it that nothing else would matter. Gary's openness had left him exposed, but that honesty had been exactly what I'd needed to drop my last doubts, and something inside me felt that new closeness with each heartbeat.

When Gary ended the kiss, he was breathing hard, and so was I.

"I'm sorry, Evie. I shouldn't kiss you like that."

I ran a finger along his jawline. "Actually, I was going to ask you to do it again."

He closed his eyes as I held his face. "If I kiss you like that again, I don't think I trust myself to stop."

Some part of me knew he was right, but I wasn't sure I really wanted to hold back. Gary made the decision for me, stepping away and bending to pick up a few books. "Do these go in any particular order?"

I wanted him to kiss me again, not put books back on their shelves, but I swallowed back that unfamiliar hunger and answered. "Alphabetical by author's last name."

He glanced at the books. "Figures."

We worked in silence, putting the books away. Sometimes our hands would touch and our eyes would meet. I spent as much time staring at his lips as I did reading book titles. The passion stayed under the surface, but only just.

"Your father had Dr. Fontaine's books?" Gary handed one to me. "I thought they were rivals."

"Maybe they were gifts. Professional courtesy or something?" I flipped through the book, then turned the pages more slowly. There wasn't a single sheet without copious notes in the margins.

Gary came closer to look over my shoulder. "I think he wrote a book, in that book."

"He's tearing all of Dr. Fontaine's theories to pieces." I skimmed through one page, then another. "Questioning the validity of his sources. Adding information where he felt the explanation was missing something. Pointing out anachronisms." I winced. "My father could be harsh when it came to British history."

Gary flipped through another of Dr. Fontaine's books. "This one too."

"If he could do this with the history of the Tudors, I suppose he'd run out of margin space if he got a copy of Dr. Fontaine's new book on the Plantagenets."

Gary shelved the book he'd been holding. "Did your dad take these notes for himself, or did he show them to others?"

"Just himself, I think."

"Evie, don't take this the wrong way, but where are you sleeping tonight?"

I thought about saying something coy but decided against it. "Probably at Aunt Janice's. That's where I've been sleeping since Daddy died. This house just seems . . . I don't know. It's hard to sleep alone when he was killed here."

Gary nodded. "Whoever killed your dad and rigged up the bookcase was able to get inside. Do you know how?"

I shook my head.

"Do the neighbors have a key?"

"No."

"Your aunt or cousins?"

"I don't think so. But . . . follow me."

I went to the entryway, where the scent of Roland's bouquet had filled the air. I yanked open the drawer in the entry table. Dad always kept his keys in that drawer when he wasn't using them. I pushed aside a few ticket stubs, loose change, a couple pens, and a pad of paper. "Daddy's keys are gone."

"Whoever killed him probably took the keys." Gary put his hand on my back, easing the sudden wariness I felt. "Let's get new locks. And until we figure out who's behind this, I don't think you should be anywhere alone."

Chapter Twenty

Letter of July 15, 1944, continued

 We do lots of maneuvers as a company, but the island isn't too big. Yesterday we were marching east, and L Company was marching north. We got all mixed up and gave the officers a real headache.

 Remember how Dad wanted me to stay in college a little longer and try to get into Officer Candidates School? I was worried the war would end before I had a chance to do my part, so I enlisted instead. I told Slingshot Ramirez about that. He was at Guadalcanal. He told me I'm crazy.

WHILE WE WERE AT THE hardware store, Gary decided Aunt Janice wasn't strong enough to defend me from a murderer who was capable of hanging my dad. After we stopped by his shed so he could pick up his homework and more clothes, we convinced Aunt Janice to join the two of us at my house. Aunt Janice and I would sleep upstairs. Gary would sleep downstairs in the parlor, by the front door.

Gary changed out the locks, and then the three of us went into the formal dining room to make our plans.

Gary took out a sheet of lined paper and a pencil. "We should make a list of everyone who might have reason to hurt your father."

I hated to think of Dad doing anything that might make someone angry enough to kill him. He wasn't perfect, but he was my father, and he hadn't deserved murder. "I can think of people who didn't like him but no one with reason to kill him."

Gary gave me a sympathetic smile. "Let's just start with the list. Add anyone with motive, no matter how small, and we'll narrow it down from there based on character and opportunity. We can start with me." He wrote his name on the paper, then wrote my name beside it with his tidy penmanship. "I have motive, because it would mean easier access to Evie."

"But you didn't do it."

"No, I didn't. But this is supposed to be a broad list."

Aunt Janice nodded. "Put me on there too. Not that I did it, but since we're listing all possibilities . . . You've planned a dozen trips, Evie, and haven't gone on any of them because you were taking care of Ernst—I wouldn't mind seeing some of those places with you. Having someone to travel with is no small thing for an aging spinster."

"But Aunt Janice—"

A chuckle from Gary cut me off.

"What's so funny?" I asked him.

"An aging spinster and a psychoneurotic Indian. Not the most impressive set of protectors."

I appreciated the lighter mood. And I appreciated all Gary and Aunt Janice were doing for me. Of the living, there were no two people I trusted more, regardless of the flippant titles they gave themselves.

"Evie, you probably stand to inherit something?" Gary asked.

I nodded. "Yes."

Gary wrote Aunt Janice down, then me, with a dollar sign next to my name. "Who else benefits in any way?"

I hesitated, but if Gary, Aunt Janice, and I were all on the list, there was no reason not to discuss all possibilities. "Dr. Fontaine."

Gary nodded. "Because with your father dead, his newest book is less likely to be picked to pieces."

"That, and Dean Roth will retire soon. Daddy was on the short list to be the next dean of the History Department. Now Dr. Fontaine is a certainty."

Gary wrote the name down, then looked up with questioning eyes. "The dean and Roland Roth?"

"Father and son." Perhaps that was why Dad had been so thrilled when Roland and I had been together.

Gary added Roland to the list.

"But Daddy liked Roland. If Roland wanted me back, he'd have a better chance with Dad as cheerleader."

Aunt Janice adjusted her reading glasses. "Maybe. But with your father dead and your boyfriend blamed for it, who better to step in and pick up the pieces?"

"Were you the sole heir?" Gary asked.

I shook my head. "He left $5,000 each to Frank and Dale. The rest to me."

Gary wrote my cousins' names on the sheet. "Nothing to Redgrave?"

"No. Although Mr. Richards from the library is hoping for a sizeable donation of artifacts and books. He'll probably get it, once I get around to sorting through everything."

"Mr. Richards." Gary wrote his name on the list as well. "Anyone else who would benefit?"

"Marge and Howard Hollingback are interested in buying the house. I don't think Daddy was interested in selling. I'm more open to the idea."

"Your neighbors?" Gary asked.

I nodded. "Or it could be a disgruntled student."

"Any names he's mentioned?"

"No, but I could ask around. If I talk to enough people, maybe a few names will pop up more than once."

Gary wrote down *students*, then a question mark. "Anyone else?"

I opened my mouth, then stopped myself.

"What?" Gary asked.

I shook my head. "I was going to say something, but it doesn't make any sense."

"Say it anyway."

"I think my friend Barbara would like to see the two of us break up. A murder could do that."

Gary wrote her name on the list. "She doesn't like me, huh?"

"The opposite problem. She finds you incredibly attractive." That wasn't so surprising. We'd liked the same movie stars when we were teenagers: Clark Gable, Cary Grant, Jimmy Stewart.

Gary stiffened for a moment, as if surprised, then he flipped the paper over. "I think we can assume the murderer is either a man or a stronger-than-average woman. Otherwise, I can't see them overpowering your dad. Is Barbara that strong?"

"No. So it can't be Barbara." That was a relief, but it didn't solve our problem. "Someone who knows a little about cars." I thought about the brake line.

"And how to tie a bowline knot with two hundred pounds on the standing end of the rope." Gary wrote *car* and *rope* on the paper.

"A Boy Scout? Or a sailor?" Aunt Janice leaned forward, her arms resting on the table. Normally, she was the one making lists, but she'd relinquished that role to Gary with grace.

Gary nodded and added her suggestions.

"It was probably someone he knew, or he wouldn't have let him in the house." It would have been easier if it were a stranger, but I had to admit that didn't seem likely.

"What if he posed as a salesman? Could have gotten in that way maybe." Gary wrote it on the paper.

Aunt Janice chuckled. "Ernst, inviting a salesman in? That's highly improbable."

Gary looked to me to confirm. "Doubtful," I said. "He usually sent them packing, with a few insults."

Gary crossed off *salesman*. "So we're looking for a man of above-average strength, knowledgeable about cars and knots, who had reason to want your father dead, and had the opportunity to kill him sometime between noon and 9:00 p.m. last Saturday."

"The earlier end of that window, according to the coroner." I assumed Sergeant Horton hadn't lied about that.

Gary put the pen down. "But what about the bookcase?"

"I think that's easy enough to explain." Aunt Janice looked at Gary. "The murderer tried to make Ernst's death look like suicide. That failed, but then the police arrested you and were certain they had the correct man. The murderer was going to get away with it. Then Evie set out to prove you innocent. If she succeeded, the police would have to look elsewhere. If the murderer could stop Evie, either by killing or maiming her and making it look like an accident, then you'd be stuck with the blame. The real murderer could walk free."

"Who could have stolen the wire?" Gary asked.

"Anyone. They could have hidden out there." I waved at the nearest windowpane. A thick grove of beech, aspen, and pine filled the view. "And the window in the study is easy to sneak in and out of."

Gary nodded and grabbed another sheet of paper. "Who knew you were trying to establish an alibi for me?"

"A lot of people. Detective Iverson and Sergeant Horton. Mr. Frye. The Murphys. Mr. Norton. Aunt Janice. My cousins. Mrs. Armellino. Mr. Baumgartner and all the other jewelers in town. Mrs. Ryder at the café and a few students from the library. And anyone they might have mentioned it to." I should have been more discreet, but at the time, I'd been worried about getting Gary out as quickly as possible, not keeping secrets from a murderer.

Aunt Janice tried to stifle a yawn.

Gary glanced at the clock, and I followed his gaze. It was nearly eleven. "Maybe after work tomorrow, I'll go visit Dr. Fontaine. And the neighbors."

"I'll come too." I didn't want anyone to give him trouble. Someone could accuse Gary of intimidation, and the police would believe them. "In the meantime, I'll get some extra sheets and a few blankets."

* * *

I had a hard time falling asleep that night. I kept thinking of all the people who might have killed Dad. When I finally drifted off, it seemed like only minutes before I woke again to a man's screams. I flew out of bed. The noise stopped before I made it to my bedroom door, but worry that the murderer was back, attacking Gary, kept me running, down the stairs and into the parlor. I wasn't sure what I expected, but when I flipped on the lights, it was just Gary.

He sat on the sofa, shirtless, leaning forward, holding his head, with the blankets askew around him. His hair was damp with sweat, and his breathing came in rapid gasps.

"Are you all right?" As I asked, I heard Aunt Janice at the top of the stairs.

"I'm sorry I woke you." Gary's voice was shaky, and he didn't look up. "Just a dream."

"Is something wrong?" Aunt Janice asked.

I walked to the foot of the stairs. "No. It's fine." I was wide awake and jumpy, and Gary was having nightmares, but no one had broken in.

I turned back to the parlor. I hadn't grabbed my robe and wore only a cotton nightgown, so I grabbed a blanket off the back of a chair and wrapped it around my shoulders. "Gary?"

He took a deep breath and looked up. "Sorry, Evie."

"Sorry? For what?"

He huffed. "For waking you up."

I sat a few feet away in an armchair. "Do you want to talk about it?"

He pushed his hair back from his forehead and took another deep breath. "I don't think you want to hear about where I was."

I wasn't sure either, but curiosity and a desire to help won out. "Where?"

The clock ticked five times before he answered. "Dresden, at least at first."

"Dresden. In Germany?"

He nodded. "I was part of a work crew in a village not far from there when I was a prisoner. They sent a bunch of us to Dresden for about a week and a half. Had us pulling the dead out of the rubble, that sort of thing. It had been bombed pretty bad. Created a firestorm." He took a deep breath. "I'd seen corpses before but nothing like that. The heat did some crazy things to the bodies."

"And you still see them, in your dreams?"

"Yeah."

"Often?"

He shrugged. "Them, or other things. More nights than not."

I glanced at the clock. The hour hand pointed to three. "What do you do when you have nightmares?"

He gave me half a smile. "Read economic theory until I'm sleepy again. Or just get up. Depends on the time."

"But how do you catch up on sleep?"

"I go until I'm exhausted, and eventually, I crash. And then I'm tardy for Professor Gerstner's 8:00 a.m. psychology class."

That explained the frequent yawns, the occasionally droopy eyelids, and the times he'd dozed off in the theater. "Do you want a glass of water or something?"

"Yeah." He stood and grabbed a shirt from a pile of clothes and slipped it over his head.

He followed me into the kitchen. I filled a glass and watched him drain it.

He set the glass in the sink. "Maybe it's just as well that I'm here tonight. It's fair that you know how broken I am before we . . ." He didn't finish his thought.

"You're not broken."

He raised an eyebrow. "Oh? That nightmare wasn't anything unusual. That's why I'm willing to sleep in a shed if it means I can sleep alone."

"I want to help." There had to be a way to make it easier for him.

His dark eyes peered at me, full of so much pain that it made me want to sob. "I know you want to help, but I'm not sure that's the best thing for you. I want to make sure you're safe, but maybe when we find out who killed your dad and he's behind bars . . . maybe then it will be time for us to back off."

"Back off?" My tears were closer to the surface now, and panic clutched at my throat. "Are you trying to give me the brush-off?"

He closed his eyes and rubbed his temples. "Evie, you're the best thing that's ever happened to me. Of course I don't want to lose you, but I'm trying to do what's right for you. I'm not whole."

"If I only love people who are whole, who will love me when I'm broken?" I'd seen enough of life to know hard times didn't last forever, but they touched everyone. Like the dynasties Dad had studied, a person's strength could ebb and flow. That was part of love, that willingness to be there through everything, including the rough patches. I reached for his hand, and he let me take it.

"Evie . . ." He held my hand in both of his. I felt tenderness and warmth and that unexplainable pull that drew me to him. "Charlie loves his wife, but that didn't stop him from punching her when he had a bad moment. I never want to do something like that to you. And Charlie had a good childhood. I think I've got a few more ghosts following me around than he does."

"I'm not afraid of your ghosts." They hurt my heart because he had suffered so much, but his past didn't make me want to leave him. "Gary, I'm not going to tell you your ghosts aren't strong or that they aren't scary. But the way I see it, they're just one more mountain for you to get over. And you've already summited more mountains that most people see in their entire lives. You can climb this one too." I stood on my toes and planted a kiss on his cheek. "If you'll let me, I'll climb it with you."

Chapter Twenty-One

August 1, 1944
  Dear Clive,
  I'm not sure how to tell you this, so I'll be direct. Mom has cancer, and there's not much they can do for her.

I LEFT GARY IN THE kitchen that night. I overslept the next morning. When I came downstairs, the blankets in the parlor were folded and Aunt Janice was in the kitchen mixing up pancake batter.

"Did Gary go to work already?"

"Yes. He said he'd come back when he finished and that he'd try to get off a little early." Aunt Janice added salt and baking powder to a bowl. "Then you can go visit Dr. Fontaine."

"Maybe I should visit the Hollingbacks this morning." A nervous sort of feeling crept over me. I wanted my father's murder solved. But I liked most of the people on that list and dreaded finding out who was capable of murder. But even more, I hated letting them get away with it.

Aunt Janice held a hand over the pan, testing it for warmth. "I think that fellow of yours would prefer you wait for him to go with you. He's worried about you."

"Did he tell you that?"

"He didn't have to tell me."

I could take Gary, but Howard Hollingback was even more old-fashioned than Dad when it came to interracial relationships, and Marge always seemed nervous around Gary, as if she were afraid he would try to scalp her. "I think with the Hollingbacks, I'll make better progress without him."

"I'll go with you." Aunt Janice added a little more milk to the batter. "I promised Mr. Redhawk I wouldn't let you go anywhere alone."

"I don't think that's his choice to make."

"No, but in this case, I agree with him. Someone killed your father. And someone tried to hurt you." She poured batter into the pan. "So I promised him I would keep an eye on you. And he promised me that he would be a perfect gentleman with you, even when you come downstairs in the middle of the night in nothing but your nightgown."

My face heated at the reprimand. I'd have to keep my robe closer to my bed. "I thought someone had broken in, and then I felt like he needed my help. Nothing inappropriate happened."

Aunt Janice was quiet, as if waiting for a confession. But I had no confession to make. I didn't regret my conversation with Gary the night before, even if it had taken place in the middle of the night. I'd pulled a blanket over my nightdress. Nor did I regret yesterday evening's kiss in the study, even if it had flirted with that invisible line we weren't supposed to cross.

I grabbed plates and silverware and put them on the alcove table. "I think if we visit the Hollingbacks and ask for information about selling the house, they won't think I suspect them. And they'll have no reason to hurt me." According to Aunt Janice's theory, someone had set the trap in the study to injure me so I couldn't prove Gary's innocence. Gary had been exonerated, so there was no longer a reason to incapacitate me. As long as no one knew I was searching for the killer, I was safe.

At least, I thought I was.

* * *

"Evelyn, how good to see you!" Marge Hollingback opened the door. "And Miss Peterson, it's lovely to see you as well. Please come in, both of you."

We followed Mrs. Hollingback to the drawing room, which smelled of pine oil and cigarette smoke. I'd been there before but not recently. Framed pictures of her grown children lined the mantel over the fireplace, with a new baby picture, not framed, leaning off to the side of one of them.

"A new grandbaby?" I asked.

Mrs. Hollingback smiled. "Yes. A boy. Arthur. Now I need to buy a new frame."

Mrs. Hollingback and Aunt Janice managed the small talk, mostly about the weather, the new grandbaby, and recent fashion trends from Paris.

I waited for a lull in the conversation before joining in. "Mrs. Hollingback, I'm not sure I want to maintain such a large home by myself. I haven't made any decisions yet, but you mentioned at the funeral that you might be interested in purchasing it."

"Oh yes. Always makes me nervous when there's a change in the neighborhood. Don't want just anyone moving in. We offered your father $15,000 for it. He wasn't ready to sell, least not yet. Howard and I are hoping to convince one of the kids to move back here. It's our dream to have all the children nearby. Julie's husband can get one of those loans through the Veteran's Administration, but if we want Ethel May or Susan nearby, we'll have to finance it ourselves."

I glanced at Aunt Janice. I had no idea what my father's home was worth or if the price offered was low or high. But they had offered to buy it before, and Dad had said no.

"Take your time thinking it over, Evelyn. We still have to convince the kids. They would have to find a job here, and that could take some time in a place as small as Maplewick."

If there was no hurry, it seemed unlikely they'd killed Dad in order to buy his property. I hadn't really thought it was them anyway. I'd planned not to discuss my suspicions with them, but Mrs. Hollingback seemed innocent enough, and I didn't think she could threaten the two of us.

"Mrs. Hollingback, were you here last Saturday afternoon and evening? Did you see anyone come to visit my dad?"

She frowned. "That detective asked us the same question. But no, we weren't here. We went to visit baby Arthur in Batavia. We got home late. Sunday morning, really."

* * *

"It seemed a fair price," Aunt Janice said when we returned to my house. "Of course, I wouldn't sell without having someone appraise it. Housing prices are climbing. That could be why they want to buy now, even if none of their children has committed to a move yet. The longer they wait, the more it will cost them."

I nodded. "I don't suppose it could have been them if they were in Batavia. Detective Iverson probably confirmed it."

"Maybe. But he had his eyes on Mr. Redhawk. He probably questioned the Hollingbacks only to see if they saw anyone visit Ernst, not to see if they had an alibi. Even then, it wouldn't be too hard to convince one of their children to lie for them."

"So you think they're still suspects?"

Mr. Hollingback was physically capable of hanging Dad, he knew about cars, and Mrs. Hollingback had seen me go inside the house only minutes before the bookcase had crashed down on me. If they were lying about their alibi . . .

Aunt Janice gave me half a smile. "Probably not. But don't cross them off the list until you've verified they were in Batavia. You might be surprised by the secrets ordinary-seeming people can carry."

I couldn't imagine my neighbors having many secrets, but maybe that was because I had so few myself. I watched Aunt Janice's expression—calm, with a hint of mystery. Did she have secrets, things I wasn't aware of despite knowing her my whole life? "Are you speaking from experience?"

She lifted an eyebrow and twisted her lips but didn't answer.

Someone knocked on the door, stopping me before I worked up the courage to press her. I went to answer it, and Aunt Janice followed.

Gary stood on the porch. "Hi."

"Hello, Gary." I studied him. His eyes drooped a little, like I would have expected from someone who hadn't slept much, but his smile seemed more confident now than it had the day before. Being free was good for him. "Come on in."

Chapter Twenty-Two

Letter of August 1, 1944, continued
Everything feels upside down, Clive. Daddy's acting like everything is normal, at least around Mom. But it's shaken him. It's shaken us all. Aunt Janice burst out crying in the middle of supper yesterday, and Aunt Shirley is so worried that she's lost weight.

I COULD TELL GARY WASN'T thrilled that Aunt Janice and I had gone to a potential suspect's home without him there to protect us, but he didn't lecture me. He never did. I liked that about him, even more than I liked his dark eyes and his full lips and his muscular arms. He took about five minutes to shower after we had lunch, and then Aunt Janice went to her hat shop, and Gary and I went to Redgrave.

"Do you think he'll be on campus on a Saturday afternoon?" Gary asked as we walked through the halls of the History Department.

"If not, we can go to his house." I'd written Dr. Fontaine's home address on a piece of paper and slipped it into my pocket before we'd left.

Gary switched the pile of books he was carrying from one arm to the other so he could hold my hand. "Are you okay?"

I nodded. "You?"

"I'd feel better if I had a sidearm. If it was him, he's stronger than he looks. Or he had help."

The door to Dr. Fontaine's office wasn't fully closed. I knocked, making the slit wider.

"Come in."

Gary released my hand, and I pushed the door open.

"Miss Hampton! What a pleasant surprise. And . . . Mr. Redhawk. I heard you were arrested." Professor Fontaine looked back at me, clearly disappointed with my choice in company. "For the murder of Professor Hampton."

"I didn't do it," Gary said.

"I suppose not, or you would still be locked away. What do you wish to see me about?" He motioned me to a chair. There were only two in the office, and he took the second.

I wasn't going to sit when there wasn't a place for Gary, but Gary nodded for me to go ahead. He handed me the pile of books, and I put them on the desk.

"Goodness. My entire collection." Dr. Fontaine peered at the stack with a smug smile. "Would you like me to autograph them?"

"These were my father's copies. I was wondering how they came to be in his library. Did you give him a copy, or do you suppose he bought them?"

"I gifted him a copy of my work on Henry VIII and Cardinal Wolsey. The rest he must have purchased." Fontaine leaned back in his seat. "I must say, it's a satisfying surprise to know he valued my work. Your visit is truly a comfort in the wake of his death."

"You didn't know he had them?" Gary asked.

"Of course not. They weren't in his office library, so how would I have seen them?"

Gary handed one to him. "So you never saw the notes he made."

Dr. Fontaine took the book and leafed through it. His face colored, and his lips pulled into a scowl. He read something on another page and then turned to his bookshelf, grabbing a second book, perhaps to use as reference. When he stopped flipping through the pages and paused long enough to read, the color drained from his face. He slammed both books shut and laid them on his desk. "Your father, Miss Hampton, was pompous, arrogant . . . and, unfortunately, usually right."

A flash of annoyance crawled across my chest, but I felt sympathy too. Dr. Fontaine had gone from the surprise of thinking his rival admired him to knowing his rival had instead ripped his work to pieces behind his back. "Your books aren't the only ones he's marked like that."

Dr. Fontaine huffed. "Why are you here?"

"Did my dad come to see you last Saturday? Or call you on the phone?"

"No." Dr. Fontaine frowned. "My son said a man called for me, but I was out at the time."

"Why did you write a book about the Black Prince?" I thought of Dad's disappointment that last day of his life. "My dad told you he was writing about him."

Dr. Fontaine leaned back in his seat. "It's not exactly easy, being in a department with someone like your father. He knows everything and wants everyone else to know that he knows everything. It's infuriating, having him act like an expert in other people's fields. For once, I wanted to show him up. The level of meticulousness he puts into his work takes time. For all his strengths, I knew I could write more quickly than he could. And I did."

Gary reached for another of the books and flipped it open. "But when you published, he would do this to it. Or more, since it's his area of expertise. He could write reviews for newspapers or journals, discredit you across the entire academic community."

Dr. Fontaine's nostrils flared. "I wanted to do something different with this book. I was tired of the Tudors. And, yes, I wanted to beat him in his own era. I didn't think he would ever read it."

"Beat him?" Gary repeated. "What type of contest were you in? I thought you were colleagues."

"Colleagues. Rivals. He always had more prestige. I'm a good professor, but I was living in his shadow."

"Not anymore." Gary folded his arms across his chest. "You must have been relieved to hear of his death."

Dr. Fontaine shook his head.

"Few people had as much reason to kill him as you did."

Dr. Fontaine sat motionless, glaring up at Gary. "What did you say?"

Gary relaxed his arms. "I said you had motive."

"Is that why you're here? To accuse me of a crime? I already spoke to the police. Do you expect to find something they missed?" He frowned. "Besides, that's not how the game works—one simply doesn't murder one's professional rivals. Does our basketball team take baseball bats onto the court and call it a win if they beat the other team unconscious? No. Killing him would be against the rules. You can't outperform someone when he's dead." Dr. Fontaine grunted. "Motive. Not as much motive as you, I would think." He glowered at Gary.

The room felt incredibly uncomfortable. I kept an eye on Dr. Fontaine's hands. He looked angry enough to tear Gary's head off. What if he had a weapon in his desk? "Gary has an alibi. I checked it myself."

"How convenient." Dr. Fontaine didn't look convinced. He shifted his glare from Gary to me. "Your father and I had our differences. But he agreed with me on one thing—that his daughter's latest choice when it came to boyfriends showed a complete lack of taste. He wanted grandchildren, not half-breeds."

I stood, furious. Curses and insults flashed across my tongue, but I held them back, knowing I had to say something logical if I wanted it to mean anything to someone like Dr. Fontaine.

Gary put a hand on my shoulder. "I think it's time for us to leave."

I gathered the books we'd brought. I didn't want them in my collection, but I didn't want to leave them with Dr. Fontaine either. More than likely, I would burn them. Or give them to students taking Dr. Fontaine's British History classes. Either way, I never wanted to see Professor Fontaine again.

We walked in silence until we were outside again. Gary led me to a bench, and we sat. I guess he could tell Fontaine's words had stung.

"I can't believe he said that," I said.

"Which part?" Gary asked.

"The part about . . . half-breeds. It's vile." I stared across the grass. "And I hate to think that Dad might have used that phrase."

Gary chuckled. "No. Your father was meticulous. I'm the half-breed. So that would make our children quarter-breeds, right?"

I made a sound that was part laugh, part sob. "It's awful. Having a little less melanin in our skin doesn't make me or Dad or Dr. Fontaine any better than anyone else."

Gary put his arm across the back of the bench and I leaned into him. "No, but it's something for you to think about. *If* we got married . . . *if* we had children . . . people would look at them differently. Race is usually the first thing someone sees. And sometimes people make assumptions and judgments because of it. You have to consider that. It wouldn't just affect you—it would affect them too."

I met his eyes. He was so calm about it. Most days, I wanted to have a family with Gary, and I had never questioned the value of any future children. But other people would, and that scared me. That doubt was harder to shrug off than the nightmares.

He shook his head. "I don't know, Evie. I'm not sure I'd be a good father anyway."

I'd watched him play catch with Sarah Murphy, I'd seen how hard he worked, and I'd felt how gentle he could be. "Why would you think that?"

"I never even met my father. And my mother was just as broken as I am. She was taken from her family when she was six, sent to a residential school, starved, overworked, abused. She didn't know how to be a mother. She didn't even know how to be part of a family. And neither do I."

"You'll learn." I didn't question Gary's inner goodness or his abilities.

His eyes scanned my face. "Are you willing to risk your happiness on that?"

"I am." I put my hand on his knee. "Gary, look at your grades last semester. No one in your family has ever gone to college before, but you're flourishing. You'll learn how to be a great father too, even if you didn't have anyone to show you how when you were younger."

"And people like Dr. Fontaine?"

There it was again—that question of if I could endure people judging my children before they even knew them. "I don't want people like him determining what's right for me and my family."

Gary ran his fingers through my hair. "If everyone was like you, Evie, the world would be a better place."

I could have said the same about him, but a glance at the pile of books reminded me why we'd come on campus. "Do you think Dr. Fontaine is guilty?" I asked.

Gary pursed his lips. "I don't think he knew your father could be such a harsh critic. So wanting to kill your father to stop him from critiquing his book seems out. But there's still the position of dean. And if he had an alibi, I would have expected him to mention it."

We walked back to my house. I was tired and discouraged. It seemed I wasn't cut out to be a detective, because even after two visits, we didn't seem any closer to determining who had or hadn't killed my father.

Chapter Twenty-Three

August 28, 1944

Dear Evelyn,

It's been weeks since I received any letters, probably because we've been on the move. We're down in Guadalcanal on maneuvers. At the end of the day, the CO of our LST leaves the bow doors open, and we go swimming in the ocean. For that little bit of time, it's like being on vacation. You should add swimming in the south Pacific to your list of things to do when you travel.

I GRABBED MY ROBE WHEN Gary's screams woke me that night. I tied the sash as I reached the stairs. I didn't care what Aunt Janice thought about my middle-of-the-night conversations with Gary. I wanted to help if he'd had another bad dream.

The front door slammed shut.

I paused on the top stair. Who had just entered or exited the house at three o'clock in the morning?

"Evie!" Gary's cry sounded desperate.

"I'm right here." I couldn't see him in the dark, but I heard his footsteps on the wooden stairs.

"Evie, are you okay?"

"I'm fine." I flipped the lights on and gasped.

Gary had made it up a few steps, and he'd left a trail of blood. He held his hand over a spot on his abdomen, and blood oozed from between his fingers. "He didn't get to you?"

I raced down the stairs without asking who he was talking about. Gary slumped to his knees and slid backward before I could reach him.

"Gary? Gary!" I knelt over him at the bottom of the stairs. His eyes were closed, and his hand had slipped from his side, revealing a three-inch-long gash in his skin.

* * *

I paced across the hospital waiting room. Aunt Janice sat in one of the chairs, knitting. She'd insisted we dress before following the ambulance to Maplewick General Hospital, which meant I hadn't seen Gary since the paramedics had carried him out.

Please let him be alive, I prayed over and over again.

We'd already spoken to a police officer—someone I hadn't met before. I'd handed him the keys to the house so he could secure the crime scene. Then I'd continued my pacing.

Finally, someone who looked like a doctor entered the room. "Are you here to see Mr. Redhawk?"

I nodded and walked closer to him. "How is he?"

"He's lucky. The knife didn't hit anything vital. Just skin and muscle. He ought to make a full recovery."

Relief brought tears to my eyes. "Thank you, doctor. May I see him?"

"He's not awake at present, but I'll direct you to his room. You're his next of kin?"

"He doesn't have any family in Maplewick. I'm his girlfriend."

He raised an eyebrow, but I didn't care what conclusion he came to, as long as he let me see Gary. "This way."

The doctor led Aunt Janice and me to a small room. Gary lay inside, sleeping, with white sheets pulled up to his chest and his arms exposed. I stepped next to the bed and took his hand for a moment, then reached up to touch his hair.

"Now that we know he'll be all right, I'll go back." Aunt Janice gave me a hug and held it awhile. "I better clean up that blood before it stains something."

"Sergeant Horton would call that interfering with a crime scene. Better make sure the police are done with it first."

Aunt Janice cupped my cheek in her hand. "All right. Call me when you need me."

I pulled a chair next to Gary's bed and sat, waiting, watching. I assumed his attacker was the same person who had cut the brake line, hung my father, and pulled the bookcase over on top of me. Had Gary seen who it was? The house had been so dark—clouds had rolled in during the night, obscuring the moon. I hadn't thought to look for an intruder until after the front door had slammed shut.

Gary's face was peaceful for the next hour or two. I listened to his steady breathing and wondered if it was the lighting or his injury that gave such a pallor to his complexion. As warm sunlight appeared in the window, lines chiseled themselves into the skin around his mouth and across his forehead.

I fetched one of the nurses. "I think he's in pain."

"Maybe," she said. "Let me know when he wakes up."

I waited, ignoring the clock when I remembered it was Sunday and worship services would begin in a few minutes. Gary moved his head once but stayed asleep. Had they given him something to help him sleep? Or was it blood loss that kept him unconscious?

Eventually, he groaned, and his eyes squeezed shut and relaxed a few times before they cracked open.

"Gary?" I whispered as I took his hand.

"What happened?"

"Someone broke in, I think. He must have stabbed you and then run out."

"Where are we?"

"At the hospital." I took a ragged breath, relieved he was awake and lucid. "You've got quite the cut in your side, but the doctor said you'll recover just fine."

I followed his gaze around the room, taking in the bland walls and the tiny window, the small table on one side of the bed, the IV stand on the other side. I moved the chair closer and brushed his hair back with my fingers.

"Did you see who stabbed you?" I'd been burning to ask that question for hours.

His lips pulled down in apology. "It was too dark. I just remember hoping he had started in the parlor, that you or your aunt weren't already dead."

The nurse chose that moment to return. She asked about his pain levels and checked the bandage on his side. "It's best if you relax. Just rest for a bit." The nurse left as quickly as she'd come.

"I hope *a bit* just means today. I don't want to miss any more classes." Gary squeezed his eyes shut.

"Are you okay?"

"Just a little sore." He forced a smile. "Evie, I'm not sure how safe your dad's house is now. Maybe you and your aunt should stay in a hotel tonight. Don't tell anyone where you are."

I nodded. "Do you suppose it was what we did yesterday? Did we make Dr. Fontaine angry enough that he came to stab you? Or tip the Hollingbacks off that we were suspicious?"

He put more pressure into his grip on my hand. "I don't know. But whoever it was is strong enough that I don't think I'll be able to stop him if he tries again anytime soon."

"Let's not worry about who it was for a bit. Let's get you healed instead. Are you hungry?"

He nodded. I helped him sit and rearranged the pillow so he could lean against the headboard. He winced slightly as he scooted into it.

I went and found the nurse, and she brought him some soup. It was past breakfast time but a little early for lunch. I was hungry and starting to feel the lack of breakfast in a dull headache, but I didn't want to leave Gary. I stayed, watching to make sure his color didn't fade any more. When he finished, I put the empty bowl to the side and took his hand again.

A knock sounded on the door frame, and Detective Iverson walked in.

Gary tensed. I felt the change in his hand, and I saw it in the quickened pulse on his neck.

"Mr. Redhawk? Mind if I ask a few questions?" Iverson kept his distance. Maybe he could tell he made Gary nervous.

Gary bit his lips, then nodded.

Iverson grabbed a chair and sat at Gary's feet. "I've been to the house and seen the blood patterns. But I'd like to hear your version of what happened."

Gary nodded and began. "I was sleeping on the sofa, and I heard a noise loud enough to wake me. A shadow lunged at me, and I knocked his hand to the side. He still stabbed me, but if I were to guess, I probably threw his aim off from something a little more vital. I kicked him and yelled, and he ran out the front door."

Iverson scribbled it all in a little notebook. "Did you recognize him?"

"No. It was too dark."

"What can you tell me about him physically? You're certain it was a man?"

Gary hesitated. "Mostly sure. He grunted a few times. It was low. And he was strong. I caught his arm for a moment before he stabbed me, but he was able to follow through with the swing anyway. I haven't met a woman that strong before."

"Height? Weight?"

"Hard to tell. Medium build. He was hunched over so I couldn't guess his height."

"Did he say anything? Make any threats?"

"No."

Iverson looked up from his notebook. "So he left. Then what?"

"I tried to go upstairs to see if Evie and her aunt were all right. Evie told me she wasn't hurt and turned on the lights. That's the last thing I remember."

Iverson glanced at me.

"He slumped over and fell down the stairs," I said. "There was a lot of blood. Aunt Janice called the hospital while I tried to stop the bleeding."

"Did you see the assailant?"

"No. But I heard the front door slam shut."

Iverson wrote more notes. "Mr. Redhawk, after he stabbed you, did you chase him? Or were you too injured?"

"I went after him. But I couldn't move too quick. Once he left, I was more worried about Evie."

"You were sleeping in Miss Hampton's parlor. Why was that?"

Gary's lips twitched, and his eyes darted over my face. "Because I didn't think Evie's aunt would approve if I slept in Evie's room."

I felt my face color, but I was glad Gary's sense of humor was back.

Gary continued, more serious now. "Someone cut a brake line in Evie's father's car, murdered her father, and pulled a bookcase over on top of her. I was there to protect her if the same man came back to try again. And it seems he did."

Iverson nodded, thoughtful.

"You didn't seem to be looking at anyone other than me," Gary said. "No suspects, no arrests. It was hard to feel safe."

Iverson twisted the pen between his fingers. "I'm sorry you were falsely accused, Mr. Redhawk. Circumstances being what they were, your arrest was logical. I have been exploring other possibilities. Given these latest developments, I wonder if perhaps you've been the target this whole time."

"Me?" Gary's eyebrows scrunched together in surprise.

"First he tried to frame you for Professor Hampton's murder. Then he tried to stop Miss Hampton from clearing your name. And when that didn't work, he tried to finish you off."

Gary ran a hand through his hair. His lips parted, and he turned to me. "Oh, Evie. I'm sorry."

"It's just a theory at this point," Iverson said.

Gary frowned. "A theory that someone is trying to hurt me, so they hurt Evie instead."

I could tell Gary was upset. I was too, but not at him. It wasn't his fault someone had killed Dad to frame him. Whoever it was had an easy task—Gary was vulnerable because of his past, and because of his race.

"Do you have any enemies?"

"A lot of people don't like me, detective. But I can't see any of them going through the trouble to frame me."

"Rivals in your classes?"

Gary shook his head. "I'm pulling decent grades, sir, but I'm not setting any curves."

"Rivals for Miss Hampton?"

Gary looked at me. He didn't answer, but I did. "I was engaged to Roland Roth during the war. We broke it off. *He* broke it off. He invited me to supper the other day, wanted to pick things up again."

"And your response?" Iverson asked.

"I told him I'm seeing someone else. He knows it's Gary."

Iverson grunted and wrote something in his notebook. He looked at Gary again. "What about Mr. Orville Brown?"

Gary's jaw tightened at the mere mention of the teacher. "Mr. Brown had a lot of victims. I'm one out of dozens."

"But you're the only one who fought back. Enough to force him into retirement."

Gary nodded. "And I don't suppose he had much saved up to live off of because I don't think the residential schools paid very well; otherwise, they wouldn't have had such a knack for recruiting scum."

"I think you had better tell me a little more about what happened with Mr. Brown."

A few muscles in Gary's face twitched. "My cousin and I didn't have much of a plan. We knew he was at a bar, so we followed him when he left. We were going to break his back—I don't know that we would have succeeded; we didn't really know how to paralyze someone. Didn't matter anyway. We clubbed him once with a stick. He cried out, and we got caught."

"What happened when you were a child, in the school?"

Gary looked haunted again, and his breathing started to come more quickly. Then he seemed to get it under control, and the muscles in his face relaxed, just a bit. "Evie, maybe you could wait out in the hall for a bit."

He was trying to protect me. I didn't like being dismissed, but there was a plea in his tone that kept me from trying to change his mind.

I went to the hospital cafeteria and ate a sandwich, which helped banish my hunger headache but couldn't do much to help with the lost sleep. I returned to Gary's room as Detective Iverson came out. His face looked haggard. I hated to think about what they'd been discussing.

"Miss Hampton." Iverson nodded his head.

"Is he okay?"

"Better than he was at the station. As a professional investigator, I try to be neutral, let the facts speak for themselves. But I almost hope that Orville Brown is the guilty party. The man deserves punishment. I'll try to locate him. Same with Roland Roth. I suppose he's staying with his parents?"

"I assume so. He didn't say. Will you keep us updated on what's happening? I'm . . . uneasy." Whoever was behind it all had tried four times, and he'd succeeded in killing once. I was worried for myself and for Gary.

"Yes, I'll let you know. I hope we'll have your father's killer in custody very soon."

"How did he get inside? I think he stole my daddy's keys when he killed him, but Gary changed all the locks."

"Someone broke the window in the back door. Probably reached through and unlocked it. But we didn't find any prints. I suspect he wore gloves." Iverson tilted his hat in farewell. "Good afternoon, Miss Hampton."

When I went into Gary's room, he was staring out the window. "Gary?" He didn't respond. Fear that he was having another episode needled through my chest. "Gary?" His breath was coming in short gasps, and sweat dampened his hair. I put my hand on his, and he jerked away. Then he winced. The sudden movement must have aggravated his wound.

I remembered Wanda Murphy and how she'd startled her husband, and for a moment, I was scared. Gary looked past me, then he looked at me. "Evie?"

"Yeah."

"I'm sorry. I was somewhere else."

"Do you want to talk about it?"

"No." He shook his head. "I'd rather be here with you."

Chapter Twenty-Four

Letter of August 28, 1944, continued
Iron Bottom Bay—that's what we call the channel. It's peaceful now, but the navy and the corps had it rough here. Frank's ship, the Helena, *took a lot of damage in these waters. But that was almost two years ago.*

GARY WAS SLEEPY, SUBDUED, AND sweet that afternoon. I stayed with him until the nurses kicked me out.

"How hard is it to get into the hospital at night?" I asked one of them.

She raised an eyebrow. "Are you planning to sneak in?"

"No. But someone tried to kill Mr. Redhawk last night. I'm concerned about his safety."

She nodded. "Several of us will be here all night. We'll keep an eye on him. I'll make sure all the windows on this wing are locked, doors too."

I watched her shuffle off, hoping she would protect Gary for me. I spoke with one of the other nurses too, assuming that two extravigilant nurses would keep him twice as safe.

Aunt Janice sat knitting in the waiting room.

"I thought you went home," I said.

"I did. But I took your car, so I came back because I didn't want you walking home by yourself."

"How long have you been waiting?"

Aunt Janice gave me a sly smile. "I assumed you would stay until the nurses told you to leave. So I came back ten minutes ago. Let's go get some rest."

"In a hotel?" I asked.

"If you'd feel safer there."

I nodded my preference. We had to stop by both our houses to gather our things, but we found a vacant room easily enough.

The next morning, I called the hospital. Gary's nightmares had given the nurses a shock, but no one had tried to attack him, and he was improving.

"When will you release him?"

"I'm not sure, miss. It depends on what the doctor says, and he's still making his rounds."

I was due back at work, and Aunt Janice had her store to run, so after a quick breakfast at a diner, we parted for the morning.

A pile of messages covered my desk when I arrived at the bursar's office. I sat with a sigh and started working through a week's worth of backlog.

Mr. Thurber offered his condolences again. Charlene wanted all the gossip about Gary's arrest and release. I put her off. I didn't feel like talking about it. She didn't ask about the knife attack, so I assumed that hadn't made the papers or the rumor mills yet.

"Miss Hampton?"

I looked up from the payment I was processing to find Mr. Thurber standing in front of my desk. "Yes, sir?"

"You should take a lunch break. It's almost one. And you have someone waiting."

The morning had flown by as if pulled by a courser. "Yes, sir. Thank you."

I finished recording the tuition payment to the correct account, then grabbed my jacket and purse. Aunt Janice had planned to spend the day at her shop, but she had an employee, so maybe she had come to see how I was doing. Or maybe Gary had been discharged. He had class at two, but there was enough time to grab something to eat together. I convinced myself it would be him, and excitement bubbled up inside me.

My face fell when I walked from the bursar's office and saw Roland Roth sitting on the bench below the massive painting of Redgrave's missionary founders.

He stood when he saw me, leaving his hat on the bench. "Evelyn!"

"Mr. Roth." I looked him over. Gary had managed to kick whoever had stabbed him, but Roland was dressed in a suit. I couldn't see more than his neck, head, and hands, none of them bruised.

"Evelyn, I told you to call me Roland. Like you used to."

"That was some years ago, Mr. Roth."

Roland frowned. "I understand if you're still angry about what happened during the war. I'll apologize again."

"That's not necessary. I've moved on. But I have a lot of work to catch up on, and I didn't pack a lunch today, so I'm in a bit of a hurry. If you'll excuse me." I walked past him.

"Let me guess. You didn't bring your own lunch because you weren't home yesterday."

I stopped. "How did you know that?"

"I dropped by. Twice. And I called several times. If you'd been home, I suspect you would have answered. You didn't even make it to church. And I think I know why."

I turned around. "Oh?"

"I suspect you were with that . . . I was going to say *gentleman*, but he doesn't really qualify, does he?"

I felt my anger flare. I was sick of people looking down on Gary because he wasn't rich and he wasn't white. "Gary Redhawk is the finest man I've ever had the privilege of knowing."

Roland walked closer to me. "That *fine man* accused me of stabbing him. The cops were asking me questions this morning."

Roland was a head taller than me. When we'd dated, I'd admired his height. But at the moment, his proximity and his size were as intimidating as a fully armored man-at-arms. The hand gripping my purse felt clammy, and my throat felt dry.

"I didn't break into your house," Roland said. "And I had barely gotten into town when your father was killed. You can ask my parents."

I took a step back, needing space. "Then you have nothing to worry about. And for the record, I was there when Detective Iverson interviewed Gary. He didn't accuse you of anything. The detective merely asked if anyone might have issue with Gary on account of me. *I* mentioned your name."

"You think I would break into your house and try to kill someone?"

"I was just answering the detective's questions."

Roland folded his arms across his chest. "Evelyn, I wanted to pick things up again. But that was before I knew he was staying at your house."

I felt my face go warm.

"You were always such a stickler on virtue . . . and now? You're not even engaged to him." The whispered words stung with unspoken accusation.

"Gary and I didn't even sleep on the same floor, let alone in the same room or the same bed. And Aunt Janice was there as chaperone." It irritated me that Roland would make assumptions about our sleeping arrangements. He had drawn the wrong conclusion, but even if he'd been right, I remembered him wanting to cross lines I wasn't ready to pass before he went overseas. Apparently, it was fine for him to try to seduce me but not for Gary to.

Roland grunted. "Well, I've seen the competition. I don't think I need to stab him to be in the running. *If* I were interested, which I'm not sure I am anymore."

"Well, if you're having doubts, and I'm certain the answer is *no*, then I see no reason to continue this conversation."

I stepped away, and he grabbed my arm. "Evelyn, don't be like this."

"Let go of me, Mr. Roth."

"Evelyn, please give me another chance."

Back when I was twenty and twenty-one, it hadn't seemed so bad to be with Roland, even when he tried to tell me what to do and how to think. But I didn't want to return to that, not after dating Gary and knowing what it was to be respected as a person instead of as some kind of ornament. "That would be like going back to buttermilk after discovering ice cream. Let go of me."

"Evelyn!" Roland's face twisted as the insult registered.

"Ahem." My cousin Frank cleared his throat. "I think she asked you to leave her alone."

Roland released me and held up his hands. He and Frank were about the same size, but it seemed Roland didn't want a fight. "I'm not looking for trouble, Mr. Bingham."

"Good." Frank crossed his arms and flexed his biceps, like he and Clive had done when they were teenagers trying to impress girls, but he looked far more intimidating now than when he was fifteen. "Maybe you should leave."

Roland nodded and grabbed his fedora as he sulked away.

"You okay, Evie?"

"Yes. Thanks for showing up. Your timing was flawless."

Frank grinned. "I heard about this weekend. Wanted to see how you were doing. You off to lunch?"

"Yeah."

"Mind if I join you?"

"That would be lovely." Having an overprotective cousin around sounded like the ideal weapon against an ex-fiancé. "Mind if we stay on campus? I've got a week's worth of work piled up on my desk."

"Sure. Does the cafeteria still have fried chicken on Mondays?"

"I believe they do."

Over fried chicken and coleslaw, I told Frank about the break-in and the attack. "Gary needed stitches, and they kept him overnight, but the doctor said he ought to make a full recovery."

"You're growing kinda attached to him, aren't you?"

"Do you approve?"

Frank had always seemed fair with Gary, more than Dad or Dale had. But he had always seemed cautious too.

"It's your choice, Evie. But with Clive and Uncle Ernst both gone, I feel it's my duty to point out that Mr. Redhawk has no safety net. Not like Roland, who can borrow money from a rich father if things get tough. And I don't have problems with Indians. I served with some in the navy, and they were good men, but not everyone feels that way."

"I've noticed."

"I'm sure you have. But what really makes me nervous is what Dale told me about how he acted in jail. If he's a psychoneurotic case, I'm not sure how safe that is for you."

"I've seen a few episodes. He doesn't get aggressive."

"It can get worse with time. And even if it doesn't, it's hard to find work if you've been labeled psychoneurotic. Then there's the matter of living with someone like that. I had a few nightmares when I got back. I think that's part of why Libby left me."

Frank's marriage had been a whirlwind wartime romance, quickly made before he'd sailed off, then quickly ended when he'd returned and they'd realized they were strangers. Dad said they were thinking about what they wanted that week, not what they wanted in a year or a decade. I suppose it was an easy mistake to make when you weren't sure you'd survive beyond the next voyage.

"Do you ever talk to her?" I'd met Libby once, and I'd liked her.

Frank frowned. "She's married to someone else now." He wiped his fingers on a napkin. "I'm not sure it's any of my business, but how serious are you and Mr. Redhawk?"

For a moment, talking to Frank was almost like talking to my brother. "When I was trying to firm up his alibi, I found out he has a ring on layaway."

"A ring? Are you engaged?"

"No. But I think we will be soon. Maybe when everything calms down and the police figure out who killed Daddy."

Frank thought for a moment. "Well, as long as he knows how lucky he is to have you, we ought to get along just fine at Thanksgiving and Easter and whenever else the family gets together."

It was nice to have people who cared about me, but Frank and everyone else were off when they made it sound like Gary was lucky to have me. "I'm lucky to have him. He's unselfish and empathetic and loyal. He's bright, and he's a hard worker. He's amazing, Frank, maybe more so because he's been through so much."

"Is he out of the hospital yet?"

"No. I called this morning before work, but they weren't sure when they'd let him out." I glanced toward the cafeteria's kitchen. Gary was normally there this time of day, cleaning dishes or mopping floors. I wished he were back there now, without a gash in his side.

Frank lowered his voice. "And what was he doing at your house in the middle of the night?"

"Trying to protect me."

"Hmm." Frank sat back in his seat. "People will talk."

"I know. But he was right. I was in danger. Or maybe he was. Detective Iverson thinks someone tried to frame him. Then when that didn't work out, tried to kill him instead."

"Iverson have any leads?"

I smiled. "He questioned Roland Roth. Roland didn't seem too happy about it, did he?"

"I certainly didn't like the way he was grabbing your arm. Clive said in a letter once that he wanted to give Roland a knuckle sandwich. He didn't say why, but I about followed his suggestion when I saw Roland in the hallway just now. Did he leave a bruise?"

"I don't think so." I felt my arm underneath my jacket, but the skin wasn't tender. "Part of me wants to believe Roland is harmless. But something about him makes me nervous."

"You watch out for yourself, you hear?"

I nodded.

"Where are you sleeping?"

"With Aunt Janice, but not at her house."

"Where, then?"

"I promised Gary I wouldn't tell anyone."

Frank chuckled. "Well, you said he was bright. I reckon you're right."

Chapter Twenty-Five

September 10, 1944

Cancer? Are you sure, Evie? I always thought nothing could stop Mom. To think that she might not be there when I finally get home . . .

I GOT OFF WORK LATE and drove to the hospital. I found Gary at a desk, signing paperwork, and walked up without him seeing me.

"Is there any way we can break it up into payments?"

The lady talking to him twisted her lips in annoyance. "Yes, but there's a fee for that."

Gary nodded. "I think I'd like to do it that way, please."

"Let me go get the form."

As she left, I stepped closer, wondering what the bill was. "Gary?"

He stood and smiled. "Evie, it's good to see you."

"I'm glad to see you on your feet." I wrapped my arms around him, trying to be gentle, and kissed his cheek. "How do you feel?"

"Sore. But it could be worse."

I stiffened, imagining Gary dead. Yes, it could have been a lot worse. I leaned my forehead on his shoulder. "I don't know what I would have done if that knife had struck something more serious."

His arms tightened around my waist.

"Mr. Redhawk, here's the form you requested." The hospital lady was back.

"Evie, could you give me a moment? Maybe meet me in the waiting room?"

I took his arm and pulled him away from the desk, then kept my voice low. "You were injured while trying to protect me, so maybe you should let me take care of your expenses."

I'd known it would embarrass him if I offered to pay and the woman heard, but his downturned lips and pinched eyes told me I'd embarrassed him anyway.

"That's a kind offer, Evie, but one I can't accept."

"Please, Gary. You might not be able to haul stuff around the grocery store or clean the cafeteria for a few weeks while it heals."

"Evie, please give me a few minutes and let me take care of it."

"But you wouldn't have gotten stabbed if it weren't for me."

"We don't know that. Based on the detective's latest theory, your father wouldn't have gotten killed if someone weren't out to get me."

"Then let me pay it, and if Detective Iverson finds out it was your fault, you can pay me back. I'll probably charge less interest than the hospital."

A hint of a smile turned his lips. He was cracking. "I think you should go to the waiting room."

"Not without you. What if the killer's out there?"

"In the hospital?"

I shrugged. "It's possible."

Gary brushed a finger along the side of my face. "Let me take care of it, Evie."

"But I want to help." I glanced at the desk. "And that lady looks tired. I think she'd rather have payment in full and be done with it. And I'd rather have your extra money go to Mr. Baumgartner than to the hospital."

His hand fell away, and his jaw slackened in surprise. He was so stunned that he didn't stop me when I walked over to the desk and took my checkbook out. I'd finished writing the check before he came over. Confusion still showed on his face as he looked from me to the pile of papers and back again. He clamped his jaw shut and seemed to give up.

He waited until we were out of the hospital to speak. "I'll pay you back."

"Okay." I should have let him arrange installments, then come back later to pay it anonymously. I'd remember that for next time to try to spare his feelings, if there was a next time.

"What did Mr. Baumgartner show you when you were in his shop?"

"He didn't *show* me anything." We'd reached the car, so I turned around to face him.

"What did he tell you?"

"He didn't mean to spoil anything. He didn't realize I was your sweetheart until later. But he said you were buying a ring. That you've been making payments since October."

I couldn't read Gary's expression. He leaned against the car, right next to me. "You've known since Friday?"

"Yeah."

He was quiet for a long time before speaking again. "Do you want it?"

Did he mean what I thought he meant? "Yes."

"And everything that goes with it?" He turned toward me.

I reached up to play with his hair, moving strands of it from one side of his part to the other. "I'm more interested in everything that goes with it than I am in the jewelry."

"You want a husband who's so poor he can't pay cash for a stay in the hospital, who wakes up screaming most nights, and who might have been the cause of your father's death?" His voice was soft, and his face was close.

"I want you, Gary."

His fingers caressed my face, and one of his arms slipped around my waist. "Do you mind if I smear your lipstick?"

I didn't need words to answer. The kiss started off gently, with soft brushes and slow nuzzles, then it continued, deeper, stronger, more urgent. Something about Gary's mouth on mine made me feel invincible and vulnerable at the same time. I needed him, and I wanted him, and he needed and wanted me too. There was Gary, and there was me, and a ticker tape parade could have marched past us, and we wouldn't have noticed because we were so swept away in each other. When he eventually pulled away, I didn't know if minutes or hours had passed, but I knew that regardless of what anyone else thought about us, my heart belonged to him.

* * *

We planned to eat supper at Aunt Janice's house, but first we stopped by Gary's shed so he could pick up a few things. Daylight was dimming, but that didn't stop me from seeing the worried expression on his face when he fingered the open latch.

"I always lock it," Gary said.

"You haven't had a normal routine for a few days. Maybe you overlooked it? Left the lock inside?"

"Maybe." Gary bit his lip. "Or maybe someone's been here."

He opened the door, and I caught a whiff of alcohol. Gary didn't drink anymore, so where was it coming from? He pulled the cord to the shed's single lightbulb, illuminating a man lying on his bed.

I inhaled sharply and moved closer to Gary, who crossed his arms and waited while the man blinked and sat up on the cot.

"What are you doing here?" Gary asked.

The man yawned and stood, stretching. "Looking for you." I couldn't tell the man's age. He might have been anywhere from eighteen to thirty-five. He was about Gary's height, with long black hair woven into two braids. He eyed me with a mix of curiosity and hostility.

He walked to Gary's desk and grabbed the sketch Gary had drawn of me. He didn't bother to unpin it from the wall—he yanked and tore. He held it out, comparing me and my likeness. "And I thought you were drawing pictures of Hedy Lamarr and adding a few freckles. Who's the broad?"

Gary's lips turned down. "Miss Hampton, this is my cousin, Otetiani Amedon."

Otetiani Amedon made me nervous, but if he was part of Gary's family, I was determined to be polite. "Pleased to meet you, Mr. Amedon." I held my hand out.

Mr. Amedon looked at my outstretched hand and let his arms fall to his side. "Gary, what are you doing? Her?" He gestured at me. "Economic theory?" He waved toward the books on Gary's desk. Most of Gary's textbooks were on the back seat of the car, where I'd put them when I'd last gone home, but a few were still present to receive Mr. Amedon's contempt.

"I told you I was taking classes at Redgrave."

Mr. Amedon huffed. "Yeah, I got the letter."

"How are things in Cattaraugus?" Gary asked.

"'Bout the same." Mr. Amedon walked back to the cot and pulled a bottle from between the bed and the wall. That explained the permeating stench of gin. He took a swig and held it out to Gary.

Gary shook his head.

"Too good to drink with your cousin? Is that what all your education is teaching you, that you're too good for your own people?"

"There's more to life than being drunk all the time."

"I'll bet." Mr. Amedon studied me again. "She your latest diversion?"

Gary's shed suddenly felt like an oven.

"You will speak of Miss Hampton with respect, or I'll ask you to leave." Gary's voice was firm.

Mr. Amedon laughed. "Hit a nerve, did I? It's not gonna work out, Gary. None of it is. Not her, not some college degree. Do you really think they're gonna give you a fair shake? Don't fool yourself. You'll never be one of them. Don't waste your time trying."

Gary turned to me. "I'm sorry, Evie. He's not always this bad."

Mr. Amedon scoffed. "Me? Bad? I'm just telling you like it is. They'll always see you as an irredeemable Indian. You're wasting your time at Redgrave. And you're wasting your time on someone like her." There was a sneer in his voice.

I got the impression that he saw me along the same lines as he saw something stuck to the bottom of his shoe: slimy and contemptible. Was that how Gary felt when people asked me why I was dating him?

Gary put his arm around my shoulders as though he could tell I needed a bolster. "I'm not wasting my time. Why don't you tell me how much money you need, and then you can take off."

"You can send me away, but it won't change anything. They won't accept you, college degree or not. Even if they did, why would you wanna join 'em? Nothing but a bunch of swindlers and treaty-breakers."

I watched Gary, wondering how he'd react. He kept his face and voice calm when he spoke. "So I should go back to Cattaraugus instead? Drink my life away, mourning the fact that we're small and powerless? No, thanks. I'll try to make it in this world instead."

"It's not *your* world. These aren't *your* people." Mr. Amedon took another sip from the bottle. "Never figured you would abandon Cattaraugus and turn your back on your own people. Guess I was wrong."

Gary was quiet for a moment. His hand slipped from my shoulder to my waist. "I wasn't doing anyone any good while I lived there—I was wasting my life. I needed something different, and this is it. I just want to be happy. Is that so wrong?"

"You could help us change things." Mr. Amedon stepped closer.

"I'm changing myself. I thought that was a good place to start."

"Changing yourself?" Mr. Amedon jeered. "With Redgrave . . . and her?" He pointed at me. He spoke again, but it wasn't English. Seneca, maybe.

I felt the tension build in Gary as he listened to his cousin. He glanced at me for a moment, then shook his head and turned back to Mr. Amedon. "What you want me to do? Be miserable because life isn't fair? Because things aren't perfect? That's not how I want to live."

Mr. Amedon didn't reply. He took another drink.

"How long are you staying?" Gary asked.

Mr. Amedon shrugged.

"I'll buy you a bus ticket tomorrow."

"Don't want me around, huh?"

"I've got a lot of schoolwork to catch up on."

Mr. Amedon glared at the books on Gary's desk, but he nodded.

Gary sighed, I think with relief. "Let me walk you to your car, Evie."

Fresh air and reduced tension greeted me as we left the shed. "I thought you were coming over for supper."

Gary looked back at the shed. "Yeah, so did I, but I don't want to bring him."

I nodded. I didn't really want Mr. Amedon around either. He was drunk and bitter, and I hated the way he scoffed at Gary's accomplishments instead of congratulating him.

Gary took my hand. "I'm sorry, Evie. He . . . he's had a rough life."

"So have you. But that doesn't keep you from being pleasant."

"I've had moments I'm not proud of. Years, actually." He looked away.

I reached up and drew his face back toward mine. "You're a good man now. That's what I care about."

He kissed my mouth, just for a few seconds, just long enough for me to know his cousin's words hadn't changed how he felt about me. "You and your aunt will sleep at a hotel tonight, right?"

"Yes. But if someone is trying to kill you, that won't do much good."

Gary glanced back at the shed. "It looks like I won't be sleeping alone."

"If he's drunk and you're still recovering—"

"There's not a whole lot of space in the shed. If someone tries to get in, he's bound to trip over one of us. And then Otetiani'll yell loud enough to wake everyone in the house."

I nodded, hoping Gary was right. The walls were sturdy enough, and it bolted closed from the inside. Breaking in would be noisy. And several able-bodied veterans lived twenty yards away. "Does he come often?"

"Three or four times a year."

"Does he always ask for money?"

Gary nodded.

"And you give it to him?"

"Yeah. He's my cousin."

"But if he's just using it to get drunk . . . that doesn't do either of you any good." Gary didn't have money to throw at his cousin's bad habits.

"It's complicated. Out here, wealth is about getting things and owning things. But that's not the Seneca way. We show prestige not by having things but by giving things. A rich man is someone who can provide for others. A lot of our traditions are gone—curbed, eroded, suppressed—but not completely dead."

I swallowed and nodded, trying to understand.

"And I feel like I owe him," Gary continued. "If I had swung that stick a little harder, I might have knocked Mr. Brown unconscious, and then maybe we wouldn't have gotten caught, and Otetiani wouldn't have spent three years in prison."

"Or you would have crippled Mr. Brown and still gotten caught, and then you both might have spent a lot longer in prison."

Gary glanced back at the shed. "Like I said, it's complicated."

"I admire that you want to help him. I just don't think giving him money for his next drink is the best way to do it, for him or for you."

Gary held my shoulders and kissed my forehead. "I'll work on some boundaries. It might take a time or two to get it sorted out, but I'll work on it. I promise."

"Okay." I recognized it was a hard promise for him to make, and I was grateful for it. "Stay safe tonight, you hear? Someone tried to kill you."

"You be careful too." Gary wrapped his arms around me, and I clung to him.

He released me, but I didn't get in the car right away. "How will I know you're all right?" Mr. Norton didn't have a phone, so I couldn't call him, and I wasn't sure where I was sleeping tonight, so he couldn't call me.

"I'll drop by your office before class tomorrow." He met my lips again, a few light brushes against my mouth that sent tingles of pleasure radiating through me.

The door to his shed opened, interrupting our kiss. Mr. Amedon stood in the doorway.

"Hopefully after I've dropped him off at the bus station," Gary whispered.

Chapter Twenty-Six

Letter of September 10, 1944, continued
We're going into action soon. I'm nervous, Evie, about that and about other things. For a long time, I've known I might not make it home, but I never thought home might change so completely while I was gone.

NOTHING UNUSUAL HAPPENED THAT NIGHT. When Gary stopped by the bursar's office the next morning, I was on the phone, so he blew me a kiss from across the room and hurried off to class. I reconciled the previous week's payments until my brain felt mushy, then sent out a few late notices. When I finished up for the day and left the office, the first person I saw was Detective Iverson.

"Miss Hampton?"

"Hello, detective. Any news?"

He frowned. "There's not enough evidence to make an arrest. I'd like to talk with Mr. Redhawk again, but he's not at home. Do you know where he might be?"

"His last class ended at about three, but I know his favorite place to study. I'll show you."

Iverson followed me to the library, and Gary was where I expected him to be. The muscles along Gary's jaw tightened when he saw the detective, but he seemed to relax when he saw me too. No one else was nearby, so we joined Gary at the table as he put his books away.

"I've done a little investigating," Iverson said. "On the afternoon of Professor Hampton's murder, Mr. Roth was with his parents most of the time but not all of it. But he doesn't seem to have been in town early enough to sabotage the car."

Gary nodded. "And he doesn't have motive for pulling the bookcase over on Evie, unless he was trying to stop her from finding my alibi. But that would have been risky. It could have killed her."

"A risk he was willing to take, perhaps? If he can't have her, no one else can either?" Iverson set his hat on the table and got out his notebook. "Mr. Brown moved to Hofeling when he retired from the Thomas Indian School."

Gary met my eyes, then turned his attention back to the detective. "That's only fifteen miles from Maplewick."

"Yes. I drove out there today and met with him. No alibi. But physically, I don't think he's capable of climbing under a car to cut the brake line or hauling a man up by his neck or yanking a bookcase over. And I think you would have overpowered him if he'd tried to stab you. He's aged. Walks with a stoop. His hands shake."

"Could he have faked it? Acted feeble while you were there?" I asked.

Iverson shook his head. "I think it was genuine. So either he's innocent— of this at least—or he has an accomplice. But I can't arrest him without evidence tying him to at least one of the events in Maplewick."

"Do you want us to find some evidence?" Gary asked. "Is that why you're discussing the investigation with us?"

"No." Iverson's answer was immediate. "I do not want either of you looking for evidence. But someone tried to kill you, Mr. Redhawk, and they succeeded in injuring you. And someone also succeeded in injuring Miss Hampton. I don't have proof it was the same person, but logic suggests it was. Who remains a mystery, so I want the two of you to take precautions. Whoever's behind all this seems persistent enough to try again."

Gary and I were silent for a few moments after Iverson left.

"Will you and your aunt go to a hotel tonight?" Gary asked.

"Yeah. And you?"

"If I bolt my shed from the inside, it's hard to break in."

That didn't seem secure enough. "But your cousin's gone, isn't he? So you'd be all alone."

"I dropped him at the station. Maybe I should borrow one of your dad's medieval weapons for self-defense."

Normally, I would have laughed at Gary's suggestion, and at the sly tone he'd used, but worry had a way of making me humorless. "Or I can get you a room." I'd sleep better knowing he was hard to find. It might get expensive but not as expensive as a funeral. I'd just planned one, so I knew. I didn't want to plan another or have one planned for me.

"I already owe you money for the hospital."

"It's worth it, to me, to know you're safe. Think about it, at least, won't you?"

Gary stood. "Yeah, I'll think about it."

His reply sounded suspiciously like *no*, but I didn't press it while we walked from the library.

"How's your side?" I asked.

"Sore."

"Mr. Redhawk?"

Gary and I turned at Professor Gerstner's call. "Good evening, sir," Gary said.

"I haven't seen you in class for a week."

"I'll be there tomorrow, sir."

Dr. Gerstner shook his head. "You've a great deal of aptitude for this subject, Mr. Redhawk. But sometimes I question your work ethic."

"Understood, sir."

Gerstner waited, as if expecting more, perhaps an apology. He sighed, then spoke again. "Mr. Murphy is doing well. I told him it was safe to go back with his family again, but we'll keep meeting. Thank you for your phone call. I love academic life, but on occasion, it's nice to have a more practical application for my work. And I was surprised at how much I enjoyed having a houseguest. Things have been too quiet since the children left."

"Thank you for helping him, professor."

Gerstner pursed his lips. "Don't let that mind of yours go to waste, Mr. Redhawk. If you apply yourself, you could go far."

Gerstner turned to go, but I called him back. "Professor, Gary hasn't been cutting class because he doesn't care or because he's not a hard worker."

"Oh?"

"Someone tried to frame him for murder. He was in jail last week until the police realized they made a mistake and released him. Then someone tried to kill him. He missed your class yesterday because he was still in the hospital."

I had Gerstner's full attention now. I glanced at Gary, but I couldn't read his face. I hoped I hadn't said more than he was comfortable with.

"I spent more time with Mr. Murphy than with the newspapers last week. I assume the real criminal has been apprehended?"

"No, sir." I hesitated. If Professor Gerstner had helped Mr. Murphy with his flashbacks, maybe he could help Gary with his nightmares. Gary needed an anonymous place to sleep, and Professor Gerstner liked houseguests. "The detective in charge of the case doesn't have enough evidence to make an arrest. But he suggested Gary take precautions. Whoever's behind it has made four attempts so far. We were just trying to figure out where Gary could safely sleep."

Professor Gerstner looked from me to Gary, and then he checked his watch. "I'm supposed to meet my wife for a show. It's a Tuesday tradition. But I don't doubt she would enjoy another houseguest. You're welcome to stay with us, Mr. Redhawk. Come by at nine thirty. Number Sixteen, Stanton Lane. Perhaps over breakfast, I can fill you in on what you've missed in our psychology class."

* * *

The next day, I got off work a few hours early and drove Gary to Hofeling. Iverson didn't want us to look for evidence, but neither of us wanted to sit around and wait for the next attack. "How did things go with the Gerstners?" I asked.

"Better than I thought they would."

I glanced at him to make sure his expression matched his words. "Good . . . I wasn't sure if I'd done the right thing. But he helped Mr. Murphy, and you needed a place to stay, and I didn't think there was any reason to suspect he's involved with the attacks."

"I was nervous when you told him, but it worked out." Gary stared out the window. "It's still strange to me when people are nice for no reason. I mean, I understand being polite, but for them to go out of their way for a stranger. I don't see that too often."

We reached Hofeling's outskirts. The sky was overcast, cloaking the old brick-and-wood buildings in gloom. Even in sunlight, I doubted Hofeling ever looked cheerful. "I guess you haven't had too many people show you kindness."

"You. Ley, when he filled out all those applications for me and made me give up alcohol. But we had a shared past, during the war. We saw and experienced a lot of the same things. And my aunt, Otetiani's mother. She would come to visit me at Thomas, first Sunday of the month. Sometimes she'd bring my mother. But that's family. They're supposed to take an interest. Professor Gerstner is different. That class is our only connection, but he still seems to care what I do with my life. No one else does."

"I care."

He put his hand on my right knee. "I know. And I'm glad for it."

There were people who cared for Gary, other than me and his family and his war buddies. Mr. Baumgartner liked him, and so did Mr. Norton and the Murphys. But for every kind person, there was someone else who made him feel unloved or unwanted.

"Here's Clafton Street." I turned left onto a residential road lined with budding trees and aging brick row homes. "Do you want me to park at Brown's place or a little past it?"

"Park where we can keep an eye on it for a while without him noticing."

Mr. Brown's address was on our left, so I parked two houses before it, on the right.

I took in the rundown fence, the crumbling mortar, and the door with the peeling paint. "It's not very fancy."

"No. But I don't think he was married, so he doesn't need much space."

It wasn't the size that failed to impress me. It was the obvious neglect. The house to the north had a fresh coat of paint on the trim. The house on the south had tulips in window boxes. But Mr. Brown's house looked almost abandoned. "Doesn't look like he's taking care of it."

Just as I was questioning if someone really lived there, an old Ford pulled to a stop on the other side of the street in front of Brown's townhome. The car, a prewar model, was much like the home—aged and uncared for.

"That's him." Gary's voice had a tightness that I wasn't used to. I turned my focus to him because the strain I heard reminded me of the warehouse.

"We don't have to do this." I put my hand on his. "We can leave it to Detective Iverson."

Gary inhaled and exhaled deeply. "It's different now. I'm not a child anymore. I can defend myself."

I watched Mr. Brown walk into the house. His coat had a patched elbow, and his hat was scuffed, with a crumpled brim. He looked every bit as frail as Detective Iverson had said. Was it all an act because he knew he was under scrutiny? "Do you want to talk to him or just watch him?"

"I don't think we'll learn much if we just sit here."

He was the one who had reason to be nervous, but fear made goose bumps form ranks along my arms and the back of my neck. "Mrs. Armellino seemed to think I was a reporter when I went to visit her. I could try that again, ask him some questions."

Gary shook his head. "He might recognize me."

"I could go alone."

"There's no way I'm letting you talk to him by yourself. Just because his taste is for little boys doesn't mean he wouldn't try to take advantage of a beautiful woman showing up on his doorstep." He ran his eyes over me. "Reporter, huh?"

"Yeah. I didn't tell her I was a reporter or that I was writing something. I just said I was investigating."

"Poor woman. I lied to her."

"Mrs. Armellino?"

Gary nodded.

"About her husband and the battle?" Gary's words had brought Cora Armellino comfort—had they been lies?

"I told her we made a gallant last stand to help everyone pulling back to Elsenborn. You know what really happened? Chaos. Panic. We were supposed to withdraw, but no one told our platoon. Don't know if they forgot or if the runner got killed, but one day we were getting hit with German artillery, like everyone else. The next day we woke up, and we were alone and about out of ammo. And then we were surrounded by Krauts."

Gary's eyes focused on Mr. Brown's house. "I told her that the last time I saw David Armellino, he was dead, lying in the snow in a beautiful little village in Belgium. That he'd taken a bullet in the head, died quickly. That he was resting underneath a bunch of pristine pine trees. He did take a bullet in the head, but only after he'd taken one in the shoulder and another in the groin. One of the medics gave him some morphine, but he still had a hard death. And he didn't die in the forest. It was on a road. We wanted to move the body after we surrendered. The Nazis wouldn't let us. Last I saw David Armellino, he had been run over by a tank."

I put a hand over my mouth and tried not to picture it. "Maybe it's better she doesn't know."

Gary nodded. "That's what I thought, at the time."

"Are you having second thoughts?"

"About what I told her? Not really. About the battle? Yeah, but that's nothing new. I think you always have second thoughts when things go so wrong." His hands flexed and then relaxed. "Armellino and I spent a lot of time together, during training, then when we got to Belgium. He was a good man. Why him and not me? Nobody cared if I made it back. A lot of people still miss him."

I took his hand. "I care that you came back."

He wove his fingers through mine. "Maybe so, but you wouldn't have liked me back then. And if Mr. Brown is behind all this and murdered your father, maybe you would have been better off if we hadn't met. I'm going to go talk to him," Gary said. "You should stay here."

"I'm coming with you." Mr. Brown had hurt Gary before. I wasn't going to let him face that monster alone.

Gary didn't argue, so we left the car and walked to the house together. I noted the pause before Gary knocked, but I didn't comment on it. His breathing was still normal, but his posture seemed more rigid than relaxed.

Mr. Brown answered the door. He didn't look like a monster. He looked like somebody's grandpa. His shoulders slumped, and his head tilted forward, like a skinny turtle with gray hair.

"Who are you?" Mr. Brown asked.

"Do you recognize me?" Gary's voice was tight, strained.

Mr. Brown sighed. "No. But a police detective came around asking questions, so I can guess you're that no-good Indian who tried to cripple me during the war."

The muscles of Gary's face tensed. I wanted to ask Mr. Brown if he was that no-good pedophile who'd molested the boys under his care at the boarding school, but I waited for Gary to take the lead.

Gary took a few deep breaths. "And what did you think of those questions? Did they hit a little too close to home?"

"I told the detective he was wasting my time."

"Are you still bitter about that attack?" Gary seemed overwrought, like at the warehouse, but he kept his breathing steady.

"Of course I'm bitter. I lost my job. And you walked free."

Gary hadn't gone free. He'd fought desperately in Belgium and been a prisoner of the Nazis. That might have happened anyway, but he had faced the consequences of his actions.

"So bitter that you decided to frame me for murder?"

Mr. Brown huffed. "You think I would waste time on an insignificant Indian boy like you? You're nothing. Your own mother abandoned you, and if you're anything like all the others I've seen go through that school, you'll turn out just like her. In a gutter somewhere, poor, drunk, and worthless. I hope you fry in the electric chair."

"How can you say that?" I said. "After what you did to those boys?"

"No one cared about those boys. Not even their parents. They had no hope, no future. They were always going to be a menace to society. The best they could do was stay out of jail, work some meaningless job. They wouldn't be fit for anything more than that."

"That's not true. And even if it were, that doesn't justify what you did." I had never felt such intense loathing for anyone before. Mr. Brown was pure evil.

Gary put a gentle hand on my shoulder. "You're wrong, Mr. Brown. I'm not worthless, and I haven't been drunk in a long time. I have a future, and I have hope, and I have love. That seems to be more than what you have at the moment."

Gary took my hand, and we left.

Chapter Twenty-Seven

September 20, 1944
Dear Clive,
I knew it wasn't going to be easy, but I didn't realize it would be this hard.
Mom's going fast. She has such a small amount of energy now, like she's aged in
decades instead of weeks. She spends hours looking at the photo albums. She stares
at your pictures for a long time, as if she knows she won't be seeing you again.

I SAT IN THE CAR, reeling.

"You okay?" Gary asked.

I nodded, waiting for my heart rate to slow. "He's absolutely vile. No remorse at all. How many childhoods did he ruin?"

"I don't know."

"He did it, didn't he? He killed my father, and he stabbed you."

Gary was silent.

"You don't think so?" I watched him. His breathing was slow and steady, like he was consciously controlling it, using it to manage whatever he'd felt.

"You're right that he's vile. But whoever stabbed me had more muscle than him. And I don't think he could have killed your dad, not the way he was hung. Doubtful he could even yank over a bookcase."

"He could have hired someone."

"Maybe. But I don't know if he would go to the trouble over a worthless Indian."

"You're not worthless. You don't believe him when he says that, do you?" I liked that Gary wasn't cocky, but I didn't want that humility to turn into depression, especially not because of something a horrible man like Mr. Brown said.

"No, I don't believe him. But look at it from his point of view. My race is inferior. Why bother? And why would he search me out now? Why not when I got back from the war? I was a lot less likeable back then, and I was drunk most of the time—easier to attack."

"Maybe he didn't know where you were until now. And then he finds out you're thriving academically and you're in a serious relationship with someone from an established Maplewick family, and he's jealous. His life is meaningless, and he wants his victims to be just as hopeless."

Gary thought about that. "From his perspective, getting me executed would be doing society a favor. But to kill an innocent college professor? That's different. I don't think he'd go that far."

I took a few more deep breaths, waiting for my body to calm down. I put the key in the ignition, but my hand shook.

"Do you want me to drive?" Gary asked.

I nodded and got out of the car. I caught Mr. Brown watching us from the window, and chills went up my spine. Gary walked me around to the passenger side and kissed me on the forehead. "Don't let him get to you."

I tried not to, but as Gary drove the car back to Maplewick, I couldn't get Mr. Brown out of my mind. "I don't think I've ever met someone so awful. It's like he doesn't know right from wrong or doesn't care. I'd be angry if someone did those things to an animal—but he hurt children! And he's not sorry!"

Gary laughed softly. "There are a lot of people like that in this world, Evie. I'm glad you haven't run into too many of them."

"Sometimes I feel so naive." There was a depth to Gary's experiences that I couldn't fathom. Many of them were hard and sad, but he'd been strong enough to overcome them. My challenges, in comparison, felt insignificant.

"You're smart, Evie. Don't let anyone tell you otherwise."

Gary's advice was wise. I wished I'd had it a decade ago.

I still remembered Clive laughing at me when I'd asked Dad for help with my algebra problems. "Those are easy-peasy, Evie. Can't you do them yourself?"

I'd felt my face go hot. I'd been trying by myself for a half hour, and I still wasn't any further than I'd been when I sat down. "I just want him to explain it again."

"I never needed help with math homework." Clive took an apple from a bowl on the countertop and ran outside.

"Never mind him," Dad said. "His teacher was a fine instructor, so talented he was hired by the university last year. Maybe your new teacher isn't quite as good."

"You okay, Evie?" Gary asked.

"Yes. No." I sighed. "I shouldn't let him shake me up like that." I meant Mr. Brown but also Clive. My brother had apologized, and we'd reconciled completely, so why did his words from over a decade ago still sting? "I should ask you that. Mr. Brown was your tormentor. Was it hard to see him again?"

"Yeah. But not as bad as I thought it might be. It helps that I'm not little anymore and he's getting old. And it helps that you were with me. I'm sorry you had to meet him, but you helped me be strong."

I studied him as he drove. I'd seen the signs: the stiffness, the strained voice, the change in breathing. "You fought off an attack."

Gary nodded. "Professor Gerstner had a few ideas. I guess they worked."

"Will you press charges against Mr. Brown?"

Gary glanced over at me, then back at the road.

That looked a lot like a *no*. "Why not?"

"It would be his word against mine. I don't know that I could get a jury to believe me over him. And going through a trial . . ."

That much I understood. Gary didn't want to talk about it, relive it in detail, especially not in front of a judge and jury, lawyers and reporters.

"The thing is, I tried to put it from my mind for a long time." Gary's hands tightened on the steering wheel. "Even now, it's more flashes of memory than a coherent account. Odd things will spark a flashback. Seeing a certain type of bed frame, the smell of licorice."

"Licorice?"

"Mr. Brown was always sucking on little pieces of licorice." Gary's lips twisted in distaste. "It's past the statute of limitations anyway. If there were still victims, it'd be different. But he doesn't have access to a dorm full of helpless children anymore. Part of me wants justice, but for now, it's enough to know that he has no future."

"And you don't trust the system."

He glanced at me for a moment. "No. And I'm not saying I know a better way, but the current setup has its flaws."

"The way your cousin was talking . . ." I trailed off. "Do you resent the United States for what's happened to your people?" A history of broken treaties and dishonest land companies colored the past, and it wasn't a pretty shade.

He didn't reply right away. "Evie, did you love your dad?"

"Yes."

"Did you think he was perfect?"

I huffed. "No. He had his flaws, and I knew that even before I started digging around to find out why someone might have killed him."

"I know my country has flaws, but that doesn't mean I don't love it. Doesn't mean I wouldn't go to war again, if I was needed."

I smiled at him, even though he was watching the road instead of me. Maybe that was what I liked most about Gary. He'd had a hard life, but he didn't dwell on blame, didn't allow himself to be classified as a victim. He could see the good, even when his country had failed him, and he was willing to sacrifice for it rather than hold out for something perfect but unattainable.

We were almost to Maplewick. Meeting Mr. Brown had shaken me up, but the tension was receding now.

"Gary—" I wasn't sure I should ask, so I stopped.

"What?"

I couldn't think of a substitute quickly enough, so I asked my original question. "Did your mother really abandon you?"

He shook his head. "We lived with my grandma when I was little. She was kind. She liked telling legends, and she made good soup, and she took good care of me. But then she got remarried, and my mother and I moved out. Never to a good situation. Lots of bottles. Lots of different men, some of them mean. A social worker decided it wasn't a proper environment for a child. And it probably wasn't. But neither was the Thomas Indian School."

"I thought New York had moved away from institutionalizing children. Changed to foster care instead."

Gary nodded. "Yeah, that's what they did for other children. Not for disabled or Indian children."

"Did she ever try to get you back?"

"She didn't think she could. The admittance papers made it sound like she was giving up parental rights, and she thought maybe the school would be better than she was." He glanced at me, then back at the road. "She grew up in a boarding school too. She learned how to sew and how to clean and how to add. But not much about how to show love. Sometimes I worry I'll end up like her."

"You can show love, Gary." I'd felt it.

He gave me a smile before turning onto Main Street in Maplewick. "Well, you're easy to love."

* * *

Gary drove until we reached Professor Gerstner's house. I left him there and drove to meet my aunt at her hat shop. Lottie Morris came out the door as I reached for it. She'd worked in my aunt's store since the end of the war, so we'd known each other a few years.

"She's helping one last customer. Mrs. Richards—she's kind of indecisive. You have a book in there?" Lottie motioned to my purse.

I grimaced. "I'm sure I can find something to do."

"How are you holding up, Evelyn?" Lottie's normal smile, the bright one she kept plastered on her face while she worked, faded into something more serious.

She was asking about Dad's death. I wondered if she knew all the other things that had happened—an attempt on my life, an attempt on Gary's life, coming face-to-face with a ghoul like Mr. Brown. "I'm trying to focus on the good. Kindness from friends. Happy memories." Remembering Gary's good-night kiss warmed me anew. Good had come with the horrible. I just had to search for it and grasp it tightly.

Lottie put a hand on my shoulder. "Let me know if you need someone to talk to or anything else. My dad died a few years ago. Different circumstances, of course. Sometimes it's just nice to remember."

"Thanks, Lottie."

She nodded. "Have a good night, Evelyn."

I went inside, where my aunt was helping Mrs. Richards narrow down the six hats she'd picked out.

"Buy them all," I suggested.

"Oh goodness. Raymond would never approve of such a splurge." Mrs. Richards tried them all on again, using the double mirrors to get a front and back view.

I went around the shop, straightening hats, smoothing gloves, placing purses and pocketbooks just so. Nothing was out of order—my aunt kept a tidy shop, and Lottie was a good worker—but it gave me something to do.

"Say, Miss Hampton, have you made a decision on your father's collections? I know Raymond was hoping to pick up a few things for the archives. And he was so disappointed not to see your father's latest reproduction."

My mind flashed back to Mr. Richards staring at the trunk of my car, where Dad's crossbow still lay in a box. "I haven't decided yet."

Mrs. Richards frowned. "It's been ten days, but I suppose if you need the time, it's best to take it." She tried another hat on. "Mmm. I'll get these two." She held them up.

Aunt Janice helped her with the purchase, then wished Mrs. Richards a good evening.

The cheerful smile on my aunt's face faded when Mrs. Richards left. "What a day. I'm exhausted."

"Too tired to cook? We could go out instead."

Despite her success in business, Aunt Janice was normally frugal. She must have been extremely weary, because she nodded. "That sounds like just the thing. Will you make sure the back door is locked?"

We went to the Ryder Café. It was Aunt Janice's favorite, and we talked about the hat shop over soup and sandwiches.

"What did you do today?" she asked as we paid for our meal and left. The sun had set, bathing the street in twilight.

"Went to Hofeling with Gary."

"Oh?"

"We were taking a closer look at a suspect." It wasn't my place to tell her about Gary's run-in with the law, nor what Mr. Brown had done to him, so I stayed vague.

"I'm surprised you didn't bring Mr. Redhawk along for supper." She had a twinkle in her eye.

"I tried to. He said he had a lot of homework to catch up on." It was getting harder to say goodbye to him. If we got married, we could merge our lives completely, and that was what I craved. He'd asked me if I wanted the engagement ring—and everything that went with it—but I wasn't sure that counted as a proposal.

"Running around after suspects. Be careful, Evie. Do you think you found him?"

"We found a man of the vilest nature, but I'm not sure he's the one who killed Daddy."

We reached Dad's car. A liquor store was visible from the café parking lot, and I did a double-take when I saw a figure standing under a nearby street light. I didn't cross the road, because I didn't want another run-in, but there was no mistaking those braids or that drunken posture.

Otetiani Amedon was still in Maplewick.

Chapter Twenty-Eight

Letter of September 20, 1944, continued

I don't mind helping Mom. She's always done so much for me, for everyone else in the family. But it's hard to see someone who was so capable need help with so much. I do her hair for her because it's too much of a strain on her arms. I put her socks on her feet because it hurts to bend down. The thick ones, because she's always cold. I have to help her shower, too, because she's too weak to do it herself.

"ARE YOU SURE IT WAS him?" Gary asked the next morning. I'd stepped into the hall when he stopped by the bursar's office on his way to class.

I nodded. Unless Otetiani Amedon had an identical twin, I'd seen him. "I'm sure."

Gary frowned. "I dropped him at the station with enough money to cover the fare. But I was running late, so I didn't see him board. I didn't even see him buy the ticket."

"Where would he be staying?"

Gary shrugged. "He could be at the shed. I haven't been there, so he'd have the place to himself. I can't figure out why he's still here."

"Maybe he wants more money."

"Well, he already about cleaned me out." Gary was quiet for a moment, then looked as if he were going to be ill. "Unless he thinks he can get money from you."

I didn't like the idea of Mr. Amedon seeing me as a steady source of income. "Do you think he'd get violent over it?" He'd been violent before, when he'd planned the attack on Mr. Brown. I doubted the three years he'd spent in prison had softened him, and addiction could drive a man to things he wouldn't normally do.

Gary's lips pulled into a hard line. "I haven't spent a lot of time with him since the war, but he wouldn't have any reason to hurt you. At least, not unless we were married."

I folded my arms across my chest. If Gary and I were married and I died, Gary would inherit all my assets. And Gary seemed to be a bit of a pushover when it came to his cousin asking for handouts. But surely not even someone as unpleasant as Otetiani Amedon would hurt his cousin's almost-fiancée.

Except he didn't like me. "What if he's trying to keep his cousin from making a mistake and marrying the wrong woman?"

There was a third possibility, but I didn't speak it aloud. What if Mr. Amedon held a grudge against Gary for the failed attack on Mr. Brown and the subsequent prison sentence? It didn't make sense for him to try to stab Gary when he had . . . unless he wasn't as concerned about money and marriage as he was about revenge.

Gary swallowed. "I'll go look for him after class. If he spent all the money I gave him on liquor, I'll buy him a ticket and see he gets on the bus. And if I find out he's behind any of this . . ."

"Gary, be careful."

"Yeah, you too." He ran a finger along my cheek before going to his lecture.

I tried to lose myself in my work for the next few hours, but it was hard to be interested in tuition and housing payments. A nagging guilt ate at my stomach. Gary didn't have much in the way of family, and I'd planted a seed of doubt in one of the few connections he had left.

What was it about Mr. Amedon that made me so suspicious? Was it because he didn't like me? Because he seemed to fit the profile of the stereotypical drunk Indian? I paused in my work, wondering if I'd been infected by the racism I'd grown up around. Was I judging Mr. Amedon based on his skin?

But I hadn't judged Gary that way. Of course, other than a traumatic past and a different skin tone, Gary wasn't all that different from any of the other students going through Redgrave on the GI Bill. He wore clean-cut hair—at least when I didn't make it crooked—and enjoyed the same types of activities the rest of the students did. He was working to better himself, and he didn't resent American society.

Mr. Amedon, on the other hand, had a blatant disdain for Maplewick. Put him in different clothes, and he could have been a Seneca scout, fighting with the colonists against the French during the French and Indian War. Or gambling on a British victory during the Revolutionary War.

I'd given Gary a chance and fallen in love. But his cousin and I had met under poor circumstances. Maybe his cousin needed a friend to talk some sense into him, drain his bottles, and bribe him with a motorcycle. It had worked for Gary. But deep down, Gary must have wanted to change. I wasn't sure his cousin had that desire, but I also recognized that I didn't know him well enough to judge.

I took an early lunch but almost retreated when I saw Roland Roth pacing outside the administration building. His shoes were polished enough to reflect sunlight, and his fedora was tipped at a rakish angle.

"Evelyn!"

An ingrained habit of courtesy made me pause. "Mr. Roth."

He came closer and put his hands in his pockets. "Evelyn, I wanted to apologize. Last time we spoke, I was not at my best."

"Apology accepted. Now, if you'll excuse me." I walked past him but stopped when he called me again.

"Evelyn, please. I just want another chance with you, whatever's gone on with that other man."

I glanced back. "You're too late. I'm in love with someone else."

"You were in love with me once."

"No. I thought I was in love with you. But really, I think I was just flattered. And afraid of being alone. And I felt you needed someone to come home to." His officer's uniform and his dad's position at the university hadn't hurt. And the war had changed things, put a deadline on our relationship, made it move faster than it otherwise would have because we were afraid we wouldn't have another chance.

"I still need someone to come home to."

"I believe there's a dance this weekend." I pointed to a nearby poster advertising the spring dance. "You could start your search there."

He frowned. "I don't want to search elsewhere. I want you back."

"I'm a different person now, Mr. Roth."

"Then let me get to know the new you."

I shook my head. "I've moved on. You moved on a long time ago too. You don't need me to fall back on."

He stepped closer. "Maybe I'm different now too. You might like the new me even more than you liked the old me."

"I have neither the time nor the desire to pursue a relationship with you."

A mischievous smile spread across his face. "Prove it, then. Let me kiss you. If you don't feel any of that old excitement, I'll move on. But I bet I can reignite a few sparks." He reached out as if he were going to caress my face in the middle of the quad.

I swatted his hand away. "Good day, Mr. Roth."

"But I need you, Evelyn Hampton!" he said as I walked away.

I ignored him. That was so typical of Roland—it was always about what he needed, what he wanted.

He followed me. "It's just that you're so beautiful, and I love you so much."

Those words triggered a memory that stopped me in my tracks, but only for a moment. I did my best to shrug off the panic that suddenly churned in my chest. "I've heard that before, Mr. Roth. Goodbye."

My heels sent clicks across the quad as I strode away. Roland might have said he wanted me back. He might even have thought he wanted me back. But I was pretty sure his efforts were more about completing a conquest than they were about resurrecting any lingering remnants of romance.

Chapter Twenty-Nine

September 25, 1944

Dear Clive,

Roland is leaving tomorrow, and all I can feel is relief. I had him bring me home early tonight. I couldn't tell Daddy why, and I didn't want to wake Mom. She already gets so little sleep. But if I don't tell someone, I'll burst.

It was supposed to be a special evening, our last together before he goes overseas—maybe our last ever. He wanted me to forget about everything else, just for a few hours. He brought a blanket and spread it out so we could look at the stars. Only, we didn't look at the stars for very long.

I didn't mind at first. I like kissing him—and with all that's been happening at home, I needed the distraction. I can't believe I'm telling you that, but I know you've kissed a few girls before. Then things changed. He was kissing me harder, and his hands were going places I didn't want them to go. I told him to stop and moved his hands away, but then he'd say things like, "I just want to show you how much I love you," and "It's just that you're so beautiful, and I love you so much." Then he'd kiss me, and we'd start the whole thing over again.

I finally pushed him away when he started fiddling with the buttons on my blouse. He wasn't happy. Said I was being a prude and ruining the evening. There was a moment when he was leaning over me, and I could feel his weight on top of me, and I was afraid he wouldn't stop. He didn't have to—he's stronger than me, and no one else was around. I told him to take me home, but I was terrified he wouldn't.

I'm torn now, Clive. I did ruin the evening. I disappointed him. But he's going away, and he might not come back. I'm not ready for a baby, especially when we aren't even married yet. And there's a feeling that it wasn't right to say yes. He made me feel so guilty for not giving him what he wants, but I don't think he understood what he was asking.

I washed the dishes in Aunt Janice's sink after supper.

Gary dried them. "Otetiani was staying in the shed. Mr. Norton thought it was with my permission. But he wasn't there last night. I couldn't find him in any of the bars, and I don't know where else to look. He might have gone back to Cattaraugus, but I don't know why he stuck around an extra two days."

I washed the last plate and stood behind Gary, leaning my head on his back and slipping my arms around his waist while he finished drying.

Roland had never helped in the kitchen. When we were dating, I'd always been excited to see him but usually a little nervous too. We did whatever he wanted—saw the movie with his favorite actors, ate whatever he was in the mood for, kissed until I told him to stop. Roland was always the focus and our dates always about making sure he had a good time. I'd usually had fun too, but Roland had never asked me my preferences or gone out of his way for me.

The butterflies I felt around Gary were different. There was a compromise in our dates, a respect for his tight budget and limited time, the occasions when we skipped the latest war movie. And they weren't always fancy. But Gary sacrificed for me. He strove to make me happy, whether it was by learning to bake my favorite type of cookie or helping me paint Aunt Janice's parlor. All his actions seemed to take into consideration how I would feel even more than he considered his own needs and wants.

I held Gary a little tighter. "You're using a different soap at the Gerstners."

I felt more than heard his chuckle. "Do you like it less or more than the stuff at Mr. Norton's?"

I inhaled deeply. "I can't decide. On the soap, or on who I think is behind all of this."

Gary turned around to hold me and kiss the top of my head. "I hope the detective is having better luck than we are."

I didn't say anything. Instead, I enjoyed the feeling of his arms wrapped around me and the sound of his heart beating. "Does anyone know you're staying at the Gerstners?"

"Just them. Given the situation, they promised to keep it quiet. And I'm parking the motorcycle in the backyard, so someone would have to look hard to find it." His fingers ran through my hair. "You haven't seen anything unusual at the hotels, have you? People following you?"

"No. And we're going someplace different tonight."

"Good. I should go now. I've got a paper to type."

"Gary . . ." A year ago, I'd discovered I could do in ten minutes what it took him an hour to peck out on the typewriter. I'd been typing his papers for him ever since.

"What? You're not at home, so the deal's off, isn't it?"

"Aunt Janice has a typewriter. Do you have it written out?"

He nodded.

"Then go get it."

Aunt Janice finished packing about the time I finished typing Gary's paper. She stifled a yawn. This was hard on her too, and I felt guilty for dragging her into it. I'd do the same for her if she were the one who needed to hide at night. But I'd been leaning on her my whole life, especially since Mom died. Did she think it was worth it, having such a needy niece?

Gary put Aunt Janice's bag in the trunk of the car for her. It was getting full. I still hadn't taken out Dad's things, and each time we went to a new hotel, I seemed to leave more stuff back there. I'd have to sort through it another night. Maybe when the killer was caught and it was safe for me to go home.

Gary pulled me into an embrace and kissed me on the cheek. "Thanks for supper and for typing my paper."

After he rode off, Aunt Janice and I drove to another hotel. There were only three in Maplewick. If the murderer wanted to find us, it wouldn't be that hard. He'd sabotaged the car once, so he'd recognize it in the parking lot.

I brushed my teeth, washed my face, and pinned my hair into rolls, trying to think of the good things I had in life—Gary, my aunt, a steady job. But I couldn't shake off a foreboding that seemed to permeate everything, the driving worry that consumed me.

We were safe, for the moment, but it seemed like it was just a matter of time until the murderer struck again.

Chapter Thirty

October 5, 1944

Dear Clive,

I read somewhere that I should keep letters to servicemen upbeat and hopeful. But right now, if I tried to write something cheerful, you wouldn't be getting any letters. There's no easy way to say this. Mom died last night.

THE NEXT DAY AT WORK, Mr. Thurber asked me into his office. I gave Charlene a wary glance as I stood to comply. He never asked us into his office.

"Have a seat, Miss Hampton." Mr. Thurber motioned to a chair. He closed the door so Charlene couldn't hear. Gary's warning not to be alone with anyone crossed my mind, but I trusted Mr. Thurber. Besides, what type of murderer would kill someone in his own office with a potential witness only a few yards away?

Maybe I was in trouble. I'd missed a lot of work lately. I wasn't that far behind—but I was behind.

Mr. Thurber sat behind his desk. Four neat piles lay on its oak surface. "Miss Hampton, I had a regrettable conversation with President Kettering this morning. He expressed some concerns about your position."

Kettering was the president of Redgrave. But why would he be concerned if a clerk in the bursar's office was a few days behind on her work?

Mr. Thurber shifted in his seat. Was he squirming? "I don't normally consider what my employees do on their own time any of my business. President Kettering seems to have a different opinion. Redgrave hasn't been a religious institution for three decades now, but Kettering feels the need to preserve the university's reputation."

I nodded, wondering where this was going.

"A rumor reached President Kettering that since your father's death, you've moved in with a man of a different race. The president doesn't approve of illicit relationships."

"It's not true." I was involved with Gary but not in that way.

I could guess exactly how President Kettering had come by the rumor. Roland Ulysses Kettering had four daughters. When he had no sons, his sister, Mary Kettering Roth, had named her second child after him. "I am dating a man of a different race, but that's not illegal in the state of New York. And we aren't living together."

"President Kettering made it clear that rumors can be just as damaging to the university's reputation as facts." Mr. Thurber looked down at his hands, crossed and resting on his desk. "He's expressed his strong suggestion that I act quickly."

"Are you firing me?" My voice sounded small in my ears.

"No. You're a good worker, Miss Hampton. But I am asking for a letter of resignation. I think you'll have an easier time finding new work if you resign *before* I can fire you."

Something twisted in my chest, and something else lumped in my throat. I wouldn't cry. I liked my job, but it wasn't my passion the way Dad's work had been his. I'd taken it only so I could check up on Dad during lunch. But I'd never been fired before. It sounded so undignified. And it wasn't fair.

Mr. Thurber continued. "I don't want to fire you, and I don't want you to resign. I'll hold the letter. If President Kettering forces me to act, I'll tell him you resigned already, I just asked you to stay on until I hire a replacement. Hopefully, this will all blow over, and then I'll return your resignation, and you can burn it. Best backdate the letter a few days. I hope we won't need it, but Kettering can be a bit unpredictable at times."

Fury made my skin hot as I typed out a resignation I didn't want to write. Either Roland had given up and was trying to punish me, or he was hoping I would beg him to intercede with his uncle on my behalf. I'd rather lose my job than ask Roland Roth for anything, especially after this stunt.

The phone rang. "Hello?"

"Miss Hampton?"

"Yes."

"This is Detective Iverson. There's been a development. I need you to come to your aunt's shop as soon as possible. Bring Mr. Redhawk, if you can."

The call cut out before I could say anything. A development could be good news, but my stomach tensed as I put the handset down in its cradle. Why meet at Aunt Janice's shop? Maybe he wanted to tell us something all at the same time.

I handed Mr. Thurber my resignation. He frowned. "I wish it hadn't come to this. Hopefully, Kettering will come to his senses, and the matter will drop."

I forced a smile, grateful he was on my side and wouldn't fire me unless he was compelled to. "Would it be all right if I left early today? Detective Iverson wants to see me."

Mr. Thurber nodded. "Maybe you can come in a little early next week to make up for it? I don't want Kettering to have any extra fuel if he makes me fight to keep you."

"Yes, sir."

I glanced at the clock on my way out. Gary would be in one of his econ classes for another ten minutes. I went to the Smithton Building and cracked one of the doors in the back of the lecture hall. The professor's voice droned on about the theories of John Maynard Keynes. I spotted Gary on the other side of the hall from me. At least he was in one of the back rows, so the professor was unlikely to notice the interruption. Someone sitting behind him glanced at me, and I mimed for him to get Gary's attention. Gary saw me and seemed to understand. He grabbed his things and left the lecture hall at the nearest exit. We met in the hallway.

"What is it?" Gary asked.

"Detective Iverson called. He said there's been a development."

"Did he say what?"

"No. But we're supposed to meet him at my aunt's shop."

Gary's lips twisted in surprise, but he nodded. He glanced back at the classroom but didn't hesitate to follow me.

"I think it's quicker if we go on foot," I said. My car was parked on the other side of campus, but if we went over to the Life Sciences Building, we could cut through it, then take the staircase from campus down to Redgrave Avenue. My aunt's store on Main Street was only a block away from there.

I didn't say much on the way. I'd been angry about the rumor Roland had started, but now I was nervous. Meeting at Aunt Janice's store suggested the development had something to do with her. She couldn't be involved. She would never hurt me. Besides, she wasn't strong enough to haul Dad's body off the ground, and she'd been upstairs when Gary had been attacked. It was disloyal to even consider it.

Maybe she'd figured out who it was. Aunt Janice was smart. Even during the Depression, her shop had turned a profit—a small one, but when so many other shops along Main Street had gone out of business, I took it as a sign of genius. I suspected Clive had possessed that gift too, but he'd never had a chance to try it out.

When we arrived, Detective Iverson was speaking with Sergeant Horton. I took Gary's hand, suspecting Sergeant Horton made him nervous. I had to pull a little before Gary followed me inside. Iverson excused himself and came over.

"Miss Hampton. I'm sorry to be the one to tell you this, but Janice Peterson died this afternoon."

Chapter Thirty-One

Letter of October 5, 1944, continued

My heart has been shattered, Clive. I didn't realize how much I depended on her until she was gone. I told her I loved her, of course, but did I tell her often enough?

MY LEGS STOPPED WORKING. I would have slunk to the floor if Gary hadn't put his arm around me to hold me up. Aunt Janice was dead? It couldn't be true.

Gary led me to a chair and helped me sit. I could barely breathe.

"How did she die?" Gary asked.

"Chlorine gas poisoning, we believe. We found empty ammonia and bleach containers in the restroom. At first glance, it looks like she was cleaning, bumped her head, and knocked the ammonia into the bleach."

Ammonia and bleach. I'd learned not to mix them when I was eight. Ammonia wouldn't get the bathtub clean, so I'd tried bleach instead. I'd gotten a headache, and my nose and throat had started to burn. When I'd complained to Clive and Frank, Clive had told me that was what I got for being stupid.

"But Aunt Janice always cleaned at the end of the day, not at lunchtime."

"We're not entirely sure the death was accidental." Iverson crossed his arms. "She's with the coroner now, but there was some bruising. Could have come in a fall. Or it could have come from struggling against an attacker."

Gary handed me his handkerchief so I could sop up my tears, then spoke to Iverson. "So, someone killed her but wanted it to look like an accident?"

"That's my initial suspicion."

Sergeant Horton came over. He ignored Gary and me. "One set of prints on the doorknob."

"And they probably belong to Mrs. Morris," Iverson said.

"Lottie?" Lottie Morris wouldn't have hurt my aunt; I was sure of it.

"Yes." Iverson sighed. "She's the one who discovered the body when she got back from a late lunch. The doorknob should have at least had your aunt's fingerprints along with Mrs. Morris's. Sounds like the killer wiped the knob clean and then made his escape."

"Was anything stolen?" Gary asked.

"No."

Gary nodded. "Of course not. He wanted it to look like an accident." Gary was worried; I could see it in the tension of his lips and the strain in his eyes.

And me . . . I felt like a part of me had died. First my mom, then my brother, then my dad, now my aunt.

Dead. Aunt Janice was dead. And Detective Iverson still had no idea who the killer was.

* * *

I sat in the shop for a long time, watching the police come and go as they conducted their investigation. Gary held me. I cried. Lottie Morris cried too. She'd been speaking with a police officer when Gary and I had arrived. She stopped to give me her condolences when the police finished their questions and told her she could go home.

"I'm so sorry, Evelyn. If I would have known, I wouldn't have gone to lunch." Her face crumpled as she fought tears again. "Your aunt was so good to me. I can't understand why anyone would do this."

As Lottie left, Iverson came over again. "Miss Hampton, I'm sorry for your loss. I'll do my best to get to the bottom of this, but I'll need your help. Did your aunt have any enemies? Anyone who might be jealous or consider themselves slighted?"

"No—Aunt Janice was an angel."

"I imagine it's connected to the other attacks," Gary said.

Iverson nodded. "Maybe, but I have to look into every possibility. Mrs. Morris left for lunch at one thirty. She returned at two thirty. Where were you during that time, Mr. Redhawk?"

Gary swallowed, and I felt him tense. I frowned at the detective. Was he accusing Gary again?

"I went to the library after work, at about one fifteen. I was there until I went to class at two."

"Can anyone vouch for your location?" Iverson asked.

The muscles on Gary's face hardened. "From two on, yes. At the library . . . Jack Dickens walked past and said hello, but I don't remember when."

A sly smile pulled at Iverson's lips. Was he gloating over Gary's shaky alibi? "So if someone were trying to frame you, why would they attack Miss Peterson while you were in a lecture where your classmates could confirm your location?"

Gary visibly relaxed. "I thought you were accusing me again."

Iverson shook his head. "Miss Peterson's death might have been an accident, but my gut tells me otherwise. I'll follow up with the other persons of interest in Professor Hampton's murder to check for potential involvement. But I also need to explore the possibility that this murder was motivated by something else. Miss Hampton, I need you to think carefully. I know it's not pleasant, but is there anyone who might hold a grudge against your aunt? Did she have a lover? A business partner?"

"She was engaged a long time ago. Her fiancé went to France in 1918 and didn't make it back."

"His name?"

I thought for a moment. "Mr. Fairfax . . . Eugene Fairfax."

"Does he still have family around?"

I shook my head. "Not in Maplewick. She lived in Albany then, met him there."

"And her business?"

I glanced around at the neat rows of hats, gloves, and handbags. Surely no one would kill over a hat? "No partner, just one employee, and Lottie was devoted to her. Aunt Janice owns this building and two others. She may have evicted someone who couldn't pay rent sometime in the last twenty years."

"Do you know where her financial documents are?"

"I can look." She'd had an office in the back of the shop, but she'd moved those things to her house when she'd wanted more space for merchandise after the war.

Iverson nodded. "I'd like to examine them. Let me know when you find them, or bring them to the station." Iverson closed his notebook. "I've got a lot of work to do. I'll be in touch. Hopefully, I'll know more once I have a report from the coroner's office."

The police finished at Aunt Janice's store, and we all left, locking up on our way out. It was a crime scene now, not a hat shop. I stood on the sidewalk, not sure what to do.

Gary took my hand. "Evie, I'm sorry."

I nodded. It wasn't his fault, even if it was part of a plot to frame him, but I knew what he meant.

"We've got to find somewhere safe for you. Until Iverson makes an arrest, I don't want you to be alone." Gary watched Sergeant Horton drive away. "Is there anyone you trust as much as your aunt? Someone you can stay with?"

I shook my head. I didn't trust anyone the way I trusted Aunt Janice. Barbara Dudley maybe, because we'd been friends since we were ten, but she was a notorious gossip. If I stayed with her, the whole town would hear about it. Plus, she thought Gary was handsome. What if she was jealous? I didn't think she was behind the attacks, but I'd feel safer on my own. There was Charlene from work, but she lived with three roommates I hardly knew. "Maybe Lottie."

"Your aunt's employee?"

"Yes. She and her husband have an extra room. They keep hoping it will be a nursery someday, but so far, it's still empty." She had offered to help, so it wouldn't be as awkward asking if I could stay with her. And maybe we could help each other with our shared grief. She and my aunt had been close.

Gary seemed hesitant. "Would she benefit in any way from your aunt's death?"

"No. She's out of a job. Aunt Janice said she paid good workers more than average so they'd have no reason to leave. Lottie will probably have to settle for something less now."

"Your aunt didn't turn the store over to employees or something like that in the event of her death?"

I didn't know, but I knew who did. "Dale drew up her latest will. We can ask him."

His law office was only a block away, so we walked. I'd run out of tears, but I caught my reflection in store windows. My eyes were red. A few people stared, but I was past caring.

Katrina Huffaker, Dale's matronly secretary, greeted us when we walked in. "What can I do for you, Miss Hampton?"

"Can I talk to Dale?"

She glanced at his office. "He's with someone now, but if you'll wait, he can see you when he's finished."

Gary and I sat in the leather waiting chairs Dad had given Dale as a present when he opened his own office two years ago. I was glad my cousin had clients, even if it meant we had to wait. Based on what I'd heard, business had been slow. I didn't think he struggled as much as Frank did with his music shop, but he had more mouths to feed.

Gary flipped through a copy of *Life* magazine containing some of Winston Churchill's war memoirs. I picked up a *National Geographic*, but a glance at the contents made it feel like my heart had been mauled by a battle-ax. The magazine included an article about the Everglades. Aunt Janice and I had talked about a trip to Florida in the coming summer, when the bursar's office wouldn't be so busy. I squeezed my eyes shut to stop a new batch of tears.

The attack on Aunt Janice made everything more complicated. Before, I had thought the targets were my father, me, and Gary. But if Aunt Janice had ended up on the killer's list . . . was anyone I knew safe? Sabotaging the car, pulling the bookcase over, and stabbing Gary had made me think that maybe the killer wasn't always out to kill—just to intimidate or maim. Dad's murder might have been an overreaction, something that escalated out of control. But now there were two murders, and there was no mistaking his intentions.

I didn't want to be alone at night. I would feel safest with Gary, but that wasn't proper, and he'd made a promise to Aunt Janice. That promise seemed like it was in even greater force now that she was dead, murdered because she'd been trying to help us.

Maybe we could elope. Redgrave's president might not like it, but he couldn't stop it. Other states had laws against interracial marriage, but not New York. We'd need a blood test, and there was a twenty-four-hour waiting period after a marriage license was issued, but we could get married tomorrow, if everything worked out just right. Then I would know he was safe, and he would know I was safe, but that didn't solve the immediate problem. I tucked the idea away. I didn't want fear to determine my wedding date.

Eventually, Dale escorted a middle-aged couple from the office and turned to me with a smile. "Evelyn, good to see you." He focused on something—perhaps my smeared mascara or my swollen eyes, and grew serious. "What's wrong?"

"Evie's Aunt Janice was killed this afternoon," Gary said.

The color drained from Dale's face. He knelt in front of me. "I'm so sorry."

"Mr. Bingham?" Gary asked. "We're looking for motive. I understand you drew up her last will. Was anyone listed who might benefit financially from Miss Peterson's death?"

Dale shook his head. "No. Evelyn was the sole heir."

Chapter Thirty-Two

November 9, 1944

Dear Evelyn,

We're back from Peleliu. I got a pile of V-mails from you, and I'm trying to wrap my head around the news. I can't believe Mom is gone. I know I should write something comforting, but right now, I can't think of anything to say.

I SPENT THE NIGHT WITH Lottie, the next morning too, as I planned my second funeral in two weeks. This one was a little easier in some ways. Aunt Janice had come with me to the undertakers when I'd arranged for Dad's service. She'd liked the white coffin, even though she thought the cherry more fitting for Dad. I knew her favorite hymn—"Amazing Grace"—and her favorite type of flower—daffodils. But the certainty that her death was connected to me, that it might be my fault, made this funeral harder in other ways.

I spent the afternoon with Gary, going through Aunt Janice's paperwork, looking for clues that might reveal a motive for her murder.

"It seems like the police should be doing this," I said as I opened another desk drawer. Aunt Janice was tidy, but she'd lived in her two-bedroom house for twenty years, and she didn't like to throw out anything that might be useful later.

"Maybe they thought you could find it sooner." Gary flipped through a ledger I'd handed him. "And they've got a lot of alibis to check."

I searched the drawer. I found a packet of letters from Clive and put them aside to read later. Then I pulled out another pile of letters, this set from the back of the drawer, bound with a yellow ribbon. My breath caught when I turned them over. They were from Eugene Fairfax, Aunt Janice's one-time fiancé. Had she still been in love with him, three decades after he'd disappeared in a trench somewhere in France? Or did she keep all her correspondence, regardless of how old it was?

I didn't expect to find anything related to a murder investigation in her pile of letters, but I was insatiably curious about her one-time romance. I unfolded one to reveal faded ink on brittle paper.

July 6, 1918

Dearest Janice,

I have reread your last letter over and over again. I am filled with anguish that I'm to blame for your current difficulty. My love for you is true, even if it wasn't self-disciplined, much to my shame. And yet, part of me doesn't regret it. Memory of our passion sustains me through all this ugliness. And to be part of a miracle with you—it's something I wanted, even if the timing is wrong. Tell everyone we were married in secret. Tell them I have the marriage certificate with me. Take my name, and when our child is born, the baby can be called a Fairfax, not a bastard. When I return, we will be married as soon as we can, and then we'll move somewhere beyond rumor. I'll make it right, Janice. I promise.

I stopped reading, shocked. Aunt Janice had been with child . . . before she was married? That would mean I had another cousin—but that couldn't be right. Aunt Janice didn't have any children. Unless . . .

"Did you find something?" Gary asked.

I handed him the letter and watched him read it.

"What happened to the baby?" Gary put the letter on the desk when he finished.

"I don't know."

"If she had the child and gave it up, and he or she found out you were your aunt's heir . . ."

I swallowed. "That would be motive."

Gary crossed his arms. "I think the letter explains why your aunt was so adamant that I promise good behavior, even when you come downstairs in the middle of the night looking like an angel in a nightgown." He offered half a smile. "She didn't want you to be in the same situation she was."

"You already went away to war. You came back."

Gary pointed to where he'd been stabbed. "This needed more stitches than anything I got in Europe."

I nodded. Sometimes it was hard to wait until marriage, especially when Gary was holding me in his arms and pressing his lips to mine. But I understood Aunt Janice's warning even better now. She'd learned from her mistake. The consequences of not waiting could be even harder. "Did you find anything?"

Gary glanced at the papers he'd been looking through. "She evicted six shopkeepers over the last fifteen years. Looks like it was always because they couldn't pay rent."

That meant there were six people who might harbor grudges. "Any of them related to our list of suspects?"

"One." Gary turned to Aunt Janice's paperwork from 1936. "A bookstore owned by Raymond Richards."

"The archivist at Redgrave's library?"

"Yeah."

Could Mr. Richards be behind it? Could he have killed my father to gain his artifacts and killed my aunt for revenge? I couldn't see anyone killing over anger at a failed career *and* passion for a new career, but I knew so little about Mr. Richards. He didn't approve of people taking notes in the pages of books, nor of his wife buying six hats in one shopping trip, but those preferences were hardly murderous. Yet, he'd wanted Dad's crossbow—I'd seen an obsession in his eyes. And he'd known I was home the night the bookcase was pulled over on me.

Gary flipped to 1947 in the ledger book. "It didn't involve an eviction, but did you know she loaned money to your cousin Frank last year?"

"No." I knew Frank's music shop wasn't doing as well as he wanted it to, but I hadn't known he'd borrowed from Aunt Janice. "Is it still outstanding?"

"She wrote 'organ' beside it and 'paid in full.'"

"But Aunt Janice doesn't own an organ."

Gary looked more closely. "Didn't the church get a new organ in February? That's when she wrote it."

I smiled, wondering if the pastor knew who had arranged for the new instrument. "She really was a good woman, even if she wasn't perfect."

"She was a wonderful woman. And so is her niece." Gary motioned to the letters. "Are you going to tell Iverson about the baby?"

I picked up the stack of letters. "Maybe I'll read through these first, see if there's anything else. I . . . She kept it secret for thirty years. And she's been like a mother to me. I don't want to ruin her reputation. I know I might have to say something, eventually, but maybe we can wait."

Gary nodded his agreement and held up the ledger. "We'll show Iverson this, nothing more, for now."

I grabbed the letters from her fiancé and the ones from my brother. Was this what Aunt Janice had meant when she'd spoken of the secrets ordinary people carried? Had anyone else known, or had she shouldered her secret burden alone for thirty years? I glanced around her house, missing her so intensely that tears came to my eyes. Gary put a gentle hand on my shoulder, and the warmth of his touch gave me courage.

I tried to return the favor when Sergeant Horton greeted us at the police station and Gary tensed up. I took Gary's hand, anger at Sergeant Horton for whatever he'd done while Gary was in custody clawing at my chest. "Is Detective Iverson available?"

Sergeant Horton lit a cigarette and shook his head. "No, he went to Hofeling."

Maybe he was checking on Mr. Brown's alibi for Aunt Janice's murder. I would have rather spoken with Iverson, but I held the ledger out to Horton. "He asked if anyone might have a grudge against my aunt. Here's a record of the shops she owns on Main Street. She evicted a few people over the years. That might be significant. Gary marked them, so they're easy to find if you flip through it."

Horton took the book and gave Gary a cold look, as if he still thought him guilty. Then he cast his gaze over me, including me in his suspicion.

"You've come into a lot of money recently, haven't you, Miss Hampton?"

I didn't like what he was implying. Did he think I was behind the murders for financial gain? "Yes. And I've lost my dad and a beloved aunt. I've also been attacked, as has my boyfriend. Are we free to go now?"

Horton nodded, but the ice in his gaze didn't thaw. As Gary and I left the station, I had to hold back a shiver.

It seemed that in some circles, Gary and I were now suspects.

Chapter Thirty-Three

Letter of November 9, 1944, continued

You aren't still planning to marry Roland, are you? If I were home, I'd smash my fist into his face. I've seen enough violence on Peleliu to last me a lifetime, but I've got enough anger left to pummel him a good one. I hope you threw his ring at him and cut his face with the diamond.

You didn't ruin the evening, Evie. He did. He wanted something he had no right to take. If he really loved you, he wouldn't have tried to force you into something you didn't want to do.

MAPLEWICK WAS A SMALL TOWN, and most of its inhabitants went to one of two churches, kitty corner from each other on Redgrave and Second Avenue. We didn't want anyone to know I was staying with Mr. and Mrs. Morris or that Gary was staying with Mr. and Mrs. Gerstner, so we met a few blocks away and walked to church together.

"Do you think Sergeant Horton will arrest us?" I asked. I'd barely slept the night before, worrying about it.

"He has to have evidence, not just motive." Gary held my hand a little tighter. "But I don't doubt he'd like to see me back behind bars."

"We both have alibis."

"Yeah," Gary said, but unease crept into his voice. He pushed a stray hair back into place and gave me half a smile. "I've been trying to come up with ideas. Who's behind this, and why? How I can protect you. I even thought about eloping so I could know you were safe at night, but I don't want you to have to give up a wedding."

My breath caught in my chest. "I thought about elopement too."

"Did you?" He cast a sideways glance at me. "And what did you think?"

"I wasn't opposed to the idea." The people I would most want to share a wedding with were dead now, other than Gary. Dad couldn't walk me down the aisle of the church, so why not go to the courthouse instead?

Gary paused on the sidewalk, and so did I. He ran a finger along my cheek. The affection in his touch and the heat that traveled into my chest convinced me that an elopement was the best idea we'd ever had.

Gary took my hand again, continuing our stroll to church. "Part of me wants to get a marriage license tomorrow. But it seems like a wedding should take place under happier circumstances. And I think if we got married in a hurry, Horton would think we were in league together, killing off your family so we'd have money."

That was ridiculous. I'd rather have my dad and my aunt than anything they could leave me as an inheritance. "I hate being under suspicion." I gazed into Gary's dark eyes and saw kindness and strength, passion and restraint. I wanted to be his wife, but I was afraid he was right. If we ran off and eloped, the police would be suspicious, and I'd probably lose my job. We had alibis for Aunt Janice's murder, but Gary had conspired with his cousin before, and we still didn't know when Otetiani Amedon had left town.

I normally enjoyed church, but that Sunday, it was simply something to be endured. Some people were kind, expressing sympathy for my losses, sharing hugs and memories. Others said the right words, but I saw the way they looked at Gary and me. They thought us guilty of murder, or, at the very least, guilty of living in sin. I didn't dare tell anyone that our sleeping arrangements weren't together, because that wasn't the kind of thing you said in church, and I didn't want to risk our safe havens.

The services ended, and Gary and I escaped out the main door. As we walked down the steps, Barbara Dudley hooked her arm through mine. "Evelyn, I absolutely must speak with you."

I nodded but kept moving away from the clusters of people scattered about, chatting in the sunshine. Barbara pulled me across the grass. I looked over my shoulder. Gary waited for me off to the side of the entrance.

"I heard about your aunt. I'm sad for you. And I'm sad for me. I liked her, and she always suggested the most flattering hats."

"She had a talent for fashion." I wondered how long it would take Barbara to get to the point. I doubted she'd pulled me away for condolences.

"I've been hearing the craziest rumors." Barbara raised an eyebrow. "Are they true?"

I sighed. Apparently, it wasn't going to take her long at all to get to the point. "Probably not, but since I don't know what you've heard . . ."

Barbara lowered her voice. "Someone said that delectable Indian moved in with you." She glanced back at Gary and twisted her lips. "How is it?"

"Gary is Seneca," I corrected her. "We have separate sleeping quarters, and that will be the case until we're married."

"Are you engaged?"

I didn't answer right away. If I said yes, Barbara would back off, but then the whole town would hear about it, and Gary hadn't officially proposed. "No."

"So, you're both seeing other people?" A smile of hope pulled at her lips.

Barbara and I had shared dolls when we were girls and secrets when we were teenagers. Her house had been a needed retreat when Clive and I weren't getting along. But we'd grown apart since the war. And even if she'd still been my best friend, I wasn't going to share Gary with her. "No, we are not seeing other people."

"Oh." She frowned, then looked past me. "And Roland?"

I huffed. "I would be perfectly content to never see Roland again."

"Then don't turn around."

"What?" I spun to look behind me. Gary and Roland faced each other. Gary's expression was calm, but his fist was clenched, and his shoulders were stiff. Roland's face was red. No one else was beside them, but heads all over the churchyard were turned to watch. Roland sneered and spat a few words out—I couldn't hear them. And then Gary swung his fist into Roland's nose.

I wasn't sure if I heard my own gasp or the collective intake of breath from those watching. I strode toward them as Roland stepped back, hand on his nose, blood leaking through his fingers.

He glared at me, then glared at Gary. "You better believe I'll be pressing charges."

* * *

"What happened?" The crowd had finally cleared away, and Gary and I had walked back to my car. I leaned against it with my arms folded across my chest.

"He was asking for it." Gary's hands were shoved in his pockets, and he stared at the road instead of at me.

"How, exactly?"

"He insulted you."

"So you punched him?"

"Yes, Evie. The words he chose were ugly—and they're not true. I'm sick of people hurting you. I don't know if Roland is behind all the attacks or not, but the least I could do is smack him when he calls you something like that."

"What did he say?"

"I'd rather not repeat it."

I shifted my arms again. "His words can't hurt me anymore. You should have let it slide."

"You're mad that I punched that jerk?" Hurt touched Gary's eyes, and disappointment colored his voice.

I forced my arms to relax. I was angry, a little, at both of them, but more than that, I was scared. "Roland is a dangerous enemy. He already almost got me fired—"

"What? How?"

"He told his uncle, the president of Redgrave University, that one of the clerks in the bursar's office had moved in with her boyfriend. President Kettering wanted it taken care of to protect Redgrave's high moral reputation. Mr. Thurber hasn't fired me, but he might have to if Kettering doesn't let it drop. And I can't imagine him forgetting about it now that you've broken his nephew's nose."

Gary's posture softened. "Why didn't you tell me?"

"It was right before my aunt died. After that, there were other things to worry about." Gary put a gentle hand on my shoulder, and most of the anger melted away, but the worry didn't. "Roland has powerful connections. And you don't. What if he charges you with assault? You could go to jail, Gary. Horton's looking for an excuse to arrest you again." That was when my tears started. Four days in jail had left Gary a numb, mute shell. What would a conviction for assault and a couple months in jail do to him?

"It was just one punch."

"He'll twist it. Make it sound worse than it was. And you have a record, Gary. That puts you at risk. So do the rumors and the fact that you're Seneca. It's not fair, but that's the way it is."

Gary ran a frustrated hand through his hair. "Maybe he's behind all of it, not just the rumors with President Kettering."

"He wasn't in town to sabotage Daddy's car."

"Maybe that was something else—a prank by one of your dad's students. Or maybe he was in town; he just kept himself hidden."

Could Roland have killed my dad and my aunt? He was capable of getting me fired and capable of getting Gary thrown in jail, but I wouldn't have thought him a murderer. "Let's see if Detective Iverson is working today."

I drove to the police station, hoping that if Iverson heard our version first, he'd be able to prevent Gary's arrest for throwing one well-deserved punch. Maybe he'd made progress on the case. If Roland was behind it, arresting him would solve all our problems.

But it turned out Detective Iverson had Sundays off, and I didn't want to talk to Sergeant Horton. We drove to my house to use the phone instead. I still didn't feel safe there, but it wasn't so bad if Gary was with me.

"Dale?" I asked when he answered.

"Evelyn, how are you?"

"I've been better." I explained what happened after church and my worries that Gary would be arrested again.

"Look, Evelyn, I want to help. But Fern's parents are over right now. They already think Fern married down. If I explain I'm trying to keep my cousin's boyfriend out of jail . . . I'll see what I can do, but it'll have to wait until tomorrow."

As I hung up the phone, disappointment pulled at me as heavy as the coat of chain mail Dad had purchased when I was fourteen. I'd counted on Dale's help, but it seemed I didn't even have his sympathy. Had he been alive, Clive would have done something to protect his sister from a murderer and keep her boyfriend out of jail. But he was gone, and so were my parents and my aunt.

I took Gary's hand. Gary would do what he could to protect me, but what would happen if the police arrested him again?

Chapter Thirty-Four

Letter of November 9, 1944, continued

Peleliu was a miserable hunk of coral in the Pacific Ocean. It was covered by land crabs, bloated flies, and Japanese corpses. It was as hot as an oven. The smell was the most awful thing I've ever experienced, and there wasn't any way to escape it.

Going in, the brass told us it would be rough but that it would be for only a few days. They were right about one thing. It was rough. But they were wrong about the timing. We fought hard for a month. My company went in with 235 men. We left with 85.

We're back at camp now, on our island of tents and mud and abandoned coconuts. Replacements were waiting when we arrived. They're easy to tell from the veterans. They all look so young. And their eyes—there's something different about their eyes. They're here, on the island, not lost in a nightmare of memory.

LATER THAT NIGHT, SITTING ON the bed in Lottie Morris's unused nursery, I read through the letters from Aunt Janice's fiancé. The last one was dated in September. He said he liked Mary for a girl's name and William for a boy. Somewhere, I might have a cousin. Mary or William. Unless the baby was adopted. Then the adoptive parents would have picked the name.

I'd never heard Aunt Janice speak of adoption before. But I remembered the whispers during the war when a member of our church congregation found herself with child without prospects for marriage. Dad had stated his firm opinion that the baby needed both a mother and a father. He'd played a role in arranging an adoption—had it been his first intervention? Or had he done something similar for his future wife's older sister? Could my cousin, now grown up, harbor resentment for Dad's role?

Another thought crossed my mind. What if Aunt Janice had gotten rid of the baby another way? Abortion was illegal, but that didn't mean it was impossible to get one. Would Aunt Janice do such a thing?

I studied the dates on the letters. Mr. Fairfax had known about the baby in July. I didn't think Aunt Janice's letter informing him could have been sent any later than mid-June, so by the time he'd stopped writing, she would have been four months along, maybe longer if she hadn't recognized her condition right away or if the mail had been slow. Mr. Fairfax's death was never confirmed. She wouldn't have suspected he was missing until October. That was too late for an abortion, wasn't it?

I hoped it was.

But if she'd given birth to the child, where was my cousin? Was an estranged family member behind the attacks, seeking revenge for perceived abandonment? Or was it Roland, even though he hadn't been in town to sabotage the car? Mr. Richards, even though his motive seemed weak? Real estate–hungry neighbors? An abusive teacher looking for revenge on a student who'd struck back?

I looked at the pile of letters from Eugene Fairfax and prayed my aunt's problems would never come to light. The last thing I wanted was to sully Aunt Janice's reputation or drag her child into the police station on charges of murder. I would keep her secret as long as I could.

* * *

I didn't go to work on Monday. I promised Lottie I'd pay her telephone bill for the month and spent the morning on the phone.

The first call was to Detective Iverson, but he didn't have good news.

"Mr. Roth may have provoked Mr. Redhawk, but there's no evidence tying him to the murders. And he has a partial alibi for the afternoon your aunt was murdered. He and his father had a meeting with Mr. Montpellier. It started fifteen minutes after Mrs. Morris left for lunch."

I could imagine the subject of the meeting—Roland was almost finished with law school, and Mr. Montpellier was the most prestigious lawyer in Maplewick. With the right kind of investment in the firm, maybe Mr. Montpellier was taking on a partner.

That wasn't good for Gary. I couldn't trust Mr. Montpellier to defend him, and unless things had changed since last night, Dale wasn't interested.

"And if Mr. Roth presses charges?"

Iverson sighed. "Then we'll have to arrest Mr. Redhawk again. But with a charge like that, the bail will be low. He might even get off with a violation instead of a crime."

The thought of Gary going back to jail—for any amount of time—made my stomach hurt. I did my best to ignore that worry and made my other phone calls to doctors and doctor's offices in Albany, asking if they had records for a Janice Peterson or a Janice Fairfax. Most didn't have records from 1918.

"And your interest in this, miss?" a receptionist asked.

"I've had a lot of family die recently. I'm trying to reach out, see if I have another cousin."

I called ten doctors or their offices, and a few promised to look through their records and call me back, but I didn't have much hope that they would find anything.

The vital records office wasn't much help either, especially since I couldn't narrow the birthdate down and didn't know the baby's name, just the parents'.

Maybe I'd have to go to Albany and search myself. Albany might be safer than staying in Maplewick, but I didn't dare leave Gary while the killer was on the loose, especially if Gary was facing charges for assault. Maybe my search was pointless anyway. Aunt Janice was smart. If she'd wanted her secret hidden, I doubt she'd left many clues.

Frustration at my slow progress burned away as I drove to the funeral, replaced by sorrow. Even on a Monday afternoon, a large group of mourners filled the church, but it brought me little comfort. The service was beautiful, but it was taking place several decades too soon.

Gary, Dale, Frank, and three of Aunt Janice's middle-aged cousins were the pall-bearers. Gary wasn't family, but she would have approved. Aunt Janice had accepted Gary more readily than anyone else in my family had, and he'd spent more time with her than any of her cousins had over the last year. Dale and Frank weren't her family either, but they were part of my family, and she'd watched them grow up.

I thought of Aunt Janice, of course, at the church and at the cemetery but also about Mr. Fairfax. What became of souls whose love had been torn apart by war? Did he have a grave somewhere in France or Belgium? Or had he survived but decided not to come home? And where was their child?

After the casket was lowered into the ground, Gary came over and held my hand. He'd borrowed Jack Dickens's suit again. He looked handsome, sober, and determined, but without my Aunt Janice, I felt lost.

At Dad's funeral, Gary had stood near me, where he could help, but behind me, where people offering their condolences didn't need to talk to him. At this funeral, I needed him closer, and he stayed by my side as each well-wisher went past.

Eventually, the crowd dispersed.

Gary guided me away from everything. "Evie, I know these last few weeks have been hard."

I nodded.

He pulled my hand up to his mouth and kissed it. "You are strong enough to come out of this."

I didn't answer right away. Did he know how close I was to giving up in despair? I clung to his hand, taking in his strength, trusting in his confidence. I felt better for a few moments. I missed my dad, and I missed my aunt, but Gary and I would get through this together.

Then I saw the police car.

Gary followed my gaze and scowled. "I always thought a real man could take a punch instead of running off to the cops."

"Gary . . ." I wanted to ask him to stay sane until I could get him out, but I wasn't sure how, so the words never came.

He squeezed my hand. "Whoever the killer is, I doubt he'll make an attempt on me while I'm in jail. But you be careful tonight. Drive around; make sure no one is following you before you go to Lottie's house."

Iverson got out of the car, and so did another officer. At least it wasn't Horton.

I blinked back tears. "I'll get you out of jail as soon as I can."

Gary's mouth pulled into a thin line. "I'll try to cooperate with the police."

"Mr. Redhawk?" Iverson stopped a few yards away from us. The other officer circled around to stand on the other side. "I have a warrant for your arrest. Again."

"Disorderly conduct?" Gary asked.

"Assault and battery."

I should have known Roland would pick the more serious charge.

"Will you come willingly?"

Gary nodded. "I punched him." The other officer turned Gary around and handcuffed him.

"Detective Iverson?" I asked. "What happens now?"

Iverson seemed genuinely sympathetic. "We'll take him in and book him. He'll be arraigned in the morning. Mr. Roth is pressing for a felony charge, but I think a misdemeanor is more likely."

"Does that include jail time?"

"It can." Iverson motioned to the other police officer, who led Gary away. "Or it could be a slap on the wrist. Depends on the judge."

Gary looked back at me, then climbed into the police car. His eyes seemed to tell me one thing: *be careful.*

"Can I give you some unofficial advice, Miss Hampton?"

"Of course." I pulled my eyes away from Gary, so I could give Iverson my full attention.

"Mr. Redhawk already has a record, and one more charge won't change that. Make a plea for disorderly conduct. If you're lucky, Mr. Redhawk will get a fine or parole and no jail time. The prosecutor is a friend of the Roth family, and he'll push for six months to a year, if it goes to trial."

I folded my arms across my chest as an icy breeze bit into my neck. "All this for one little punch in the face."

"Do you know why Mr. Redhawk punched him?"

"Mr. Roth said something insulting about me. Gary wouldn't say what, but I hear rumors are going around."

Iverson frowned. "The rumors may be partially my fault. I suggested the two of you take precautions. When you both stopped going home to sleep . . ."

"People jumped to the most likely conclusion, even though it's not true."

"I'm sorry. I was trying to protect you. I didn't mean to sully your reputation."

I took a deep breath, grateful for his honesty. "The truth is, I don't care what other people think anymore." I was tired of trying to project the right image, sick of living up to expectations other people had set for me. I was ready to live my life the best I could and ignore what everyone else thought of my efforts.

Iverson nodded. "Judge Farrow has daughters about your age. And Judge Crandall's son was in the army." With those tips ringing in my ears, Iverson walked back to the patrol car.

I watched them drive away. I missed my dad, I missed my aunt, and I was terrified that the next time I saw Gary, he'd be different.

The cemetery was mostly deserted, and I was suddenly very, very alone.

Alone and vulnerable.

Chapter Thirty-Five

December 12, 1944
Dear Clive,

I remember your letters from last year, how you said Christmas was differ-ent in a place like San Diego. It was different for us, too, with you gone. But we told ourselves in another year or two, the war would be over, and you'd be back, and we'd celebrate extra hard to make up for it. This year will be harder because Mom's gone, and she's not coming back.

I FOLLOWED GARY'S ADVICE AND drove around, taking the long way back to Lottie's house. That night, I tossed and turned on the mattress in the nursery. How was Gary holding up? And what would happen the next day? Dale had agreed to attend the arraignment, but he'd sounded less than enthusiastic about it.

Eventually, I switched on a lamp and read through some of Aunt Janice's letters from Clive.

Dear Aunt Janice,

You were right. You always are. Evie's not so bad, especially now that she's not tattling on me for sneaking home after curfew. I took your advice, and I've been writing to her every week. She writes back at least that often. It's nice to have a friend instead of just an annoying little sister. I didn't realize how much I needed that friend until I gave her a chance. Her letters are entertaining, insightful, and they make me happy. She's a lot smarter than I ever gave her credit for.

Tears blurred my eyes, and I couldn't read any more for a while. Aunt Janice had been behind the reconciliation with Clive. She'd given me a precious gift—repairing a rift that had cut at me for years. I still grieved for my lost family members, and I still worried about Gary, but I had hope too. Love couldn't be destroyed by disease or a noose, by poison or a Japanese weapon. It was lasting, sustaining, and powerful, even from beyond the grave.

Roland Roth had managed to threaten my job and get my boyfriend thrown into jail. And someone had killed my dad and my aunt. They'd taken a lot from me, but they couldn't rob me of my family's love. Love like that was immortal.

* * *

"I think we should fight the charges." Dale folded his arms across his chest as we sat together in the courthouse early the next morning. "It was just one punch, and it was provoked. No jury will lock him away for that."

"But Roland is a Roth, and he's been meeting with the most prestigious lawyer in town about joining his practice. Gary is a Seneca with a previous conviction for assault. He won't get a fair trial." It would be like a serf hoping for mercy when accused by a lord.

"You don't know that."

Dale was right. I didn't know, not for certain, but I wasn't willing to risk it. "I want him out of jail as soon as possible. You saw what it did to him before. I think we'll get a better deal from a judge than we will from a prosecutor trying to impress the Roth family."

"Oh, and when did you graduate from law school?"

I didn't answer. He sounded like Clive, before the war. Maybe it had been a mistake to call my cousin. Iverson's warning that I shouldn't let it go to trial weighed on my mind—I wasn't going to ignore his advice.

"I'm sorry, Evelyn. I just don't like the idea of my cousin dating a man with a criminal record."

"He already has a record."

Dale grunted. "He was a minor for the last conviction. He's an adult now—it's different. Although punching Roland is small compared to all the rumors I've been hearing. Fern's mother heard them too. She's appalled."

"The rumors are false, started by Mr. Roth. Maybe I should sue him for slander."

"Be honest, Evelyn. Where have you been sleeping since your dad died?"

I thought I'd come to the courthouse as an observer, but apparently, I was being judged. "Not with Gary."

Dale kept his eyes on me for a long time, as if trying to decide if he believed me. "Fine. I'll pass your suggestions on to Mr. Redhawk when I meet with him. Ultimately, it's his decision. Sometimes charges like this can get cleared up at an arraignment. At the very least, we should get him out on bail."

"I'll pay whatever I need to."

Dale stood. "I'll see what I can do."

I sat in the courtroom through a few other arraignments—one for shoplifting, another for domestic violence. Judge Crandall was lenient with the shoplifting case because it was the teenage boy's first offense. He was sterner when it came to the man accused of beating his wife—it wasn't the first complaint, and he was accused of breaking her arm.

The bailiff announced Gary's case, and a deputy led a handcuffed Gary into the courtroom, still wearing his housemate's now-rumpled suit. I held my breath as I studied him, then relaxed when he met my eyes. He seemed tired and stiff, but he recognized me.

Gary was placed under oath, and the charges against him were read. Assault and battery. The judge asked if Gary understood the accusation.

"Yes, Your Honor."

"You have the right to plead 'guilty' or 'not guilty' to these charges. If you plead guilty, you will be giving up the right to a trial by jury and the right to confront and question witnesses against you. Do you understand these rights?"

"Yes, Your Honor."

"Would you like to plead guilty or not guilty?"

Dale put his hand on Gary's arm, stopping him from answering. "My client would like to plead guilty to the lesser charge of disorderly conduct. You'll find the statement he made to the police yesterday among those papers. My client is a successful student at Redgrave, and he served honorably in the army during the war. He's been a model citizen during his time in Maplewick. The incident on Sunday was provoked."

The judge read through a single sheet of paper and asked the prosecutor if he had any objections.

"No, Your Honor."

"Mr. Redhawk, do you plead guilty or not guilty to the charge of disorderly conduct?"

"Guilty, Your Honor."

"In light of this, I will issue sentence." The judge sorted through his papers again, taking his time to review everything. "Mr. Redhawk, you are sentenced to six months' probation and a $150 fine. If at any time you violate the terms of probation, your sentence will be four months in the county jail. Are you able to meet the fine?"

"He is, Your Honor," Dale said.

After a few whispers between Gary and Dale, the judge dismissed the case.

The outcome was bittersweet. Gary had a new conviction, and he was on probation, but he didn't have to go to jail.

As I walked the half block to the bank, I started to second-guess my push to get the case resolved today. I could have posted bail, and he would be out of jail anyway. But a trial was unpredictable. Roland had a dozen witnesses that Gary had punched him, but I doubted any of them had heard the insult. I loved Gary, but I knew him well enough to recognize he wasn't at his best in front of large groups. He'd have a hard time garnering sympathy from a jury, especially if Roland turned on his well-practiced charm.

Someday, in some way, I was going to get back at Roland. As I withdrew $150 cash from my savings account, it occurred to me that marrying Gary was probably the best way to do that. I didn't know the terms of Gary's probation. If it prohibited travel outside the state of New York, then I supposed that meant we'd have to go to Niagara Falls for our honeymoon.

Last I heard, Niagara Falls was among the best honeymoon destinations in the world.

* * *

Gary was still stiff when I hugged him.

"Are you okay?" I asked. The fine was paid, he was free, and the terms of his probation had been set, but he seemed uptight, on edge.

"Just give me a little time."

I nodded. "Should I take you to the Gerstners' house?"

"Please."

We drove in silence. I didn't mind quiet most of the time, but this felt uneasy. "I'm sorry, Gary. I wanted you out. I thought pleading guilty would be best—a dozen people saw you punch him. And the Roths have influence."

Gary sighed. "You didn't do anything wrong. I'm glad it's done. I just wish I would have walked away when he came up to me on Sunday."

That would have been ideal, but I was grateful Gary had tried to stick up for me, whatever Roland had said. "I think I'm going to buy you a new suit. You always get arrested when you borrow that one."

"Evie . . ."

We'd reached Stanton Lane, so I pulled the car over, but not right in front of the Gerstners' place. I glanced at Gary. "What?"

He looked away. "You don't need to buy me clothes. I already owe you for a hospital bill and now a fine. I will pay you back. It'll just take some time."

"I think our relationship has moved past paying each other back, don't you?"

"I don't want to leech off my girlfriend."

"Fine, I won't buy you a new suit." Hopefully, there wouldn't be any more funerals anytime soon and no need for something black.

He squeezed his eyes shut and rubbed his forehead. "Evie, I don't mean to sound ungrateful. I just . . . A man's supposed to take care of his own. I should be helping you out, not the other way around."

I'd hurt his pride. Again. I hadn't meant to. "If I needed money, and you had it, I know you'd help me. Why should it be any different when our roles are reversed?"

"I don't know. It just is." He turned his gaze on me, and instantly, his face went contrite. "Don't be sad, Evie. I'm not angry at you—I'm just disappointed in myself."

"I don't think you did anything wrong."

Gary swallowed. "I better get going so I can make it to class on time."

"I can wait and drive you."

"You should probably get to the bursar's office before Roland gets you fired for falling behind in your work. I'll stop by at six." He opened the door and gave me a smile. Despite the gesture, I detected sadness in his eyes and defeat in the set of his shoulders. "Thanks for getting me out of jail. Again."

Chapter Thirty-Six

Letter of December 12, 1944, continued

I miss Mom so much, Clive. Dad is quiet now. He spends a lot of time in his study, but when I tell him it's time to eat, I find him staring at the bookshelves or out the window. He's not doing any work. It's like the grief has broken something inside of him, and I'm not sure how to fix it.

"Miss Hampton?" Mr. Thurber stood in front of my desk later that afternoon.

"Yes, sir?"

"Can you run along to the library and pick up something from Mr. Richards?"

"I'd be happy to, sir."

I wasn't sure what Mr. Richards would have for Mr. Thurber. Did they keep old tuition receipts in the archives? I didn't really care, because Gary was probably studying in the library, and I wanted to see how he was doing. He'd come out of jail sane but defeated in some way.

When I got to the library, Gary was where I thought he'd be. I didn't want to startle him, so I stood in front of the table, waiting for him to notice me.

He looked up, then smiled. "Aren't you supposed to be at work?"

"I'm picking up something from the archives."

He glanced at the papers strewn in front of him. "Let me finish this problem, and I'll walk you back."

"I'll meet you in a few minutes." As I headed for the stairs, the practical part of me said I should have left Gary alone. He had a lot to catch up on. But he had class in twenty minutes anyway. Twenty minutes wasn't that hard to make up, was it? And it was good to see him in his normal routine, no longer looking beat down by an arrest and an arraignment.

Mr. Richards's office was in the basement. Only dim lightbulbs showed the way through row after row of towering filing cabinets and shelves piled with neatly labeled boxes. Scaffolding was set against one of the walls, probably to restore the damaged ceiling above it, but no one was working on repairs. It wasn't the library's best-looking section and included no desks or tables for students to sit and study at. The poor lighting was good for the preservation of old documents but not for a student's eyes.

I wondered if Mr. Richards would put Sir Redgrave down by his office or up with the history books. It seemed a shame to hide a suit of armor in the archives. Maybe when I donated it, I could specify that it be placed where more students would see it.

Something creaked behind me, and I turned around. What was that? It didn't sound like footsteps or mice. More like groaning metal.

It was probably just the pipes. The plumbing had been added after the library was built, and exposed pipes were visible on this level. Any time someone used the restroom on the floor above, the pipes made noise.

I heard it again and stopped. Something wasn't right.

The lights flickered out. There were no windows, so blackness consumed me.

Something rustled beside me, I felt a shove, and then the back of my head crashed into something hard.

* * *

"Clive, I'm stuck! I can't get down!"

Clive stood below the big oak tree at Uncle Melvin and Aunt Shirley's house. He looked up at me, laughter from his eleven-year-old lungs sounding in my ears. The laughter held mirth but no sympathy. "Maybe you shouldn't have climbed up there, then."

Frank glanced from Clive to me, then back again. "Should we help her down?"

Clive huffed. "No. Maybe now she'll learn to leave us alone instead of pestering us. Come on, now's our chance to lose her."

"Clive! Frank! Don't leave me!"

I kept calling, but they ignored me. They walked back to the house, and after a few minutes, I saw them pedal away on their bikes. A feeling of complete abandonment swept over me. It wasn't fair that Clive had a cousin his exact age. They never let me play with them!

I didn't want to stay up in the tree all day. Mom and Aunt Shirley had gone shopping, and Dad and Uncle Melvin, probably Dale too, would be holed up in Uncle Melvin's woodshop, trying to reproduce an English longbow.

If I wanted to escape the tree before dark, I'd have to get myself out.

I clung to a branch at chest height and tried to lower my foot to a limb a few feet down. My black Mary Jane barely reached. I shifted my weight and knelt on the branch. The one below was a long way down. I wrapped my arm around the branch and willed my feet to find some type of hold. How had I gotten up here in the first place? The bark caught my dress and hair, scratched my skin. I loosened my grip, getting closer to the target branch, but I still couldn't touch it. I'd have to drop . . . and land on it.

I squeezed my eyes shut, hating Clive and Frank for leaving me trapped. I'd just wanted to play with them, and they had made it look so easy, climbing up and down like monkeys, but my arms and legs weren't as long as theirs.

"One," I counted to myself. "Two . . . three." I let go.

I didn't land on the branch.

I fell to the ground with a scream, knocking the back of my head on the way down.

Blackness and pain overwhelmed me.

Everything shifted to a scene fifteen years later.

Moonlight made the sidewalk outside Redgrave's Student Union Building sparkle like sand on a beach, and music from the band playing at the Homecoming dance drifted outside through cracked windows. A cool breeze whisked the heat from my skin. Gary took his suitcoat off and slung it across his shoulder.

We followed the sidewalk away from the crowd, and suddenly, we were alone.

"Is it better out here?" he asked.

"Much." The inside of the Student Union Building had been stifling. So many students and so much jitterbugging. I ran a hand along my neck, wondering if my hair was still in place.

"You look gorgeous tonight, Evie."

I felt heat rush to my cheeks. I wasn't even wearing a new dress, just an old one Aunt Janice had helped me alter to include a more flattering neckline. "You don't look so bad yourself."

Gary's dark eyes were absolutely mesmerizing as they stared at me.

"A penny for your thoughts?" I asked.

One side of Gary's lips pulled up. "I think they're worth more than a penny."

"If that's the case, then I think I need to hear them."

He reached out, slowly, and tucked a stray bit of hair behind my ear, then let his fingers trail down to my jaw. One of his fingers brushed lightly across my lips, and I could barely breathe at the spellbinding sensation it sent along my skin and down my throat. "I'm just trying to decide if I should take this beautiful moment and leave it alone. Or if I should take a risk, and maybe make it perfect."

In my heels, I was the same height as Gary. I followed his glance from my eyes to my lips and knew what he was asking. "I think it's a good night for risks."

He leaned toward me, and I couldn't figure out why my head hurt so much. The dance floor had made me warm, but it hadn't given me a headache. It was Homecoming weekend, 1946, and Gary was about to kiss me for the first time.

"Evie? Evie? Can you hear me?"

A steady pain hammered on the back of my skull, one of my thighs ached, and my left shoulder felt sore. Where was I? I wasn't a little girl stuck in a tree, and I wasn't on a date with Gary. I'd gone to the library to get something for Mr. Thurber and then . . .

I opened my eyes and groaned. The light was too bright, and it made the pain in my head worse. The rest of my body felt as though someone had used it for jousting practice. Gary knelt beside me on the floor. Above me the scaffolding looked broken. I hadn't been anywhere near the scaffolding, had I?

"Evie?"

"What happened?"

"The scaffolding collapsed, and the tool box fell on you. At least, that's what it looks like."

"But I was on the other side of the basement." I picked out a hammer, a wrench, thick copper pipes, and a heavy-looking toolbox scattered around me. I squeezed my eyes shut again. "Collapsed scaffolding—that sounds a lot like a falling bookcase."

"Yeah." Gary's voice was quiet. Worried. "I had someone call Detective Iverson. Who knew you were coming here?"

"Just Mr. Thurber and Mr. Richards. And you. Maybe Charlene."

"Mr. Richards. The guy who wants your dad's artifacts? Whose bookstore couldn't earn enough to pay the rent your aunt charged?"

I heard footsteps. Gary shot to his feet and moved in front of me as if to protect me.

"What's going on?" The male voice sounded slightly familiar, but I couldn't put a name to it. "What's this mess?"

Gary moved slightly, and I caught sight of Mr. Richards. "This mess? It's a crime scene. You lured Evie down here and tried to kill her!"

"What?" Mr. Richards seemed to notice me for the first time. "Miss Hampton, are you hurt?" He tried to get closer, but Gary blocked him.

"Stay back," Gary said. I hoped he wouldn't throw any punches, because that would probably violate his probation terms.

"I'm just trying to see if she needs help."

"If you dare lay a finger on her—"

"What seems to be the problem, Mr. Redhawk?" I recognized the new voice immediately. Detective Iverson.

"Someone tried to kill Evie." Gary spoke without turning away from Mr. Richards.

"Well, I certainly didn't," Mr. Richards said.

"Only a handful of people knew she would be here," Gary said. "That scaffolding isn't on the way to your office. Someone dragged her over and planned to kill her, then make it look like an accident."

Mr. Richards's face grew pale. "That's absolutely beastly. But I didn't know Miss Hampton would be down here."

I tried to sit. Gary saw and knelt beside me again, putting a hand on my back to support me. I didn't feel strong enough to stand yet, so I stayed on the floor, surrounded by screwdrivers and clamps. Iverson had brought Horton too, and a few students stood further back, watching. I turned to Mr. Richards.

"Mr. Thurber said I was supposed to get something from you. I was under the impression that he arranged it with you over the phone," I said.

"Me?" Mr. Richards looked flabbergasted. "No. I haven't spoken to Mr. Thurber since your father's funeral."

Iverson cleared his throat. "Mr. Richards, I'd like to ask you a few questions. If you would please come with me." He glanced down at Gary and me. "Miss Hampton, when you're feeling up to it, perhaps you could join me in the bursar's office? I'd like to get a statement from you."

I nodded. Iverson and Mr. Richards left. Horton and most of the students stayed.

"Let me feel." Gary's hand brushed lightly against my hair. His touch was gentle, but I still winced. "Sorry. I don't feel any blood, but maybe we should get you some ice."

"How long was I out?"

"I'm not sure. I followed you after I packed my things. I got a little panicky when I came down the stairs and heard something crash." He cradled my cheek in his hand. "I should have come with you from the start. I'm sorry."

"It seemed like a safe enough errand." I scanned the basement. Several staircases led in and out. There was something I wasn't remembering, but the more I tried to grasp it, the more it eluded me. "Maybe you should get to class." He was probably late already.

Gary frowned. "You're more important than a class." He helped me to my feet. "We've got to solve this before one of us ends up dead."

Fear surrounded me as if I'd been dropped into a dank medieval moat. I felt the knot on the back of my head, then clung to Gary's arm. I winced as I put weight on my leg, but nothing was broken, just bruised. We ignored the onlookers and left Sergeant Horton to his investigation.

When we got back to the bursar's office, Detective Iverson was speaking with Mr. Thurber and Mr. Richards.

"I didn't call you," Mr. Richards said. "What would I have in the archives for the bursar's office?"

"You did call, thirty minutes ago, and you asked me to send Miss Hampton to retrieve something from your office." Mr. Thurber jabbed his finger at Mr. Richards's chest.

"I did not call you. I don't even have a phone in my office."

Iverson held up a hand. "What was Miss Hampton supposed to be picking up?"

"He didn't say." Mr. Thurber's mouth twisted to the side sheepishly.

"Of course I didn't say." Mr. Richards's voice rose in volume. "Because I wasn't on the phone."

Charlene stood on the edge of the conversation, listening with interest. "Excuse me, sirs."

"Yes?" Iverson said.

"We could ask the school operator who placed a call to Mr. Thurber at 1:30."

"Can you see to that, Miss Jones?" Mr. Thurber asked.

She nodded. We all watched while she made the call and spoke with the operator. "Yes, thank you for the information." She hung up and looked at the rest of us. "It was made from one of the pay phones outside the cafeteria." That meant anyone could have made it.

Iverson turned to me. "Did you see anyone you recognized while you were going to Mr. Richards's office?"

"Just Gary. I assumed he would be studying, so I stopped to say hi."

Iverson glanced at Gary. I hoped he wasn't going to accuse him again. "Which stairs did you use, Mr. Redhawk?"

"The north ones."

"Did you hear anything?"

"A crash. So I started running."

Mr. Richards huffed. "On metal stairs. No doubt you scared the real culprit away. Perhaps a bit of stealth would have been wiser."

Gary frowned and folded his arms across his chest.

"It's hard to say," Iverson glanced from Gary to me. "Mr. Redhawk undoubtedly scared the man away before he could be identified, but if that also kept the man from swinging one of those tools into Miss Hampton's head, then he may have prevented a murder."

Iverson finished up his questions and left, convinced someone had impersonated Mr. Richards on the phone. Mr. Thurber seemed more comfortable with an imposter than with the alternative, that one of his colleagues had tried to kill one of his employees.

I sat at my desk, gratitude for Gary shadowed by pain from my injury and fear at the knowledge that someone had almost killed me again.

Chapter Thirty-Seven

January 19, 1945

Dear Evie,

We're at Guadalcanal again, for maneuvers. It's good training for the replacements. For me too, I guess. I think about Frank a lot here. And about you. I'm sorry I was such a bad brother growing up. And I'm sorry that even though I might be able to make it up to you, Mom won't be able to see me do it.

We got along some of the time, didn't we? Like that day Mom and Aunt Janice made all those pies for a church social and I wasn't tall enough to reach them. But you were light enough that I could boost you up, and we feasted on apple pie. I wish there had been more times like that. I thought of our stolen pie the other day when Slingshot and I snuck into the Seabees chow line. They had hot food, fresh salad, and ice cream. Lots of ice cream. I'm sure they noticed our uniforms, but they didn't say anything, just served up big helpings for us. Almost as good as that apple pie we snitched when we were little.

I DIDN'T GET ANY REAL work done that afternoon. My head throbbed, and so did a few other places. Gary refused to leave my side, which I didn't mind, but I felt guilty that he was missing class.

"Evelyn, you've got a call," Charlene said.

I picked up the receiver. "Hello?"

"Evelyn, it's Lottie."

"Hi." I purposely didn't say her name. I trusted Charlene, but it was better if I didn't give out any clues about where I was staying.

"A lady called from Dr. Zimke's office in Albany. She wants you to call her back."

The phone calls to Albany seemed as if they'd happened a week ago, not a day ago. I'd almost forgotten about them, but I took down the name and two phone numbers. I didn't want to make the call in front of Charlene, so I had Gary drive to my house after work, and I made the call there. The first number just rang and rang—probably the office, and it was probably closed. The second number went through.

"Hello?"

I swallowed. "I'm trying to reach Estella. It's Evelyn Hampton. I believe we spoke yesterday."

"Oh, yes." Her voice was friendly. "I wasn't working for him at the time, but Dr. Zimke has been practicing medicine in Albany for forty years. I found records for Mrs. Janice Fairfax—Dr. Zimke saw her three times. A prenatal exam. Then influenza. Then a birth. Dr. Zimke didn't remember Mrs. Fairfax, but he says he was a little ragged that winter, what with the outbreak of the Spanish Flu. The notes say the baby was born early and lived less than an hour. Probably complications with the flu."

"I see." Poor Aunt Janice. She had carried the baby and made plans for a future with her fiancé, and then she'd lost them both. "Was it a girl or a boy?"

"A girl."

Mary. Even if she'd lived for only an hour, even if she'd died five years before I was born, even if she was illegitimate, I had a cousin named Mary. I blinked away tears. "Thank you, Estella."

I was sober as I hung up the phone. Gary seemed to sense my mood and wrapped his arms around me.

"She had a little girl," I whispered. "But she died the day she was born." I leaned into him, needing his strength. "In some ways, I'm relieved. Given her situation, I was worried that she'd had an abortion. But she was preparing to love that baby." I inhaled deeply. "And whoever is behind this isn't Aunt Janice's child."

"It will be easier if it's someone we don't like, like Mr. Brown. Or someone I'm jealous of, like Roland Roth."

I cracked a smile. "You don't need to be jealous of him." I stood on my toes to kiss Gary. I'd intended it to be quick, but once our lips met, I found myself lingering in that warmth and sweetness. Heat blossomed where his left hand held my back and where his right fingers caressed my neck. I felt like I could kiss him forever. Was this how Aunt Janice had felt with Mr. Fairfax? Had she loved him this much and then lost him?

I drew back, heartbroken over my aunt's loss and terrified of losing Gary. Someone had tried to frame him and kill him, and we still didn't know who.

But why would Mr. Brown kill my aunt? And would Roland try to kill me? He was trying to punish me, but he knew Iverson was watching him. I couldn't see him risking anything illegal. Ever since Iverson had suggested it at the hospital, I'd assumed Gary was the one with the murderous enemy. But now I wasn't so sure.

"Gary, I don't think you're the target. Otherwise the murderer would have made Aunt Janice's death a clear homicide and done it when you weren't in class. And he would have killed me outright in the library without bothering to make it look like an accident."

He was quiet for a few moments, thinking over my suggestion. "But that would make you the target. And you don't have any enemies, do you? Other than an angry ex-fiancé?"

I shook my head. Detective Iverson had already asked me that. "No one that I can think of. Maybe I made someone angry at work. I send out most of the bills for tuition and on-campus housing, but I can't imagine anyone killing over that. Roland's upset, but he wants me back, so he'd want me alive, wouldn't he?"

We didn't say anything for a time. I was the connection between all the attacks. My dad, my boyfriend, my aunt. All the people I was closest to.

"Someone was in the basement with me." That was what I'd forgotten. "The lights went out, and someone pushed me. I hit my head."

Gary's lips drew into a tight line. "The lights were on when I came down."

"He didn't want me to see him. He could have stabbed me or strangled me—instead, he risked my survival because he wanted it to look like an accident. But he needed the lights to pull over the scaffolding and dump the tools on me. If you hadn't come . . ." If Gary hadn't come, whoever had been down there would have slammed the toolbox or the wrench into my head. It would have looked like bad luck—the scaffolding breaking and tools falling on me at just the wrong angle.

"So it's someone you know." Gary held his thought, shuffling from one foot to the other. "Evie, what's your net worth?"

I glanced at Gary, surprised. We rarely talked about money. That was something that would have to change if we got married, maybe if we were going to solve the case. "Clive had me as beneficiary on his life insurance. That's $10,000. Daddy had another $10,000 in the bank—that will go to my cousins. The house is worth about $15,000, plus about $25,000 he had in stocks and bonds. That's mine. Aunt Janice's house is smaller—maybe $9,000." I'd seen tax assessments on all her properties when we looked through her paperwork, along with bank statements, invoices, and receipts. "Then there's her business. She owns three shops on Main Street, and there's the inventory in her store, plus her checking and savings accounts—probably around $40,000."

Gary whistled and leaned back against the wall. "No wonder you can loan me money for a hospital bill and a fine. You're probably worth close to $100,000. Do you have a will?"

"No." I'd never needed one. I was twenty-four, and I worked in an office. Until someone had cut the brake line on Dad's car, I hadn't thought death was likely anytime soon.

"So if you died, who would that money go to?"

"Nearest kin."

"Your parents and brother are dead. Do you have living grandparents?"

"No. No aunts or uncles either, not now. It was just Aunt Janice on my mom's side. Dad had a brother, but he died in the navy. That left just him and Aunt Shirley."

"Frank and Dale's mother?"

"Yeah. There was a girl too. Mabel. But she died almost twenty years ago. Scarlet fever."

"And their dad?"

"He and Aunt Shirley got in a car wreck. Two and half years ago. Killed both of them. Daddy took it really hard."

"So the only people who would benefit financially from your death are your cousins, Frank and Dale."

"Yeah . . . but they wouldn't hurt me. And they wouldn't kill my dad or my aunt." I'd known them my whole life. Things hadn't always been smooth when we were little, but on the whole, they'd been nicer to me than Clive had been, up until he'd enlisted. "It's not like I'm a millionaire."

"No. But $100,000 could look tempting to a lot of people."

It was enough to buy ten houses. More, if they were small. I could understand that it sounded like a lot to someone who got $50 a month from the GI Bill. It was a lot. But it wasn't enough to kill over—was it?

Gary fiddled with a pen on the entry table. "Dale drew up your aunt's will, so he knew who she had specified as heir."

I nodded, hating where this was leading but knowing I had to follow it out. "And he's never liked you. He offered to defend you when you were arrested for murder, but he was hoping to get you life imprisonment on account of insanity. He didn't have a lot of faith that he could clear your name. Maybe he didn't want you proven innocent—maybe he just wanted inside information about the investigation. And this morning . . . he was reluctant to help. Originally, he wanted to push you toward a jury trial. But he did help, in the end."

"If he wanted me dead, getting me out was in his best interest. Does Dale have money troubles?"

"Maybe a little. But Daddy left him $5,000. That's more than most people earn in a year."

Gary's lips turned down. "But if he thought you were getting married soon, he was on a deadline. It would be hard enough to kill off your father and your aunt—making you rich. Harder if a husband's involved. Even if he killed your husband first, there might be complications or delays when another family was involved." Gary swallowed. "I'm sorry, Evie. I didn't mean to trigger all this."

"It can't be one of my cousins." I folded my arms across my chest. I'd said the words, but I didn't believe them, not completely, because I didn't think anyone else would benefit from my death. "Maybe it's a random sociopath trying to make my life miserable. Like Roland, only Roland is sticking to legal methods, and this other man isn't."

Gary didn't look convinced. I wasn't convinced either. A stranger wouldn't have needed to turn the lights off in the library basement.

I sighed. "So, Dale. Or Frank."

"Or both, working together."

"I guess I can dig around to see if they have alibis." It wouldn't be hard to talk to them, but emotionally, it would have been a lot easier if it had been Roland Roth, Raymond Richards, Lawrence Fontaine, or Orville Brown.

Chapter Thirty-Eight

February 23, 1945

Dear Clive,

When we were younger, I wanted to be your friend so badly, but the harder I tried, the worse I made it. It's good to remember the times when we weren't fighting, even if they were rare. Do you remember when I lost my first tooth? We were in the backyard, and I dropped it in the grass. I was devastated. You searched until sunset, and then you brought it to me.

I WAS STILL BEHIND AT work, but a lingering headache and a restless mind hampered my productivity the next day. I couldn't stop thinking about who was behind the murders, and I didn't like the conclusions I was drawing.

Roland had made a nuisance of himself, but for all his flaws, he was smart. If he was behind the deaths, he wouldn't draw attention to his vendetta by openly spreading rumors to get me fired and provoking Gary into a fistfight. Plus, there were only fifteen minutes when he could have killed Aunt Janice. Nothing was more important to Roland than his prestige; I didn't think he'd risk being late to a meeting with Mr. Montpellier.

For a few days, I'd been sure it was Mr. Brown. But why would he kill Aunt Janice, unless he could somehow blame it on Gary? And how could a man so frail pull over a bookcase or hang a man or hold the door to a restroom closed while chlorine gas killed the woman trapped inside? Maybe I'd just wanted it to be him because I knew there was evil in his soul. With any other suspect, it meant someone I'd thought was good was instead a murderer. And if it was a cousin . . . then someone I loved had betrayed me.

I called Detective Iverson on my lunch break, but he didn't want to discuss the investigation over the phone. Maybe he didn't have any leads. Or maybe he didn't trust me.

I asked Mr. Thurber for another afternoon off. He didn't hide his annoyance, but he relented. "I'm sorry you've had such difficult circumstances lately, Miss Hampton. But the first week of the month is our busiest time. And if President Kettering comes around looking for an excuse to fire you . . ."

"I know, sir. I can work extra tomorrow or come in on Saturday." At least I could if I was still alive. I wanted to keep my job, but now that Dad was dead, my biggest reason for working at Redgrave was gone.

Mr. Thurber nodded and went back into his office. Charlene gestured to the piles on my desk and lowered her voice. "No one except Mr. Thurber will mind if they wait another day."

I smiled my thanks and gathered my things, wishing I could somehow pack extra courage into my handbag.

Gary waited for me outside the bursar's office. He opened his arms, and I snuggled next to him. I couldn't pack courage in my handbag, but I could gather a little from Gary.

His arms relaxed, and we walked to Dad's car. We drove to First Avenue and parked near Dale's law office. Gary took my hand and gave me a smile of encouragement as we got out. I guess he knew how hard this was for me.

I pulled the door open to see Dale's wife, Fern, speaking to Mrs. Huffaker. "You haven't seen him all day?"

"No, Mrs. Bingham. He never arrived at the office."

Fern looked up at me. Even with three little boys, she always managed to put her hair in pin curls at night and smear on a little lipstick before she left the house, but today, her hair was limp, pulled into a simple bun, and her lips were bare. "Have you seen Dale?"

"Not since yesterday at the courthouse."

Fern's knuckles turned white as she wrung her hands. "He was upset about something last night. He left after supper, didn't say where he was going. He never came back."

I met Gary's eyes. Dale had gone missing at about the time we'd started to suspect him.

"And he never came into the office this morning?" I asked Mrs. Huffaker.

"No. I thought he was ill. I've been fighting a cold all week. I assumed I'd given it to him and he just forgot to call."

"Fern, did he say what was upsetting him? Where he was going?"

Fern shook her head. "No. I could tell he was troubled, but he wouldn't say why. I thought maybe a case had gone wrong."

"Have you reported his disappearance to the police?" Gary asked.

Fern's eyes widened in shock. "Well, no. Surely it's nothing involving them."

I wasn't so sure. Had Iverson questioned Dale, and had fear of suspicion caused him to flee?

Gary shifted his weight. "Mrs. Huffaker, do you mind if Evie and I look through his appointment book? Maybe there's something there that would give us a clue."

Mrs. Huffaker handed the book to Gary, and he went into Dale's office, with me in tow.

"Did you call him yesterday?" he whispered.

"No. Did you?"

Gary shook his head. "So if neither of us tipped him off that we were suspicious—who did?"

"Detective Iverson? Maybe he figured it out at the same time we did."

Gary leaned out into the hallway. "Mrs. Huffaker, Mrs. Bingham, do you mind if I make a phone call? I think we should inform the police."

I didn't hear any protests. As Gary made the call, I looked through Dale's appointment book. He was a new enough lawyer that his days weren't full. Nothing yesterday afternoon when I'd been attacked in the library. Nothing from noon until three the day Aunt Janice had been killed. I'd visited him at work often enough to know he usually kept the door to his office shut. It would have been easy enough to slip out the back of the building without Mrs. Huffaker noticing, especially if she was feeling a little under the weather.

Dale could have cut the brake line. He and Fern had bought a new car last year, but until then, they'd made do with one that seemed in need of repairs every other week. He'd had to replace the spark plugs before they could come for Thanksgiving, fill the radiator before they'd left on the Fourth of July. He'd done enough work to know the basics of brake lines and how to sabotage them.

Dad would have let Dale inside. He would have trusted Dale until the rope was around his neck. Dale had been there when the wire had disappeared from the bookshelf. He was strong enough to pull down scaffolding, overpower Aunt Janice, and stab Gary. He'd never approved of Gary.

And if I died, Dale would be about $50,000 richer.

When Detective Iverson arrived, I listened to his questions for Fern. She didn't say anything I hadn't already heard. Dale was worried about something, but he hadn't said what. And he'd disappeared.

"Is anything gone?" Iverson asked. "His toothbrush? A change of clothes?"

Fern's lips pursed in surprise. "No. Just our car. And his hat and wallet, the normal things he takes whenever he leaves the house."

When Iverson finished, I motioned for Gary to show him the appointment book, but I didn't want Fern to hear the accusations.

"Fern, will you take a walk with me?"

Fern nodded, but Gary looked worried. "Evie, I don't know if that's such a good idea."

"We'll stay on First, near the other offices. I promise."

Fern huffed as we went outside. "He's a little controlling, isn't he?"

I looked back at the office. "Who? Gary?"

"Can't you take a stroll without his permission?"

"Of course I can. He's just worried because someone's been trying to kill me."

Fern slowed her pace as we passed an insurance office with frosted windows. "Someone's been trying to kill you? Someone killed your father . . . but surely you're not still worried about that. Dale thought it was your beau."

"It wasn't Gary. Nor was Gary behind Aunt Janice's murder or the attempts on my life."

Fern stopped walking altogether. "Your aunt's *murder*? I thought her death was an accident?"

I shook my head. Fern was busy with her boys, so she didn't always read the paper, but I was still surprised she hadn't heard the truth.

"And someone tried to kill you?"

"Yes." Dale hadn't told her about the bookcase? He'd been there right after. At the time, I'd thought he didn't believe me. But maybe his silence was evidence of a guilty conscience. The library was more recent—I hadn't told Dale. If he was innocent, he might not know, but if he was guilty . . .

Fern gasped. "You think Dale's behind this."

I opened my mouth, but I couldn't answer.

Tears formed in her eyes, and she shook her head. "He can't be. He wouldn't do something like this. I know he wouldn't."

She ran back to Dale's office.

llowed, hearing the end of Mrs. Huffaker's statement. "No, I leave

hin   one when he's inside his office."

n held her hand up to her throat.

rson glanced at her, then back at Mrs. Huffaker. "And from your

de   ou can't see the back door?"

s. Huffaker frowned. "No."

n you hear it?"

shook her head.

son walked down the hall and opened the door. Nothing squeaked

aled. Depending on the time of day, the door was shaded, so it

't affect the office lighting.

Mrs. Bingham, will you have a seat?" Iverson asked.

Fern reluctantly sank into one of the leather waiting chairs.

"Are you and your husband in any financial difficulties?"

"No more than most people, I suppose."

"Meaning?"

Fern sighed. "We have three children in a two-bedroom house. The yard is teeny, and the boys are wild. I've been telling him we need more space. He says we can't afford it. But he wouldn't have killed for money. I know he wouldn't have."

Chapter Thirty-Nine

March 28, 1945

Dear Evelyn,

The truth is, I couldn't find your tooth. It's probably still in the backyard. Mom saved all of mine, and I found them one year when I was looking for Christmas presents. She hid stuff in her sock drawer sometimes. That's where the teeth were. So I took one of mine and picked the scab on my knee so I could make it bloody, and then I passed the tooth off as yours. I guess it was a lie, but I still remember your smile, so I don't regret it.

I'm on a troop ship now, part of a big convoy. We're hitting something big, and we're hitting it soon. I can't say much about it in a letter. I know where we're going because we saw maps during training. The maps didn't have names, but a buddy found a National Geographic article with a picture of the same coastline.

We've heard how bad the Marines have been chewed up on Iwo Jima. I fear the enemy will be just as hard to root out where we're going.

I THOUGHT I WOULD SLEEP better that night, now that the police were looking for Dale. They might not have enough evidence to arrest him, but they would at least question him. Then maybe this whole nightmare would end.

But I didn't sleep, not well. I tossed and turned on the mattress in Lottie's spare room, torn between worry, fear, and anger. How could Dale kill my dad and my aunt? When it came to my brother and my cousins, Dale had always been the kindest of the three. He was older than Clive and Frank and hadn't delighted in pestering me like the other two had. Had his polite exterior held a soul so cold that it could slam a wrench into a trusting cousin's head and knock the life out of her?

What would happen to his family? Fern had graduated high school, but she didn't have many skills that would serve her outside the home. And his three little boys—would they grow up knowing their father was a murderer?

Beyond my worry over Dale, something else was unsettling me, but I didn't know what. I'd felt that way before, when the Japanese had bombed Pearl Harbor, even before I'd heard the news on the radio. And I'd felt it every day from when the marines had hit Okinawa until we'd gotten the telegram confirming Clive had been killed in action. Something was wrong.

A dull headache caressed my temples as I drove to work, listening to the radio, wondering if a new war had been declared. But the radio mentioned nothing unusual.

Gary waited in the hall outside the bursar's office. That was our deal, at least until the murders were solved. He would meet me before his first class so we each knew the other was okay.

But Gary wasn't okay, not this morning. Angry scabs crossed his left cheek and chin, and a cut above his eyebrows showed stitches.

I gasped as I ran up to him. "What happened?" I touched his arm, and he winced.

"A car banged into the back of my motorcycle. I flew off."

I swallowed hard. "But that . . . that could have killed you."

"I think that was the intention."

"Did you see the car?"

"It was late, and I hit the sidewalk pretty hard. A Buick, I think, dark paint."

Dale drove a navy-blue Buick Roadmaster. "Did you see the driver?" I asked, still hoping that despite all the evidence, somehow, Dale wasn't the murderer.

Gary shook his head. "I think I blacked out. I would have been easy to finish off, but a couple saw me and ran over. Your cousin Frank too."

"He was there?"

"I landed about twenty yards from his store." Gary walked toward a bench, and I followed him. When he sat, I joined him, sitting as close as I could.

Gary could have been killed. Just like that. I grabbed his hand none too gently. "Why didn't you call me?"

"I wasn't by a phone, at first. Frank offered to call, but I didn't want to tell him where you were."

"It's got to be Dale, not Frank. It was his car, and why else would he have disappeared?"

Gary's eyes flicked over my face. "I didn't want to risk it."

"Did you go to the hospital?" I raised my hand to examine the scrapes and bruises on his face but stopped short of touching him. The road had torn significant portions of the skin away, and it looked raw and tender.

"Yeah."

I nodded. I would stop by the hospital to take care of the bill, if Gary hadn't already paid it. "But after that? Couldn't you have called me when you were released?" I sounded like a nag, but he was the most important person in the world to me. No one else came anywhere close, especially not now. When he was hurt, I wanted to help, to at least offer comfort.

Gary ran a finger along the edge of the bench. "I got a little shaken up at the hospital." The muscles of his face tightened. "Sergeant Horton was there, asking questions. Someone was speaking German and smoking home-rolled tobacco, and I felt like I was going to throw up. Some poor nurse came at me a little too fast with a rag, and I bolted."

I closed my eyes, picturing Gary running through the hospital, trying to escape. "Did you think you were somewhere else?"

"Yeah."

"But they stitched you up, so you must have come around again."

"Mrs. Gerstner saw my wrecked motorcycle and asked around. Professor Gerstner showed up at the hospital and helped talk some sense into me."

I put my hand on his shoulder, but he didn't relax at all. "That must have been so scary."

Gary huffed. "Scary? No. It was pathetic. I'm pathetic." He stood. "Look, you've got to get to work, and I've got to get to class."

I hurried to my feet as he stalked away. "But, Gary—"

He glanced back, giving me a forlorn smile. "I'll see you around or something." He paused but only for a second, not long enough for me to catch up to him. Then he was gone again, his shoulders slumped and his pace uneven.

I hated Dale. Running into Gary and knocking him off his motorcycle was bad enough. But even more than he'd hurt Gary's body, he'd injured his spirit, and that part of Gary was still fragile. Like my mom's favorite porcelain vase—precious and beautiful but easily damaged.

I wanted to run after Gary to tell him I loved him anyway, that he'd be strong again soon, that one episode didn't make him pathetic. But I was late for work, and he was late for class, and I didn't think he was ready to hear it yet.

* * *

I spent the morning processing payments and worrying about Gary. The anxiety and the fear had to be eating at him the same way they were eating at me. How hard had he hit his head? Had he been wearing his helmet? First the arrest, then the accident. Add in the attack on me, and it was no wonder he hadn't been able to stay calm last night.

How long until the police found Dale so I could stop living in fear that Gary would end up dead? Knowledge that Dale had killed Dad and Aunt Janice—and that he'd tried to kill Gary and me—left a festering wound in my chest.

Lunch hour arrived, and I contemplated going to the hospital to take care of Gary's bill and ask about what had happened. But they might not tell me. And I doubted they'd have much sympathy for him. They couldn't understand all he had been through—lately and in the past.

I skipped lunch and went to the Tillman Building on campus. It was isolated, but no one would expect me to go there, so it didn't feel unsafe. I climbed to the third floor and knocked on Professor Gerstner's door.

"Come in."

I turned the knob and stepped inside. Dr. Gerstner's office wasn't so different from my father's. Shelves full of books lined the walls, a window let in plenty of cloud-shadowed sunlight, and stacks of papers covered the surface of the desk. But where Dad had medieval helmets and weapons, Professor Gerstner had a model of the brain, a fish bowl, and a variety of small machines.

"Miss Hampton? What can I do for you?" He motioned to a seat, and I took it.

"I, um . . ." I wasn't sure how to best broach the subject. "Gary said he had an episode last night, after someone knocked him off his motorcycle."

"Yes."

"Can you tell me what happened?"

Professor Gerstner pursed his lips. "You spoke with him already?"

"Yes, but he didn't say much. He was in a hurry to get to class, and I think he was ashamed of whatever happened."

"Perhaps he told you as much as he wants you to know. He values his privacy."

I bit my lip as the gentle rebuke hit me. "I'm not trying to pry. I just want to help. I'm worried about him, and I'm to blame for what happened last night, for just about everything bad that's happened these last three weeks. It seems only right that I should share his burden."

Gerstner leaned back in his chair, studying me. "How are you to blame?"

"I'm the target. Someone killed my father and my aunt, and he's trying to kill me, and he's trying to kill Gary."

"What is the nature of your relationship with Mr. Redhawk?"

I took a deep breath, gathering my thoughts. "We've been dating for eighteen months. Hasn't he . . . hasn't he ever mentioned me?"

"We speak about the bad things from his past, not the good things from his present. I'm aware the two of you are acquainted, but we haven't discussed it at great length. How serious would you say your relationship is?"

I almost told the professor that Gary valued his privacy, but I wanted Gerstner's help. "We're not officially engaged, sir, but I think we're both planning to get married."

"Oftentimes, people who have experienced trauma in their past have difficulty showing affection. Have you found that to be the case in your relationship with Mr. Redhawk?"

I took my time answering. Gary had never told me he loved me, unless I counted the time he'd asked about it when he was still getting his head back together after his first release from jail. But even when he didn't say it, he showed it in his kindness, in his concern, in his kisses. "No, I've not found that to be the case with Gary."

Gerstner nodded.

"Professor, what happened at the hospital?"

"By the time I arrived, they'd given him something to sedate him. He sat with a blank expression while they stitched the gash above his eye and disinfected the rest of the cuts."

I'd seen that blank expression, and it terrified me. "Because of what they'd given him?"

"I'm not sure. One of the nurses said it took considerable effort to restrain him, so they gave him a higher dose of whatever tranquilizer they had on hand." His lips pulled into a frown.

"You didn't approve."

He had been staring out the window, but he turned back to look at me. "He's been making progress. But that could all unravel quite easily at this point. His head was injured in the accident, then they drugged him.

That's a double vulnerability. I wish things could have gone differently last night."

I thought of the broken posture I'd seen on Gary this morning and wished the same thing. "Do you think he'll regress?"

"Perhaps. He's always been reluctant to cooperate with me. If he hadn't seen Mr. Murphy strike his wife, he might never have agreed to it. But I think he sensed he might be dangerous. Maybe it was concern for you that pushed him into giving my techniques a chance."

"Will your techniques work?"

Professor Gerstner took one of his machines and placed it on the desk between us. It reminded me of a telephone switchboard, only smaller and with more wires. He pointed to the mass of cords, most of them coated in red or black. "The mind is a bit like a switchboard. Trauma can rewire things."

I nodded, watching as he moved some of the wires around.

"Once someone has experienced trauma, they react differently. Internal responses are changed. They react to danger—even the hint of danger—much more strongly than someone who hasn't experienced trauma. Sometimes it leads to aggression. Sometimes it leads to isolation. Sometimes it leads to depression or numbness."

"And those changes, are they permanent?"

"Not always."

"So you can fix it, whatever's wrong in his head?" I leaned forward, willing him to say yes. I wanted Gary to be happy so badly.

Gerstner frowned. "I don't know. But sometimes we can rewire it again. Mr. Murphy, for example. Next time he's startled, instead of growing violent, I expect he'll turn inward. I don't know that it's much better for him, but it's better for his wife and children."

"And Gary? Sometimes it seems like he's in so much pain."

"Mr. Redhawk is a difficult case. He watched his best friend die in battle, then saw the body desecrated. That alone would be difficult to deal with. Add in time as a prisoner of the enemy, and it's even more complex. But what he went through during the war pales with the effects of his childhood. Abandoned, institutionalized, and abused. Quite frankly, I don't know if those things can be overcome. They affected him while his brain was developing. Were you my daughter, I would probably warn you away. Mr. Redhawk's brain has been rewired so many times that it's difficult for a doctor of psychology to make sense of. For someone like you . . ."

I swallowed back the tightness in my throat. "But I love him, Dr. Gerstner."

He watched the goldfish swimming in their bowl for a few moments. "As I said, were you my daughter, I'd warn you away. But Mr. Redhawk needs someone he can feel safe with. Were he my son, I'd pray quite fervently that you would stand by him."

"I intend to."

A soft smile played on Professor Gerstner's lips. "That's the thing about love, isn't it? It doesn't always make sense. Sometimes it doesn't even seem to be for our own good." He stared out the window again. "I married my wife, knowing she had cousins with hemophilia. But I loved her. That didn't stop me from fretting as each of our children learned to walk, didn't stop me from nearly going mad checking their bruises, seeing if they were normal or if the bleeding seemed worse than what's customary."

"And your children? Do they have hemophilia?"

"No. All three are healthy. As are the handful of grandchildren we've been blessed with." He leaned forward. "But the fear was there for years. And if you marry Mr. Redhawk, you'll have to deal with that fear far longer than I did. There will always be a chance that his brain won't react to something the way it should. Little things—a smell, a sound, a pattern on the wall—might break loose a memory of something he's tried to push away. He'll have to deal with each horror as it comes. And that will be a challenge for him and for anyone trying to help him."

Gerstner sat back in his seat and gave me a sympathetic smile. "I'm not saying you shouldn't marry him. But I think you should know what you're getting into before you make that decision."

* * *

The relief on Charlene's face when I returned to the bursar's office told me I didn't have time to think about Gary right then. "I think half the school was in here during lunch." She waited for me to sit, then stilled her hands. That wasn't like Charlene—she was usually doing at least three things at once. "The police called. They found Dale Bingham's car near the border and suspect he's fled the country. They're working with the Canadian authorities to find him."

That seemed to confirm his guilt. The crimes were solved. Case closed. If only solving the murders made the pain go away.

"Your cousin was behind it?" Charlene asked.

I nodded, running my finger along the pile of academic journals Professor Gerstner had lent me.

"I'm so sorry, Evelyn. That makes it even worse, doesn't it?"

A stocky young man came into the office—a freshman, by the looks of him. Charlene waved him over to her desk. Maybe she knew I needed a moment.

Piles of undone work covered my desk, but I called the police station, hoping for more details.

"I'm sorry, Detective Iverson is out. Can I take a message for him?"

I left my work and home numbers, even though he already had them. Then I hung up and tried to focus on my job. I hadn't had time to eat lunch, so a dull headache arrived by two and grew as the afternoon progressed.

Worse than that was the ache in my heart. Dale had killed Dad and Aunt Janice. I supposed it was about the inheritance money, but nothing could be worth all the lives he'd damaged or destroyed—including his own. At least it was over now. But the consequences couldn't be wrapped up so easily. I thought back to my conversation with Professor Gerstner. I loved Gary. But I was worried about him and about the wounds in his mind— made worse by Dale's treachery. Could I handle that mix of love and fear for a decade? For a lifetime?

"Evelyn, there's a call for you."

I glanced at the clock as I took the phone from Charlene. It was only 4:40, but the overcast sky made it feel later.

"Evie?"

I recognized Frank's voice. "Yeah?"

"I think Mr. Redhawk is having another of his episodes. He's bad, Evie. Doesn't recognize me, won't talk, acts like he's scared of me. I think you better come. He's not being aggressive, yet, but I'd hate for him to get that way."

Poor Gary. First the arrest, then the motorcycle wreck, then the incident at the hospital. Now this. "Where are you?"

"If you keep on Redgrave Avenue past the city limits, it turns into a dirt road. There's a warehouse three miles out, on the left. On the way to the junkyard. That's where we're at."

I felt like my stomach had just been tied in knots. It couldn't be the same warehouse that Gary had looked at for Mr. Norton . . . could it? There wasn't much else out there, so it had to be the same place. Gary had been at his most vulnerable there. "What are you doing at the warehouse?"

"He came to look at his motorcycle, and I offered him a ride to get a new part. I was just trying to help, then this happened. Hurry, Evie. The longer these episodes last, the more damage they do." Frank hung up.

I held the phone in my hand a little longer than necessary. Should I tell someone where I was going?

If Dale was in Canada, I could go where I liked while trying to clean up the problems he'd caused. And if Gary was having a bad episode, it was best to keep it quiet. He had it hard enough without everyone thinking he was a psychoneurotic case. Maybe he was, a little, but the term sounded more serious than it was. I'd convince him to get in the car with me, we'd drive around until he calmed down, and then we'd visit Professor Gerstner.

I often finished whatever I was doing before I left for the day, but I left an account only half reconciled and clocked out. "I'm sorry," I told Charlene. "There's an emergency out at the old warehouse."

I grabbed my handbag and the pile of journal articles. I couldn't run well in heels, but I got to the parking lot as fast as I could and sped my way out of town. I had to find Gary and help him, and the sooner I managed that, the better.

Chapter Forty

April 1, 1945

There's something about fear, Evie. Before we landed at Peleliu, I didn't know what to expect, and I was scared. But in a few hours, they'll give us a hearty breakfast of steak and eggs. Then they'll have us climb into our landing craft to attack another island. This time, I know what to expect, and this time, the fear is worse.

I DOUBLE-CHECKED THE MILEAGE ON my odometer, hoping I was mistaken, but it was the same warehouse with the same bleak weeds in the yard and the same coiled wire on the fence. Why had Gary come here again? I understood driving to the junkyard to get a part for his motorcycle, but why stop at the warehouse? Or had simply driving past it been enough to cause problems? He'd done well when it had come to managing his trauma around Mr. Brown, but revisiting a place like this was asking for trouble.

Tension made the muscles in my neck and shoulders ache. I tried to relax as I got out of the car, but the wind picked up, making the trees sway with an ominous rhythm. The air sent chills along my arms, and something else, some deep worry, made my guts feel like ice. I didn't like this place. But there was nowhere I wouldn't go for Gary.

The door to the warehouse was unlocked, so I pushed it open.

"Gary? Frank?" I thrust aside a few spiderwebs and flicked the light switches on. The electricity hummed, and the lights began to glow. It was just as dusty as I remembered it, and the stale air tickled my throat. Hazy shadows blurred the outlines of old crates. Everything looked green in the murky light—dim and spooky.

At the far end of the warehouse, descending from the rafters, was a hangman's noose.

Something shifted behind me, and strong hands gripped my wrists, yanking them behind me.

"What the—?"

Rope bit into my wrists, pulling them together roughly, despite my struggles.

"If you relax, this will all be a lot easier."

I knew that voice. But why was Frank binding my hands? "What's going on? I thought you said Gary was here."

"I'm just tying up a few loose ends. Literally and figuratively."

I caught a glimpse of his face as he pushed me forward. The expression was hard, something I'd never seen from him before. And it was terrifying. "You're working with Dale?"

"Your coworker shouldn't believe everyone who calls in and claims to be the police."

"You left the message with Charlene?" I could barely breathe. "You killed Dad? And Aunt Janice?"

"You never were the brightest kid, were you, Evie? Too coddled and naive to understand anything important. Some things never change."

"But you . . . you . . ." I couldn't finish. He'd accepted Gary more than any of the other men in the family. He'd defended me when Roland had started getting a little rough. How could he be my protective cousin *and* a murderer? "How could you?"

"See, that's the exact sort of trite thing I'd expect you to say." He pushed me forward a little more. I walked where he directed me—it was either that or fall to the ground. With my hands bound behind me, I wouldn't be able to catch myself. "There's your precious Indian." Frank shoved me past a pair of crates.

Gary lay on the ground, bound in chains—the big chains from the back office, the ones that had sent him into his first episode almost three weeks ago in this same warehouse. I couldn't see his face. His body was curled up on itself, and his hands were pulled over his head, like he was cowering.

"Gary? Gary, are you all right?"

He didn't respond.

I turned on Frank, helpless but furious. "What did you do to him?"

"I told him that Dale had you but I knew where he'd taken you. He cooperated well enough, until we got here. Then this was sufficient to keep him in line." Frank pulled out a revolver. His hands were gloved. To prevent leaving fingerprints? "Once I chained him up, he went crazy again. Pathetic. Don't know what you ever saw in him. But you're pathetic too, so maybe it was a good match after all. Too bad you'll never get to see if it would have worked."

"You're going to kill us." It wasn't a question. I knew.

"Don't have much of a choice now, do I?"

I could scarcely wrap my head around the revelation that someone who had known me for so long and so well was behind all the deaths. "Why are you doing this?"

"Why?" His exasperation was thick. "Money, honey."

"This is all about money?"

"Your brother and I were going to go into business together after the war. We'd been planning that music store for a decade! And we were supposed to put each other down as the beneficiaries on our GI Life Insurance policies so that if something happened, our dream could still go forward. That was our agreement. But your brother broke it! He put you down instead, and then he went and got killed, and I was left without a partner and without any seed money. That $10,000 payout should have been mine!"

He waved the gun around as he spoke. I took a step back, but he took a step closer.

"After the *Helena* sank, I wasn't rescued for eleven days. She was torpedoed at night, and as soon as dawn came the next morning, the two destroyers picking up survivors had to scram before Jap planes showed up. I ended up in a life jacket, trying to push a raft full of wounded sailors to an island. I almost died, but I held on to that dream. Clive and I were going to have a music store, just like we'd always planned. That dream kept me alive, kept me pushing after the current took us away from one island and landed us on another, where we had to hide in the jungle so the Japanese patrols wouldn't get us. And then Clive died, and I found out he'd double-crossed me in favor of his whiney little sister."

Frank shoved me again. "Clive didn't even like you! Growing up, he was always complaining about spoiled little Evie not doing her chores right and tattling on him and poking him and annoying him about out of his mind. He hated you! Why would he leave you money when he hated you and I was his best friend?"

"He didn't hate me. We reconciled, after he left." We'd become friends through our letters, smoothing out the annoyances and mending the fissures.

I'd bared my soul to him, and he'd confided in me. "He said he wanted me to have options."

Frank huffed. "Options? You didn't even need the money. You're almost twenty-five, and you haven't been anywhere. A month ago, you still lived with your dad and worked at a boring job and ran around with a crazy Indian for a boyfriend. That money should have been mine, but he gave it to you instead, and you weren't even doing anything with it!"

"Then why not ask me for a loan?"

"Your dad wouldn't loan me any money. Why would you? He'd probably tell you not to. And you'd obey him, like you have with everything else, except that Indian. Your aunt loaned me money, but when things took longer to build than I thought they would, she wouldn't loan me any more, and she wouldn't forgive my debt. If Clive had lived, she would have given *him* more money. I'm making Clive's dream a reality, and your aunt was charging me interest."

"Is that why you killed her?"

"It sure made it easier. Dale said that if she died, you'd inherit. I would have waited. Years, if needed. But then it looked like you might get married, and I knew I had to act. Your dad had to die, or he would have gotten your money instead of me. If I was going through all that work, why not make it so I'd never have to worry about money again? I'd make you nice and prosperous, and then I'd finish you."

His greed staggered me, but even more, it was his unequivocal justification that unnerved me. "And Dale? He'll get half of it. Did he really go to Canada?"

Rage crossed Frank's face. "Dale's as bad as Clive. He came to me, asking questions. I told him he could have half the money, but he threatened to go to the cops. I was solving all his money problems, but my own brother chose you over me!"

Dale hadn't chosen me over Frank. He'd chosen right over wrong. "What did you do to him?"

"I'll give him one more chance to change his mind. But if he won't, I'll have to kill him."

"He's your brother!"

"I have to. If he talks, I'll be executed for murder."

"You won't get away with it. Detective Iverson will figure it out."

Frank raised an eyebrow. "He hasn't figured it out yet. Why would he figure it out now? Especially when I'm leaving him an obvious solution."

Frank grabbed my arm and pulled me toward a scuffed table. "Detective Iverson will find a confession on this old typewriter. Go ahead, read it."

I looked at the paper sticking out of the top of the dusty Underwood.

Evie and I were behind it all. We knew if we killed Professor Hampton and Miss Peterson, Evie would be rich. Evie didn't lie, not completely, when she reported my alibi. We were together, just at her house instead of in town. Things got complicated when I was arrested. The episodes Iverson and Horton witnessed were real enough, but guilt played its role too.

Evie pulled the bookcase over on herself. She wasn't supposed to get hurt, but it was heavier than she thought. We figured it out a little better in the library. I pulled everything over, then she lay down and pretended to be hurt.

My stab wound was a little more serious than planned, but we had to make it look like we were innocent. I saw a lot of people recover from worse during the war. It was a sacrifice I was willing to take for a payout that big. The motorcycle accident was just that—a random hit-and-run. But it helped our plans, so we made sure everyone knew about it.

I didn't mean to kill her. One moment, I was hauling a Nazi guard up by his neck, getting my vengeance. Then everything was quiet, and it wasn't a Nazi; it was Evie.

I wish we hadn't done it. Once we started, we had little choice but to continue. We had to keep going, or we'd be found out. We came here because we thought no one would look for evidence at an old warehouse. But the pull of this place is too strong. I went crazy, and I killed her. I did care for her. Evie was half the incentive. Money was the other. Now I won't have either. I won't be a prisoner again or face the chair. So you'll find my confession and my dead body.

Gary Redhawk, May 6, 1948

I read the words and hoped no one would believe them. But if Iverson had no other suspects, why wouldn't he? Gary was horrible at typing—he wouldn't type a confession; he'd write one. Would Iverson know that? Would he bother to ask? Even if he did, would anyone other than me be able to tell him?

"What evidence are we hiding?"

Frank smirked. "The knife that stabbed Mr. Redhawk. Your dad's missing keys. The tool I used to cut the brake line. The wire that pulled the bookcase over."

He had thought of everything.

I was going to die. Gary would be blamed for it. And then Gary would die, and Dale would disappear. Frank would be rich, and no one would ever suspect he was behind it all.

"I'm not experienced enough with coroners to know how accurately they can pinpoint time of death. So, ladies first." He glanced at Gary, still huddled in a ball and wrapped in chains. "I'll take care of him after. Suicide by gunshot. With a handgun purchased by his cousin nine days ago." Frank held the revolver up.

"Why would Mr. Amedon buy a gun for you?"

"Because I offered him enough money to stay drunk for a month if he did. I saw Mr. Redhawk dropping him off at the bus station. Obvious enough that there was a connection, one the police would notice. Funny thing is, he wasn't so thrilled that his cousin was dating the wrong type of girl. I could have told him that the girlfriend's family thought the same thing about her choice."

That was why Otetiani Amedon had still been in Maplewick. Frank had distracted him, and he'd probably been too drunk to buy a ticket after that. But Iverson would check the weapon for fingerprints. Frank's gloves would keep his prints off it, but maybe Gary's prints would be absent too. That would make Iverson suspicious, wouldn't it? But even if Iverson had doubts, that suspicion was unlikely to lead him to Frank, and it wouldn't save me or Gary.

"Gary!" I had to try one more time. "Gary, I need your help."

I stepped away from Frank, but that was closer to the noose. My eyes darted to the door. Could I make it past him without getting shot? I hated to leave Gary, but Frank wanted me dead first, so that meant Gary still had time. And Frank wanted me dead by hanging, so he didn't want any bullet holes in me.

I couldn't die without a fight.

I sprinted for the door. Having my hands tied slowed me more than I'd expected, and my heels didn't help, but desperation spurred my legs on, across the dusty concrete and around the old crates.

I wasn't fast enough.

Frank grabbed my arm and pulled me toward him, then dragged me toward the noose. "I was hoping you'd do that. The police will expect to find signs of a struggle. You won't bruise the right way if I hit you after you're dead."

He pulled me past Gary.

"Gary, please!" I didn't know why I was calling to him again. Even if he weren't in chains, he couldn't help me. His mind was somewhere else. He'd said he was making progress with Professor Gerstner, and I'd seen him fight it in Hofeling, but Gary's ghosts were stronger here than they were elsewhere, and this week had brought him one blow after another.

"Frank, don't do this. I'll keep it a secret. I won't tell anyone you're involved. And I'll give you everything. I'll deed the houses over to you, the businesses too. You don't have to kill me to get the money. I swear I won't tell." I would move into Gary's shack if I had to, live on nothing but what I earned if giving up my inheritance would keep us both alive.

Frank glanced back at Gary. "He knows too. And he's not in full control of his mind, so I can't trust him. And if Iverson doesn't have a suspect, he'll keep digging. He might find something, especially if he follows your money. He hasn't caught on to me yet, but he's not a dullard. Plus, I don't trust you. You always let it slip when you saw Clive and me sneaking out."

"That was a long time ago. I can keep a secret now."

"For decades? No. You would always have something to hold over my head. I might have trusted Dale to keep quiet. I'd have to give up the shop and leave the country, because he might change his mind, but I could start again somewhere else. But you? I can't live with you as a constant threat. Can you imagine that? Trying to sleep every night, knowing that if one word leaked to the police, I'd be arrested and executed?"

"So you'll live with three more murders on your conscience instead?"

Frank's scowl deepened, and his voice gained a rough edge. "You don't know what I saw during the war. When the *Juneau* sank off Guadalcanal, we left her behind. No one thought anyone survived an explosion that big, but there were a hundred men in the water. And they stayed there for eight days. Only ten were rescued. Wasn't that murder—abandoning them to sharks and starvation? But we thought it was necessary because a Japanese sub was after us. Sacrifice a few so that the rest might live. Isn't this the same thing? I'm just sacrificing a few so I can live my dream—the dream you and your brother robbed me of."

"No, it's not the same! You think Gary's crazy? You make Charles VI look sane! This isn't war! Nothing's sinking!"

"My shop is sinking. I need money to save it."

He grabbed the noose and brought it toward me. Coarse fiber ends curled outward from the thick rope.

I went limp, forcing my muscles to relax so completely that they no longer supported me. Frank still had me by one arm, so I didn't crash to the floor, but my neck was no longer high enough for the noose.

Frank swore. "Stand up and face your death like a man."

I wasn't a man, and I wasn't about to stand up and meekly submit to the noose. I kicked him in the shin with the narrow heel of my shoe.

He swore again and brought the revolver around, pointing it at my forehead. "I can type a different confession. I wouldn't have to change much, just the weapon."

Frank whacked the back of my head with his revolver, and mottled bursts of light and shadow blocked my vision for a few moments. He yanked me up and slipped the noose around my neck, then tightened it. The rope dug into my skin, and it was hard to breathe.

"Frank, please." The sound of my strangled voice startled me.

Frank turned away and strode to the other end of the rope. He kept his back to me, perhaps to ease his conscience, and hauled on the rope.

My toes lifted off the ground, and the pressure from the rope went from snug to a chokehold. No matter how hard I tried, I couldn't breathe. I kicked in a panic, but it didn't do any good.

I was suffocating.

Fading.

Dying.

In a blur of movement, something plowed into Frank and knocked him to the floor. I dropped to the ground and gasped for breath. The rope wasn't hanging me anymore, but it was still tight enough to strangle.

Two men wrestled on the ground a few yards away from me. Frank. And Gary—chains still clutched his legs, but somehow, his hands were free. He swung his fist into Frank's jaw and Frank fell back.

Gary hobbled over to me and pulled the rope around my neck loose. Then he freed my hands. That was all he had time for before Frank dove onto him and shoved him into one of the crates. I heard something crack as his body crashed into the wood.

"Run, Evie! The gun's not loaded."

I didn't know how he'd partially escaped the chains or how he knew Frank's revolver wasn't loaded, but I believed him. Gary had sounded desperate but sane.

I slipped the rope from my neck and scrambled to my feet. Then I sprinted for the door. I heard grunts and groans behind me and turned back to see Frank knee Gary in the side, right where he'd been stabbed. Gary's cry echoed through the warehouse. I wanted to go back and help, but after skipping lunch, getting pistol-whipped by my cousin, and then being partially strangled, I was dizzy. I was more liability than asset until the room stopped spinning.

I reached the door and glanced back to see Frank swinging the butt of the handgun into Gary's head. Gary collapsed. Frank swung the revolver toward me, and it looked like he pulled the trigger, but nothing happened. He swore and aimed again, but by then, I was outside.

Chapter Forty-One

Letter of April 1, 1945, continued

I'll admit it. I'm scared to die, Evie. But more than that, I'm scared of disappointing my squad mates, scared of not living up to all that I'm supposed to be. More than anything, I want to be brave when the times call for courage.

I WAS A COWARD. I'd left Gary partially chained, still recovering from a stab wound, to fend for himself against a man who was trying to kill him because of me. I had to find a way to help him. But first, I had to catch my breath.

I dashed away from the entrance and hid in a thick copse of overgrown bushes and leafless birch trees. Breathing hurt, probably because my neck was bruised and swollen. I still fought light-headedness, but my eyes were focused now.

Frank appeared in the door of the warehouse. "Evie!"

I didn't answer. The warehouse was isolated, so no one but me would hear his shouts. The car keys were tucked in my jacket pocket, but Frank was closer to the car than I was. And could I drive away without Gary? Frank wanted me dead first, but after their scuffle, I doubted Gary's body was in the right condition for a believable suicide. Frank might cut his losses and finish him off. But his first priority would be my death.

Frank's previous attacks had all been carefully planned. Would he be able to improvise when things went wrong?

I hoped not.

When his plan to sneak in and murder Gary had gone awry because the locks were new, he'd broken the window and done it in a room where no one would hear. But that was something simple. This was finding and killing someone, then making it look like a murder-suicide.

I couldn't fight Frank. He was stronger than me. He was probably smarter than me too, but this time he didn't have a plan. His revolver was empty—or it had been a few moments ago. He'd thought it was loaded, so what had happened? Would he have spare cartridges in his pocket?

I needed a weapon.

I didn't own a gun, nor had Dad.

But unless Gary or Mr. Frye had moved it, Dad's reproduction of a fourteenth century Genoese crossbow was still in the trunk of the New Yorker.

A portion of Dad's long and involved lecture echoed through my mind.

"It took a great deal of strength to load a crossbow. Sometimes the bowmen would have hooks attached to their belts. They'd bend down, hook the string, and then stand. Or they would lie on their backs and put their feet on the bow arms and pull the string back in that manner. Then the winch system came along. Still took a lot of strength. And time—that's why English archers were so effective during the Hundred Years' War. They could shoot six arrows a minute. A crossbow could maybe do four—more likely three, two even. I cheated on this model. The windlass uses the best of modern technology. A child could wind and load it."

A weapon lay in my trunk, one that shot from a distance, one I was strong enough to use.

I just had to get there.

"I'll make a deal with you, Evie," Frank called. "Your boyfriend is still alive. For now. I'll have to burn the warehouse to hide the damage I gave him. He'll burn alive, Evie. Is that what you want? Or something a little more merciful? Your choice. Either way, I'm going to win. Before this night is over, you'll both be dead. But death doesn't have to be horrible. Cooperate, and it will be easy, for both of you. A bullet instead of the noose. Quick, painless. Then no more worries."

Hatred flared so strongly that I contemplated grabbing a nearby tree branch and running at Frank with it. But he might have found his spare rounds. And while dying bravely might be noble, I was more interested in living.

Frank glanced back inside. He seemed satisfied with whatever he saw and began circling the warehouse.

The moment he disappeared around the corner, I left my hiding place. I walked as quickly as I could without making the gravel crunch. The warehouse was big. It would take him a long time to go all the way around it. I should have time to get the crossbow, arm it, and find cover.

My hands shook as I unlocked the trunk. Red welts lined my wrists from Frank's ropes. I glanced at the driver's side door. I could get in the car, speed away, and hope the police arrived before Frank killed Gary. But I couldn't risk that. I'd already lost Dad and Aunt Janice. I couldn't lose Gary too.

The crossbow was still in its box, with a dozen bolts. I took one and slid it into place, then wound the wench.

"You should have left when you had the chance." Frank strode toward me, his revolver held in front of him with both hands. Was it loaded now? I'd thought he would take longer, but he was coming from the same side of the warehouse he'd disappeared behind. Maybe his car was over there, with spare ammunition.

I fumbled with the windlass. He was at the wrong angle to see the crossbow. I wanted him to get closer because I hadn't practiced and I wasn't sure how accurate I'd be. And it would take precious seconds to load the next bolt. A revolver could get off multiple shots a whole lot faster than a crossbow.

I needed to keep him talking. "Maybe you should have gone to the bank and asked for a loan like a reasonable person." I sounded terrified, and I was.

"I did. They denied it."

"Something through the GI Bill?" It provided small business loans for veterans.

"They wouldn't give me another one." He stopped ten feet away. Maybe that was as close as he would come.

I held the end of the crossbow. The second I lifted it, Frank would see it. He'd pull the trigger on his revolver before I had a chance to position the crossbow, let alone loose a bolt.

"Gary, look out!" I yelled.

Frank turned his head to look at the warehouse just long enough for me to pull the back of the crossbow tight against my shoulder. I pulled the release as his face turned back to me, anger in the lines of his mouth and hatred in his eyes because Gary hadn't made an appearance. I'd bluffed, and he'd fallen for it.

The bolt hit Frank's chest, high and to the right of where I'd aimed. He lurched backward, and his hands jerked. He shot, and the bullet struck the open lid of the trunk. I grabbed another bolt and ducked behind the car.

Gravel crunched beneath Frank's shoes as I wound the winch again. An expert crossbowman could shoot every fifteen seconds, but I wasn't an expert, and it wouldn't take Frank that long to walk around the car.

He came into view. Blood stained his shirt, and his movements were slow. I gripped the crossbow and ran. The warehouse would give me a place to hide long enough to finish winding it.

A shot sounded, and something snarled into my leg. I crashed to the ground. The crossbow slid from my hands, and pain seared my left calf.

"Only someone from your family would use a crossbow in 1948."

"It worked for Joan of Arc." I turned to face him.

Frank huffed, then winced. His movements were even slower now. He kept the revolver pointed at me but held it with one hand instead of two. His left hand pressed the skin around the bolt, trying to control the bleeding.

"You should pull that out as soon as you can. A lot of wounded men died of infection back then." I scooted back toward the crossbow.

"So I can bleed to death? I'm not stupid, Evie. I'll wait till I'm at the hospital. I'm not sure what I'll tell them, but I'll think of something. Maybe Mr. Redhawk went crazy, used a revolver on you and a crossbow on me. If I burn the warehouse with both your bodies, they might never know the difference."

My hand touched the crossbow. I hadn't wound it all the way. It would still shoot; it just wouldn't be as powerful. But Frank was close, and he wasn't wearing chain mail. The bolt didn't need its full force to do the job.

I couldn't distract him again. I just had to hope he'd be slow.

I grabbed the crossbow and whipped it around. I loosed the bolt and prayed it would strike. It hit him in the ribs as he fired. The shot sounded loud in my ears, but he missed.

The revolver tumbled from his hands. I scrambled toward it, ignoring the gravel that dug into my skin and the mass of pain in my calf.

Frank collapsed to his knees and reached for his weapon.

I dove and gripped the revolver before he did. His fingers grasped weakly for the gun, but I tugged it away.

I scurried back, not wanting him to tackle me in a desperate burst of last-minute strength. I tried to stand. I stumbled, then hobbled. The pain flared stronger than anything I'd ever experienced before, and the scene before me tilted and doubled before merging back into focus. Somehow, I managed not to collapse.

I pointed the gun at Frank. How had it come to this? Two cousins shooting at each other until one could barely walk and the other could barely breathe.

The whistle that accompanied each inhalation told me the second bolt had pierced Frank's lungs. I'd thought I'd feel satisfaction when the murderer was caught. But I just felt empty inside. So many deaths. And what for?

There was just death. And a permeating sorrow.

"Where's Dale?" I asked.

Frank's voice was weak. "In . . . crawl space."

"In your store? Your house?"

Frank didn't answer. His eyes closed, and the wheezing grew stronger.

I took a few steps back and sat for a moment, looking at the mess on the back of my leg. I put the revolver down and took my jacket off to fold and wrap around the wound. I winced as I pulled the knot tight, but I wasn't done yet. I couldn't bleed out, not now.

I struggled to my feet again, with the gun, and tried putting more weight on my injured leg. The bullet must have missed the bone. The pain was excruciating, but I was able to limp forward.

I had to check on Gary.

Those steps were the hardest of my life, physically. And in other ways too. My father and my aunt had died because of me, because Clive had tried to do something kind. If Gary was dead, I wasn't sure I wanted to survive.

Inside the warehouse, moving was a little easier. There were crates and boxes to use for support. I tried to hold back my whimpers as I forced myself to move despite the pain. With each step, the throbbing turned to a sharp stab, and I felt dizzy and nauseated.

I finally crossed the warehouse and knelt next to Gary. His face was marred with fresh cuts. Blood dripped from a gash on the side of his head, but I felt a pulse. I dug in his pocket for his handkerchief and pressed it against the largest wound. I did my best to be gentle. He didn't stir.

I held the handkerchief there, trying to catch my breath and process all that had happened. I needed to find a phone. My left leg was weak, and I didn't know if it would hold in the clutch. Even if I could drive, I wasn't strong enough to drag Gary to the car. I wouldn't leave him alone with Frank, even a dying Frank, even if I was just driving to get help.

Frank had to have called me from somewhere nearby. Had he meant it when he'd said they were at the warehouse? I prayed the telephone in the back office was still connected to something and limped toward it.

The old thing was attached to the wall and had a separate ear and mouth piece. I cranked the magneto and gasped in relief when I heard an operator at the telephone exchange come on the line.

"Operator? I need an ambulance. And the police."

Chapter Forty-Two

Late April 1945

Dear Evelyn,

We landed on Okinawa on April 1. They said we can tell you that now because it's all over the news. The landing wasn't contested. All the replacements think we were snowing them about what battle is really like, but the scuttlebutt is that it's really hit the fan in the south of the island. And that means we'll be sent there before it's over. The Japs will fight hard, and I have a feeling I'll have to do my part to pry them off this island.

I'm writing you from a destroyer escort anchored near the tiny island of Takabanare. We made a landing here to ensure there weren't any Japs who could attack us from the rear, but it's been more like a camping trip than a battle. It's like our own private island. I swam out to the ship for some hot chow and some V-mail forms.

It makes me sad that it took a war to bring us together. When I get back, I'm going to be the brother I always should have been. And whatever your dreams are, I'm going to help you achieve them. If I don't make it back . . . I don't like to think about that possibility, but after Peleliu, the odds aren't just numbers. They're memories. If I don't make it back, I've made sure you'll have options. Be happy, Evie, whatever you decide to do, however you decide to live.

Love,
Clive

GARY AND FRANK WERE BOTH alive but unconscious when the police arrived. Gary's condition had stayed the same, but Frank's was deteriorating.

"Don't know if he'll last long enough to stand trial," Detective Iverson said after speaking with the ambulance driver.

"And Gary?" I watched Sergeant Horton and the man from the hospital load Gary's stretcher into the back of the ambulance. Frank was already inside.

"He'll need stitches, and he'll probably have a concussion, but the bleeding is under control. Give him a little time, and I think he'll recover."

I nodded. Gary was going to survive. That was what I cared about the most. As for Frank . . . I hated to think I had killed someone, especially my cousin—my brother's best friend—but he hadn't given me much of a choice. Still, Frank had known Clive better than anyone. If he died, I would lose another little bit of my brother.

I handed the revolver over to Iverson, glad to be rid of it. "Frank said he paid Otetiani Amedon to buy it for him. That's Gary's cousin from Cattaraugus. And Frank confessed to kidnapping his brother, Dale. He said he's in the crawl space, but I'm not sure if he meant his store or his house."

"We'll find him. But first, let's get you to the hospital."

I handed over my keys and accepted Iverson's help to the New Yorker, wincing as I climbed inside. I gritted my teeth and held my breath each time we passed over a pothole on the way back into town because each bump in the road sent a jolt of pain through my leg.

"What will you do now?" Iverson asked.

What would I do? I could sleep without fear of someone killing me, but with everything that had happened, I wasn't sure I'd be able to sleep in peace. "I guess for now, I'll take care of Gary. And he'll take care of me. And we'll move on from there."

"I wish I could have solved this case sooner." Iverson pursed his lips. "Frank Bingham was cautious, clever. No fingerprints, no witnesses, common materials. He didn't make any mistakes." The hint of a smile slid across his face. "Except messing with the wrong woman. You're strong, Miss Hampton. Keep that inner strength, and you'll do well."

I didn't feel strong. I felt beaten and damaged.

The hospital was a blur of activity. I spotted two nurses with Gary, then another nurse pulled me into a room and swabbed my leg with iodine. About an hour later, a doctor came in, extracted the bullet from my calf, and left me with a dozen stitches.

The nurse told me I could stay longer, so I rested on the bed, letting time pass as I tried to push away all the horror I'd seen the last three weeks. I wept, for my father, for my aunt, and for my cousin who had become a monster. I cried because it had happened, and I cried because it was over. I'd grieved before, but I'd kept part of my emotions bottled up. Now they were all released, in a stronger vintage.

I woke the next morning, somehow surprised to see sunshine through the window. My world had been turned upside down, but the sun had still risen, and life would continue.

None of the nurses had woken me to send me home overnight. Maybe my leg was worse than they'd told me. I flexed my foot, testing it, then decided to rest it longer when the pain grew from a knotted ache to a burning stab.

A soft knock drew my attention. Gary stood in the doorway, wearing a pair of hospital pajamas.

"Gary! You're okay!"

He glanced over his shoulder before stepping inside. "I don't think I'm allowed to get up yet, but they said you were here, and I wanted to see you." He came over and sat next to me on the bed. He stared at my bandages. "They said Frank shot you."

"It's not serious. I probably could have gone home, but I guess I fell asleep, and no one woke me." I studied his face. It had looked bad yesterday, even before Frank had clobbered him. Now it looked worse—more cuts, deeper bruising. "There was a gash on the side of your head. It looked deep last night."

He twisted his head so I could see the line of stitches above his right ear. The skin around it was cropped to the scalp. "This makes the haircut you gave me look pretty good."

That brought a smile to my face. "How long will it take your hair to grow out?"

"A month, maybe." He brought a hand up and cradled my face with such tenderness that I almost cried. Gary was alive. I was alive. And no one was trying to kill us anymore. "So I was thinking that maybe when I have a decent haircut and you can walk without limping, we could get ma—"

"Mr. Redhawk? Mr. Redhawk!" Someone in the hallway sounded upset.

Gary frowned, and his hand fell away. "Guess I got caught escaping again."

A nurse barged into the room. "I believe you were instructed to stay in bed, Mr. Redhawk. You have a serious head injury. You assured me this morning that you were no longer a flight risk."

Gary stood, then put one hand on his head and the other on the wall, as if he needed help balancing. "Uh, I think I need to sit down." He sank into a chair. "I'll go back soon, I promise. I won't leave the ward." He gave me a wink.

The nurse put her hands on her hips and seemed ready to argue, but then Detective Iverson appeared in the doorway. "Mind if I ask these two a few questions?" He showed the nurse his badge, and she nodded.

"It's a police matter. I'd like some privacy with your patients, please."

The nurse left with a scowl on her face.

Iverson pulled another chair around and sat near the foot of my bed. "Miss Hampton filled me in on most of what happened last night, but I still have a few questions. How did you end up at the warehouse, Mr. Redhawk?"

"Frank pulled up in his car while I was walking to the administration building. He said Dale had Evie, but he knew where he'd taken her. He made it sound like if we didn't hurry, we might be too late. So I got in the car with him. He drove to the warehouse."

"And once you were there?"

"He pulled a gun on me. And it took me until then to realize Evie and I had suspected the wrong brother. He chained me up, and I pretended to have a fit so he wouldn't notice when I unloaded his revolver."

"You what?" Iverson asked.

"I, uh . . . well, I used to be good at picking pockets and that type of thing. He got distracted trying to untangle the chains using only one hand. I didn't think I could snatch the pistol away without it going off. He had the barrel shoved into my stomach. So I slid the cylinder out and ejected the rounds." Gary glanced at me. "Sorry I couldn't do anything about the rounds in his car. I heard him call you. I hoped you wouldn't come, but I figured you would."

"And then?" Iverson asked.

"When he wasn't standing over me with his revolver, I scrounged for something useful. Took forever to find anything I could use to pick the locks. By the time I got my hands free, he was about to kill Evie, so I did my best with my legs still chained."

"You saved my life." I'd known that, but I hadn't known how hard he'd had to work to do it.

Iverson set his notebook down. "So the psychoneurotic episode was a ruse?"

"That one was. I knew Evie was depending on me. And I guess the nightmare before me was stronger than the nightmares behind me."

Iverson stood. "Well, I'll leave you two alone. Frank Bingham didn't last the night. So there won't be a trial."

Frank was dead. The weight of that knowledge felt heavy, like a block of stone meant to be hurled from a trebuchet, but I didn't know how to get rid of it. I'd killed my cousin. But if I hadn't, he would have killed me and Gary and Dale.

Gary put his hand on my elbow, and I had the impression that he knew all about difficult decisions and hard consequences and how guilt and sorrow and relief can all swirl together, not mixing but blending into a potent blur of emotions.

"Is Dale all right?" I asked Iverson.

"Sergeant Horton found him. He's home with his family now. I'll interview him after I've gotten statements from the hospital staff."

"The nurse wants to send me back to my room, so feel free to take your time," Gary said. "She's the one I tried to run away from after the motorcycle accident. I don't think she trusts me."

"I suppose Frank was behind that too?"

Gary nodded. "If Dale went to see him, Frank would have had his car. He had just long enough to drive past, park, and come back. When he saw a few people helping me, he decided to join in the rescue instead of finishing me off. If I'd told him where Evie was sleeping, he probably would have killed her that night." Gary looked at me. "I almost told him."

I took his hand and squeezed it. "But you didn't. You kept me safe, even when it hurt you."

Iverson cleared his throat. "I'll take extra care interviewing the nurses and doctors about the nature of your injuries, but I won't be able to keep them out of here for long."

"Understood, detective," Gary said. "Thank you."

Iverson nodded. "Good luck to the two of you."

The detective left, and Gary moved to sit beside me on the bed again. "Are you all right?"

I shrugged. I glanced at my hands, half expecting to see blood on them.

Gary took one of them and held it. "You didn't do anything you need to feel guilty about. You were reacting to evil. If you hadn't shot him, he would have killed you, then me, then Dale."

I nodded. My head knew he was right, but my feelings were taking awhile to reach the same conclusion.

Gary squeezed my hand. "Thank you for saving my life."

"Thank you for saving mine."

He stared at me for a long moment. "I have a couple confessions, Evie."

Something about his words seemed to lighten the mood, and I needed it to change, so I responded in kind. "A couple concussions, or a couple confessions?"

"Both." Mirth tugged at the corners of his mouth. "I'm not sure I can pull all A's this semester."

That almost brought a laugh out of me. The movement was there but not the sound. "If your grades suffer on account of your being framed for murder, stabbed, hit by a car, and almost clobbered to death in a warehouse, I won't hold a slip in GPA against you. I assume you'll still have high enough grades for the GI Bill, but if not, I've just come into a considerable amount of money, and I'd be happy to fund your education."

He chuckled. "I don't think I'll lose funding. But it's nice to have a safety net. Thank you. And there's another confession." His fingers played with the ends of my tangled hair. "I know I said I'd given up thieving, but there's one more thing I'm aching to steal."

"What's that?"

"Your heart."

My lips drew into a smile. "Gary, you stole that a long time ago."

His fingers moved to my neck, his touch so light that it didn't irritate the bruising there. "Then do you mind if I smear your lipstick?"

"I don't think there's any still—" I didn't finish my sentence, because I had better things to do, like respond to Gary's mouth, which moved over mine with a sweetness and a thoroughness that scattered the pain of the past and gave me hope for a beautiful future.

Epilogue

May 15, 1945

  Deeply regret to inform you that your son Private Clive E Hampton USMC was killed in action in the performance of his duty and service of his country. No information available at present regarding disposition of remains temporary burial in locality where death occurred probable. You will be promptly furnished any additional information received. To prevent possible aid to our enemies, do not divulge the name of his ship or station. Please accept my heartfelt sympathy. Letter follows.

  A.A. Vandegrift Lieut General USMC
  Commandant US Marine Corps

I STOOD NEXT TO GARY in the cemetery. One of his arms snaked around my waist, holding me. Some days, that was the only place I felt safe— in his arms. The soft spring breeze stirred the fragrance of the flowers I held—daffodils for Aunt Janice, irises for Mom, and roses for Dad.

The cuts and bruises on Gary's face had all faded, and his hair had grown out where they'd clipped it for his stitches. I could walk normally now, but I had a scar. Time didn't erase all wounds, but for the two of us, the last month had brought a measure of healing, physically and emotionally.

Professor Gerstner said trauma wasn't as damaging when it didn't inter- rupt the body's natural fight or flight cycle. Being held down and abused or being stuck in a foxhole, unable to move—the effects of those were more likely to linger. I'd fled, and I'd fought. That hadn't stopped nightmares from visiting me, but their intrusions were rare. I'd talked with Professor Gerstner, voiced what had happened, and recognized it as part of the past. He said that was important, being able to organize events into a narrative rather than a collection of disjointed fears.

Gary pulled me into him and brushed his gentle lips against my forehead. He smelled like citrus and cedar. "I'll give you a few minutes alone."

I watched him meander through the cemetery. A bench sat beneath a tree near Aunt Janice's grave, and I suspected he would go there. I would join him in a while.

I looked down at the headstone in front of me, my dad's. Beside it was my mom's. And somewhere on a little island in the Pacific, my brother's body rested. Dad had started the process of repatriating Clive's remains, so someday he would be here beside them, and then I would put flowers on his grave. For now, I put bouquets next to my parents' headstones.

"I'm getting married this summer," I told them. I looked down at my left hand, where the ring from Mr. Baumgartner's jewelry store hugged my finger. It had dozens of small diamonds, set to look like a feather because Gary said I made him feel like he could fly. I loved it. And I loved how the man who had given it to me had sacrificed for it.

Gary was changing his major to psychology. He said there were other people like him, haunted by the past, in need of help. He met with Professor Gerstner from time to time, going over his ghosts. Often, he put his memories down on paper, sketching the things that haunted him. He'd shown me some of them: a fearful child clutching shorn braids, a snow-covered battlefield, tall gates topped with barbed wire, a forlorn soldier lying on a stained mattress, piles of rubble where a city had once stood. He would show me, and then he would strike a match and burn the paper. The smoke would curl into the sky and dissipate and fade, just like he hoped his memories would. Other drawings, he didn't show me. I saw only the match and the dark smoke.

He still lived in his shed and would until the wedding.

I'd sold my aunt's house to Mr. Norton. I'd sold my dad's house to Dale and Fern, keeping it in the family. Dale had been bound and bruised when the police found him, but he'd made a quick recovery, physically. The horror of what had happened—and what had almost happened—was still raw, for all of us.

I'd moved into an apartment and decorated it with my dad's favorite books and what was left of my mom's favorite china. When we got married, Gary would move in with me. And when he was done with school, we'd move on, leaving Maplewick and all its memories behind us. A new town, a new start. Someplace where I wasn't surrounded by memories of a murderer and his victims.

Gary questioned me sometimes, wondering if I really wanted a man plagued by ghosts, a man who still woke up screaming at night, a man who'd never been part of a functional family. I told him that any man who could march through hell and emerge an angel was good enough for me. Then he'd tell me he wasn't feeling so angelic at the moment, and then he'd kiss me.

And for now, that seemed to be good enough for both of us.

Notes and Acknowledgments

THIS PROJECT STARTED ONE MORNING, far too early, when I needed a distraction from the pain caused by a herniated lumbar disc. I'd been mulling the plot and the characters around in my head for a while, and my sciatic nerve kept preventing a normal night's sleep, so the first draft came quickly—this is by far the fastest book I've ever drafted. Then I played with it, revised it, and polished it. I hope you've enjoyed it.

This story doesn't have as much history as most of my other books (which, no doubt, played a role in how quickly I wrote it), but here are a few notes for curious readers.

During WWII, mail from home was enormously important for keeping up servicemen's morale, but letters and packages had to compete for cargo space with troops, ammunition, food, and other war supplies. To reduce cargo space devoted to correspondence, the US government promoted V-mail, or Victory Mail. V-mails were written on a standardized form, photographed, turned into microfilm, and then reprinted closer to the recipient's destination. A single bag of V-mail film could take the place of thirty-seven normal bags, and travel time was usually shortened.

The Thomas Indian School really existed. Unfortunately, the description of what happened to students there is all too accurate, though Gary's experience is based not just on Thomas but on common patterns found in other Indian residential schools.

Information on the *USS Helena* and the *USS Juneau* is based on fact. Readers wishing to know more about what Clive's WWII experience would have been like might wish to read *With the Old Breed: At Peleliu and Okinawa* by E.B. Sledge (it's one of my favorites). I placed Clive in the same battalion (3rd), regiment (5th), and division (1st) that Sledge served in. Gary's war experience was as a member of the 99th Infantry Division. A fictional version of his time as a POW is included in one of my previous novels, *Defiance*, where Private Redhawk appears in a supporting role.

Ambulances weren't as widespread in the 1940s as they are today. Some hospitals had them; some didn't. Since Maplewick, its hospital, and its university are all fictional, I decided to include things like ambulances and train stations when they benefited the story. Other than the made-up locations, I've tried hard to be true to the late 1940s. I apologize for any mistakes I may have made.

Inflation has a way of making monetary values from the past seem less than impressive today. For reference, $100,000 in 1948 would be over $1 million in early 2019, when this novel went to press. The GI Bill's $50 a month would be roughly $522.

I owe a big thank you to my marvelous test readers: Kathryn Andrus, Melanie Grant, Ron Machado, Kathi Oram Peterson, Charissa Stastny, and Linda White. Their suggestions and enthusiasm were vital to this project.

* * *

If you enjoyed this book, I would be very grateful for your review on websites like Amazon and Goodreads. Reviews can be as simple as "I liked it," and are a key component to any book's success. They help readers determine if a book is a good fit for them, encourage sales, and open the door to future marketing opportunities.

About the Author

WHILE GROWING UP, A. L. Sowards devoured her parents' collection of murder mysteries. Most of them weren't historical . . . but some of them were old enough that they felt like it to a teenager. Perhaps it was inevitable that she would eventually write a historical mystery of her own.

A. L. Sowards grew up in Moses Lake, Washington, then came to Utah to attend BYU and ended up staying. Now she's a busy mom, with three young children and a head full of story ideas. She enjoys reading, writing, learning about history, and eating chocolate, sometimes all at once. As an author, she is known for heart-pounding action, memorable characters, careful historical research, and clean love stories. Her novels include a Whitney Award–winner and several Whitney Award finalists.

For more information, please visit her website, ALSowards.com, or find her on Facebook, Goodreads, Instagram, and Twitter.